When
the Beast
Ravens

By E. Rose Sabin from Tom Doherty Associates

A School for Sorcery
A Perilous Power
When the Beast Ravens

When the Beast Ravens

E. ROSE SABIN

STARSCAPE

A TOM DOHERTY ASSOCIATES BOOK
NEW YORK

This is a work of fiction. All the characters and events portrayed in this book are either products of the author's imagination or are used fictitiously.

WHEN THE BEAST RAVENS

Copyright © 2005 by E. Rose Sabin

A Starscape Book
Published by Tom Doherty Associates, LLC
175 Fifth Avenue
New York, NY 10010

www.starscapebooks.com

ISBN 0-765-34759-8
EAN 975-0-765-34759-6

First Starscape edition: January 2006

Printed in the United States of America

0   9   8   7   6   5   4   3   2   1

This one is for my sisters and brothers:
Barbara, Carole, Evelie, and Patty
John and Bill

LESLEY SIMONTON SCHOOL
FOR THE MAGICALLY GIFTED

HEADMISTRESS
Miryam Vedreaux

FACULTY
Aletheia—Specialist in Interdimensional Concourse
Mistress Blake—Gifting Mistress, Expert in the
Development
of Supernormal Gifts
Mistress Dova—Professor of Arcane Rites and Esoterica
Master Hawke—Professor of Alchemy, the Mandala,
and the Healing Arts
Master San Marté—Professor of Ethics
Master Tumberlis—"Old Tumbles"—Professor of the
History and Philosophy of Metaphysics

STUDENTS
First Year

Women:
Omiya Asaba
Sindia Carroll
Maridel Denham
Lana Harper
Jenna Jacobs
Elaine Keller
Debra Larkin
Shadoe Quinn
Analise Richmond

Men:
Carl Crane
Eran Drake
Dwayne Echols
Todrick Hanes
Viad Morig
Lybrand Sartori

Second Year

Women:
Yvonne Bolte
Giselle Dorr
Ferene K'Sere
Chantal Navarese
Vanita Trask

Men:
Kelby Carter
Troy Cavender
Joel Feldor
Marcos Matarin
Reece O'Shannon
Lisander Whitley

Third Year

Women:
Lina Mueller
Coral Snow
Petra Stratigeas
Rehanne Zalos

Men:
Gray Becq
Oryon Brew
Jerrol Fyfe
Davy Geer
Kress Klemmer
Fenton Rhoze
Nevil Santomayor
Britnor Wythyn

"MAIDS"
Veronica Crowell
Tria Tesserell

*   *   *

DEMONS
Ghash
Grimgrist
Gruefell

OFFICIALS
Millville Peace Officers
Chief Officer Telpor Ardrey
Adjutant Lewis Canby
Mr. Drake Shardan

Provincial Council Members

LESLEY SIMONTON SCHOOL

When
the Beast
Ravens

1

THE RETURN

Rehanne was excited, and eager to share that excitement with Gray. Summer break was over; a new school year was about to start. Her last year. She anticipated that it would be a good one for her. She hoped it would be good for Gray as well. Last year he'd been so moody, so often depressed, but she resolved to do all she could to help him regain his formerly sunny nature—starting with a cheery greeting as soon as he stepped off the bus that was due to arrive in less than an hour.

She had come a day early to fix up her room, greet her friends and catch up on their news, and relax before plunging into the daily routine of classes and study assignments. Her new roommate, Chantal Navarese, had gotten in this morning.

Rehanne had expected to room with Petra Stratigeas, her previous year's roommate. She and Petra had gotten along well; she scarcely knew Chantal. But she learned that each of the third-year women had been assigned a second-year roommate.

Rehanne had seen her new roommate only briefly. When the younger girl arrived, Rehanne had left Chantal to unpack and arrange her things and had gone off to spend time with Petra.

When the time approached for Gray's bus to arrive, Rehanne returned to her room to freshen up before going to meet him. She was greeted by the sight of her roommate on hands and knees, rump in the air, face near the floor.

"What are you doing, Chantal?"

The girl swiveled around and peered up through the long blond curls that had fallen in front of her face. "I've lost a good diamond earring. You've got to help me find it."

"Sorry, I don't have time. Gray's coming in. I have to meet the bus." Rehanne went to her dressing table and picked up her comb.

Chantal straightened and brushed her hair from her eyes. "Be careful where you walk," she snapped. "You could step on it and break it. I've *got* to find it. It's very valuable—and it's not mine."

"Whose is it?" Rehanne asked, not really caring but trying to show some interest for politeness' sake. Her mind was on Gray, not her roommate's predicament.

"It's my mother's—a family heirloom. And . . . and she doesn't know I have it." Tears spilled from Chantal's hazel eyes. Her long lashes closed and opened like butterflies' wings. "Please, please help me."

If the foolish girl had stolen her mother's valuable earrings, she deserved to suffer. But the tears aroused Rehanne's sympathy. Chantal's distress seemed genuine and deep. Rehanne glanced at the clock. The bus was scheduled to arrive in five minutes, but it always came late. She could spare a few minutes to help her roommate. She didn't want their year together to get off to a bad start.

"How big is the earring? What does it look like?" As she asked the questions she got down on her knees and searched around her dressing table and desk.

"It's a small silver filigree crescent with the diamond in its center," Chantal replied. "Here, I'll show you the other one." She scrambled to her feet, went to her dresser, and took a small object from a silver tray, held it out for inspection.

Rehanne caught her breath. The description had been accurate but had not captured the earring's delicate beauty. She touched the tiny crescent with the tip of her finger, admiring the intricate silver lace that cradled the gleaming, many-faceted diamond.

The missing earring had to be found, but it could have rolled anywhere; the light was poor, and the floor held the summer's accumulation of dust. Blast Chantal! How could she have been so careless?

They searched and re-searched every inch of floor, pulled apart the bedding on both beds, looked through dresser and dressing table, emptied drawers. Every time Rehanne protested that she must leave to meet Gray, Chantal's wails persuaded her to stay a little longer. Her hands were dirty, her face was probably as smudged with dust as Chantal's was, her skirt was wrinkled from crawling around on the floor, and her clean white blouse had lost its freshness. She was thoroughly disgusted with Chantal, and with herself for yielding to the girl's entreaties.

"Are you positive you lost it here in the room?"

Chantal answered with an emphatic nod.

"Tell me what happened."

"I wore the earrings to lunch. I wanted to impress . . . someone."

The coy admission would have amused Rehanne had she been in a better mood. Chantal's unrequited passion for tall, handsome Kress Klemmer was well known.

Her brow furrowed with the effort of remembering every detail, Chantal continued. "After lunch I came back here to write my parents, to let them know I got here safely. I didn't have time last night. I took off both earrings, put them in the tray on my dresser, and sat down at my desk to write. I'd written one page and started on a second, when I spilled ink. I couldn't find a blotter, so I ran to the washroom for a sponge, came back, cleaned up the ink, and had to rewrite the second page. When I finished the letter, I was going to go mail it. I went to put my earrings on. And I could only find one." She walked to her dresser and stared at the single earring in the tray. "The other one is not in this room. Someone must have come in and stolen it while I was in the washroom."

"Chantal, that's ridiculous. Who would steal one earring? They were together; a thief would have taken both of them."

"Well, it can't have disappeared into thin air. If no one took it, it has to be here somewhere. We've got to keep hunting."

"There's nowhere else to hunt." Rehanne looked at the clock and gasped. "Gray must be here by now. He'll be wondering where I am."

She rushed from the room, furious with her roommate for detaining her and with herself for having wasted so much time. Gray had tried to be cheerful in his letters through the summer, but she could tell he was still depressed, still floundering with no sense of purpose. She knew, too, how hard it was for him to trust people after what happened.

But he trusted her. And she'd let him down. Not a good way to start their final year at Simonton School.

Gray walked through the double doors, stopped in the foyer, and set his suitcase down. He took a deep breath, inhaling the familiar stale smell, feeling the dust-dryness of the place. The bare wood floor was scuffed and dirty; the low-watt bulb in the ceiling fixture scarcely penetrated the gloom. Simonton School hadn't changed.

He'd expected Rehanne to be waiting when he got off

the bus in front of the school. But maybe she hadn't known when he'd be arriving. He picked up his suitcase and entered the formal parlor. The uniformed peace officer lounging against the wall just inside the door was an unexpected sight; usually the Millville authorities ignored the school.

The peace officer glanced in his direction and looked away, his gaze roving about the room. He showed no interest in Gray, yet Gray found his presence unsettling.

Veronica, the school maid, scuttled past him, a short, plump woman with eyes like raisins. "Ignore him," she muttered without stopping.

Trying to follow that advice, Gray scanned the faces of the few students who sat chatting in the parlor. Three young women, two young men, all unfamiliar. First-year students, looking very young and more than a little scared. He should talk to them, encourage them. He knew how daunting the first days at Simonton could be.

He did not speak to the students. Instead, his gaze wandered to the portrait hanging on the wall over the mantel— a portrait of a young man in the dress of the past century. He had always found it depressing, with its dark wood frame, the subject's red hair dull against the dark background, face partially in shadow. It seemed odd that the artist had chosen to paint his subject in such somber tones, with so little highlighting.

He felt a kinship with that youth for whom the Lesley Simonton School for the Magically Gifted was named, who perhaps had been so darkly painted to reflect a darkness of spirit. So might a present-day artist capture Gray on canvas.

But he was dawdling, hoping that Rehanne would come. Headmistress might be able to tell him where Rehanne was and why she hadn't kept her promise to meet him. He might as well report in and get his room assignment.

Not that he was eager to settle in. He regretted coming back. No, Simonton School hadn't changed.

He had.

2

MEMORIES

On his way to the stairs leading to Headmistress's office, Gray nearly collided with Kress. "Watch where you're going," the blond youth said and shoved Gray, pushing him into someone behind him.

That person growled and spun Gray around. He found himself face-to-face with Jerrol, another of the conspirators. With his thin face, long nose, and close-set eyes, third-year student Jerrol Fyfe had always reminded Gray of a ferret, and never more than now, with his face contorted with anger. Keeping a tight grasp on Gray's arm, Jerrol drew back his other hand, clenched into a fist, ready to strike.

Gray dropped his suitcase and doubled his own fists to fend off the unprovoked attack. It would feel good to release all his pent-up tension and anger by beating Jerrol senseless.

Before either he or Jerrol could land a blow, Veronica reappeared and stepped between them, pushing them apart with surprising strength for a small woman.

"Now, now, gentlemen," she said, "you are choosing a very poor way to begin the new school year. You certainly do not want to draw the attention of the peace officer, who is hoping to see just such a display as you nearly put on."

Gray dropped his arms to his side and cast a quick glance at the peace officer. The man didn't seem to be looking at him, but it was hard to be certain.

"You take care," Veronica told Jerrol. "You should have learned not to get involved in things that don't concern you."

With a snarl, Jerrol released Gray's arm and backed away.

Turning to Gray, she said, "Headmistress is expecting you, Mr. Becq. Please report to her office immediately."

"That's where I was going when Kress and Jerrol pushed me." Gray found himself shaking with anger.

"Good. You may report this incident to her."

Gray nodded and picked up his suitcase. He wouldn't report the incident. Why bother? But if Kress or Jerrol or any of the others pushed him any further he'd light into them and damn the consequences. Veronica wouldn't always be present to stop him, and Wilce wasn't here this year to intervene, either.

His former roommate had often used his gift of peace-bringing to calm Gray's rage and restore reason. Wilce would remind Gray that he'd suffered the same treatment and could forgive. That those responsible all regretted it. That Headmistress had punished them by greatly reducing their power. That Oryon, who had instigated the whole plot, had changed and was not the same person.

But Kress, Oryon's staunchest supporter, had not changed. Now it looked like Jerrol had not. The restriction of their power meant little to Gray. His power had always been limited to creating lovely but ephemeral art out of scraps of material. That talent was of no use in confronting even the diminished power of the others.

And Wilce was gone, graduated on schedule last year despite the time he'd missed the year before. Gray should have graduated, too, but because of the unspeakable thing that had darkened his life and robbed him of joy, he had missed most of his second year and had been forced to repeat it. It was no consolation that both Oryon and Kress had also been made to repeat their second year. That only meant that in this third and final year, he was forced to face again, day in and day out, in classes, at meals, on work detail, those whose actions two years ago had consigned him to weeks of unspeakable horror.

Last year, besides Wilce, he'd had Tria to help him through—Tria, who'd rescued them from the Dire Realms and of whom the others were afraid because of her exceptional talents. Because of those talents, Tria had graduated a year early.

So this year he had only Rehanne. She'd persuaded him to return when he wanted to drop out. "You can't let them defeat you," she'd said. "You can't overcome a thing by running away from it. I'll be here," she'd promised. "When it gets rough, we can talk it out."

It was rough already. Why wasn't she here?

He climbed the stairs, halted at the second floor landing, and set down his suitcase. When he knocked on Headmistress's door, he heard her call, "Come in, Mr. Becq."

He opened the door and advanced to stand in front of a desk piled high with papers and books. The woman behind the desk was uncommonly tall, and though her face was in shadow, he knew its features well: dark and piercing eyes, long straight nose, thin lips that rarely smiled, sharp chin, high cheekbones that along with the eyes suggested a western coastal heritage. Most students found her intimidating. Gray rather liked her.

"Welcome back, Mr. Becq," she said. "I trust you had a pleasant summer."

"I spent it working in my parents' store," he answered

noncommittally, not caring to explain that nothing was pleasant anymore. Probably she knew that.

"You'll be wanting your room assignment," she said. "I've left you in your old room. Your roommate will be Reece O'Shannon."

"Reece! He's back?"

"After a year of thinking matters over, Mr. O'Shannon decided to return. He is on probationary status as a second-year student."

Gray felt numb. Reece had left after his first term at Simonton School, left because he'd been involved in the trouble that had changed Gray's life. Reece had played only a minor role; he hadn't really understood what was at stake. Gray didn't hold it against him, not consciously. But to room with him, his presence a constant reminder of what Gray wanted desperately to forget . . .

So they were *all* here—all those who had conspired to summon the Dire Women, who'd let those abominable creatures capture him and Wilce, carry them off to their hellish realm, and transform them into beasts. All of them: Oryon, Kress, Jerrol, Britnor, Davy, Fenton, and Reece. Here. Free and unscathed. Lina, too. Her actions had set the thing in motion. And she'd blocked his single opportunity to escape. How could they expect him to act as though nothing had happened, to return to the easy camaraderie of classmates?

"Here is your key." Headmistress's voice broke through his dismal thoughts. The large orange gem in her ring sparkled as she reached through the light of her desk lamp to press the key into his hand.

Against his will his fingers closed around it. With no conscious volition he found himself walking to the door, picking up his suitcase, and marching down the hall to his room. He reached the door, inserted the key in the lock, and only then remembered he had not asked Headmistress about Rehanne.

Reece was not in the room, but he had left ample evidence of his presence. Clothes were strewn over one bed and tossed into open dresser drawers. Candy wrappers and other trash littered the floor around the wastebasket. One shoe lay on its side in the middle of the space between the beds. Gray traced a sour smell to a wet towel wadded up under a desk. Reece would not have arrived earlier than yesterday, but already he'd reduced the room to a shambles.

Gray swung his suitcase onto his bed and snapped it open. He stood staring at the neatly folded contents. The task of transferring them to armoire and dresser drawers called for more energy than he could summon. This place wasn't his. Reece had marked the territory; let him keep it. Gray wanted only to find Rehanne. She could lighten his mood.

He slammed the suitcase shut and fled the room.

He checked again in the parlor, met only the nervous gazes of the first-year students. The peace officer had left. Gray stepped outside to assure himself that Rehanne wasn't waiting for him, unaware that the bus had come and gone.

Disappointed, he wandered back to the library. It hadn't officially opened for the new session, but Coral and Petra were inside, dusting shelves and arranging materials for the fall classes. When he poked his head in the door, Coral looked up and waved.

"Hi, Gray. Welcome back. Where's Rehanne?"

"Don't know. I'm looking for her. I thought she'd meet the bus, but she didn't. You don't know where she is?"

Petra stood up from dusting the lower shelves and wiped her arm across a sweaty forehead. Her broad face wore a worried frown. "That's odd. I know she planned to meet you. She was talking about it at lunch. I can't imagine why she wouldn't have gone."

Britnor popped out of the rear workroom with a stack of

books. "Got these mended." At the sight of Gray he stopped in midstride. "Oh, hi, Gray," he said with a tentative smile. "You know Reece is back? Heard you and he'll be rooming together. You seen him yet?"

"No. I'm looking for Rehanne." With that curt reply Gray turned and left.

"Haven't seen her. Sorry," Britnor called after him, sounding crestfallen.

Gray was sorry, too. Sorry he'd run into Britnor, sorry he was behaving so badly. Even though he didn't feel like making small talk, he could have responded politely to Britnor's attempt to be friendly. But he was still angry about his earlier encounter with Kress and Jerrol, and he was troubled about Rehanne.

Dining hall and kitchen were deserted; the kitchen crew had completed the after-lunch cleanup, and supper preparations had not yet begun. He walked through the empty classroom wing and exited onto the quadrangle between the buildings. The rosebushes were in full bloom. Their sweet smell might have softened his mood had he not seen Lina and Oryon standing by the fountain, her hand resting on his arm as they talked. Gray didn't trust those two, never mind that they'd both lost most of their power to the Dire Women, and Headmistress had decreed that they would not regain it until they proved worthy.

They were alone on the patio. Gray stayed only long enough to make sure of that before retreating inside, a red haze of rage clouding his vision.

That was how it had started. Lina, flirting with Oryon, teasing Kress, creating a friction that had burst into a power struggle. Then Kress and Oryon had joined forces in a bid for power that led them to summon the Dire Women and entrap Wilce and Gray.

He trudged past the empty classrooms and headed for the

stairs. Two first-year students strolled toward him, looked at his face, and quickly stepped out of his way. He used to have a reputation for friendliness and helpfulness; now he was developing the opposite reputation.

He reached the stairs and placed a foot on the first step. "Gray!" The glad cry stopped him, lifted his gaze to the upstairs landing.

"Gray!" Rehanne shouted his name again and bounded down the steps and into his open arms.

His arms closed around her, hugged her to him, letting the solidness of her, the warmth, the sweetness draw out the poisons like a poultice on a festering wound. Her hair was soft against his cheek. He breathed deeply of its clean fragrance, brushed his lips across its silky smoothness. When he could release her and step back a little, his hands on her wrists, and look into her face, into those wonderful turquoise eyes, the rightness of the school came back to him and settled around him like an old familiar jacket. He took a deep breath and smiled. It was, after all, good to be back.

"I've been looking for you," he said, finding his voice. "I thought you'd be waiting when the bus came."

"I meant to be. It was Chantal's fault. I'm rooming with her this year, did you know?"

He shook his head, tried to remember. "First-year last year?" A vague picture swam into his mind. "Little busybody. That the one?"

Rehanne sighed. "That's the one. Pries into everybody else's business but keeps her own a secret. I can't figure out why Headmistress put us together."

"She must have had a reason. What did Chantal do?"

"She lost an earring. A valuable diamond earring that belongs to her mother. She begged me to help her hunt."

Her explanation stunned him. "You couldn't meet me because you were looking for an earring?"

"Oh, Gray, please don't be mad." She moved closer, put her hands on his shoulders. "She was crying and carrying on, practically in hysterics. I *couldn't* leave her like that. She swore she lost it in our room, and I kept thinking we'd find it. I didn't expect to take so long about it."

"And did you find it?" He kept his voice level, masking the hurt that she'd let such a trivial thing keep her away.

She wasn't fooled. Worry lines creased her forehead. She placed one hand against his cheek. "I know I should have walked out. But I couldn't. I just couldn't . . . I don't know why . . . I . . ." She stopped and bit her lip. Her hands dropped to her side.

"It's all right," he said quietly. "It's not important. Forget it."

She didn't speak, and he drew away from her. "I need to unpack," he said. "The room's a mess. I'll see you at supper."

She nodded, eyes downcast, not moving when he brushed past her and went upstairs.

In his room he transferred clothes from his suitcase to dresser drawers, hung shirts and trousers in the armoire, shoving aside Reece's things to make room for his, performing the tasks mechanically while his thoughts remained fixed on Rehanne.

He shouldn't be angry with her; he should go down, find her, and apologize. She'd been helping her roommate, nothing wrong with that. It was an example of her kind-hearted ways.

But an earring! She'd broken her promise over such a silly trifle. Valuable it might be, but it wasn't hers and she hadn't been responsible for its loss.

An earring. For another, darker reason that particular excuse had upset him.

Two years ago he'd escorted Rehanne to the Midwinter Ball, the most important social event of the school year. It was a tradition for the men to buy a date gift to present to their date at the crowning of the King and Queen of Winter, before the final dance of the evening. In Gray's pocket had resided a tiny, carefully wrapped package. He'd checked after each dance to make sure he hadn't lost it. The gift had been earrings, expensive ones, but he had his own funds, money earned working in the hardware store. And he'd wanted to give Rehanne something very special.

Oryon and Kress arrived late to the dance, escorting masked women. After one dance, their partners had removed their masks to reveal skull faces. Dire Women! In the ensuing panic, the Dire Women snatched Wilce and Gray, carried them off to their demon realm, and transformed them into loathsome beasts. And in that awful place the little gift had been lost.

His hands clenched. He crashed a fist against the dresser, kicked the bedpost, hurled the empty suitcase to the floor, then stood in the middle of the room shaking until the violent rage subsided into icy resentment.

He picked up his suitcase, latched it, and set it aside to be stored in the attic. The mess Reece had left on the floor offended him. He kicked the shoe under Reece's bed, threw the wet towel out into the hall, and gathered up a handful of trash that included three red and silver candy wrappers. Sitting in his desk chair, he methodically reduced the candy wrappers to tiny scraps.

He tossed the bright shreds into the air. His power held them and sculpted them into a crescent moon of silver filigree the size of his fist. A needlelike knife pierced a small, pulsing crimson heart in the center of the crescent, and blood dripped through the delicate lacework.

The macabre sculpture hung in the air, the embodiment of his defiance. Scarcely breathing, he counted the seconds. "Six, seven, eight, nine, ten . . ."

He'd reached thirty-two when the room door opened, breaking his concentration. Reece burst in, stopped, stared at the floating artwork, mouth agape.

The bloody crescent quivered and slowly burst into fragments that drifted down like tainted snow.

More than thirty-two seconds. None of his creations had lasted that long before.

Gray bent and scooped up the debris as Reece eased around him.

"Man, I'm sorry I left things in a mess. I meant to get back and clean it up before you got in, but . . ." His voice trailed off into confused silence.

Gray shrugged. "It seems like everyone's good intentions got sidetracked. It doesn't matter. I don't plan to spend any more time in here than I have to."

He tossed the red and silver scraps into the wastebasket and walked out of the room.

3

PROBLEMS

Rehanne took refuge in the library. She sank into a chair, rested her elbows on the table, and propped her chin on her hands.

"Gray's looking for you," Petra said, coming to stand beside her. "He was worried."

"He found her," Coral called from the desk, saving Rehanne the trouble of explaining.

Petra clucked sympathetically and settled into the next

chair. "Poor Coral was almost flattened by the anger and depression he was broadcasting. I guess being home for the summer didn't help him."

Rehanne shook her head.

"And now he's dumping that poison on you." Coral joined them at the table and placed a hand on Rehanne's arm. "You mustn't let him do that. You can't heal him, and he *can* infect you. I'm sensing the same wrong vibrations I got from him, only not as strong. But they'll get stronger if he does this every time you're with him."

Rehanne gazed at the two, willing them to understand. Her closest friends at Simonton School, they were a study in contrasts. Coral had the fine, delicate features of a porcelain figurine, her short, smooth, dark hair impeccably trimmed and shaped to emphasize her high forehead and long, slender neck. Petra was stocky, big-boned, square-faced, with the ruddy complexion of a country woman, though in fact she came from Kannia, a key city of Delta Province, where her father held a high government position.

So different in appearance, yet so alike in their thinking. They had supported her all last year in her efforts to help Gray. Now they both seemed to be turning against him.

She said, "He was upset because I didn't meet the bus. He was right: I should have been there. I tried to explain, but the excuse *did* sound silly." She told them about Chantal's lost earring.

"That's odd," Petra mused, frowning.

"What's odd?" Rehanne asked when her friend did not continue.

"The earrings belonging to her mother," Petra answered and hesitated again. "I shouldn't tell you this. I'm not supposed to know it. She comes from a very poor family. She's here on a scholarship. I can't imagine her mother owning valuable diamond earrings."

"She said they were an heirloom."

"I suppose that's possible," Petra said slowly. "But in that case . . ." Her voice trailed off and she shook her head. "I really can't say more. But I can't believe that Chantal's mother would have inherited valuable jewelry."

Rehanne didn't pry. She didn't care where Chantal had gotten the earrings. One was lost, and Rehanne had searched for it when she should have been meeting Gray, and her absence had hurt Gray, and the reason for it had angered him. She had to find a way to make amends, to make things right again. That was all that mattered.

"I don't think it will change anything, but I can probably help you convince Gray that he shouldn't blame you for being late," Coral said.

Grateful that Coral at least was willing to focus on the real problem, Rehanne listened intently to Coral's explanation: "You may have noticed that I avoid Chantal as much as possible. Because I'm an empath, I can't stand to be around her. She's a reverse empath."

"Reverse empath?"

Coral nodded. "Everyone leaks emotions that an empath picks up. I'm much better than I used to be at blocking, but I can't shield out anything from Chantal. She projects everything—and not just to me. If you're near her you'll feel what she does—the stronger the emotion, the more she broadcasts it. So if she was really upset and obsessed with finding the earring, she'd have passed that feeling on to you. That's why you couldn't tear yourself away. You experienced her panic. You needed to find the earring as much as she did—maybe more."

Rehanne's relief at being given a way to justify her actions to Gray gave way to horror as the full implication of Coral's revelation hit her. "All year long, rooming with Chantal, I'll have to feel everything she feels!"

"You don't have to, Rehanne," Petra said. "You have the talent to suppress her emotions when they get out of control. That's probably why Headmistress assigned you to room with her."

Rehanne chewed a fingernail as she considered Petra's suggestion. "You know I never use that talent," she said.

"You may have to," Petra counseled. "It's your best defense."

"It's not fair." Rehanne's teeth ripped off her nail at the quick.

Grimacing, Coral asked, "Which is more reasonable: to put her with someone who has a defense but may choose not to use it, or to put her with a defenseless person who has no choice?"

She was right, though Rehanne hated to admit it. Britnor's timely entrance from the workroom spared her the need to comment. He came up to them scratching his head, his thick hair in wild disarray. He acknowledged Rehanne's presence with a quick nod before addressing Petra.

"There's one book on the 'To Be Mended' list I can't account for. All the rest are checked off, but I don't remember ever seeing this one. I've looked all through the workroom, I've checked the book cart and the shelves in here, and I can't find it."

"What's the book?" Petra asked.

"One I never heard of, though I suppose I'll be blamed if it's missing. It's called *Transformations, Transmutations, and Transmogrifications*."

Petra shook her head. "I don't know anything about it. No books are checked out to students until classes start, and if it's on the mending list, it has to have been here at the end of last year. I'd guess a faculty member took it. They're supposed to leave a note, but some of them get careless. I wouldn't worry about it."

Britnor continued to look distraught. "I had to beg Headmistress to put me on the library staff this year. She didn't feel I'd earned the privilege. But Nevil didn't want the job, and all the other third-year guys . . ." He ended the sentence with a shrug.

Rehanne understood. All the third-year men except Nevil Santomayor had been involved in the plot that had resulted in Gray's captivity and transformation.

Transformation. The title of the missing book. Could it have anything to do with—?

But, no, that was silly. That had happened two years ago, and the book had only now turned up missing. As Petra said, a faculty member had probably borrowed the book and forgot to leave a note. She was getting as paranoid as Gray. Maybe Coral was right: he was infecting her.

Unwilling to return to his room after supper, Gray wandered through the first-floor rooms, avoiding the others who stayed downstairs. He'd sat with Rehanne at supper and she'd whispered to him about Chantal being a reverse empath, as if that explained everything. Maybe it did. He wasn't angry anymore; he told her that. But the coldness didn't go away. Rehanne felt it; he couldn't conceal it. They lingered in the parlor only a few minutes before Rehanne excused herself and went upstairs. He was driving her away and knew it and couldn't stop himself.

The library was locked, the corridor outside it dark. He sat on the floor in the shadows for a while, trying to sort things out. Maybe he should admit he'd made a mistake in coming back, repack, and go home. Except that things wouldn't be any better there. His folks would probably let him work in their hardware store. They loved him and were worried about him and would welcome the chance to keep an eye on him. But he wasn't good for business; his surliness had driven away customers this summer. He'd tried to be courteous and pleasant, but the darkness within always managed to creep out at inopportune times.

The windowless corridor was hot and stuffy. With nothing resolved, he got up and rambled aimlessly through rooms and corridors. The few students who remained downstairs were seated in the parlor, so he stayed away from that room. He roved to the patio doors and cursed to find them locked. "Place is like a prison," he muttered.

He tried the various classroom doors. Most of them were locked, but one yielded to his push. He went in, closed the door, turned on the light, and explored the room, not looking for anything, merely trying to occupy his mind with inconsequential observations. He gathered several pieces of chalk from the chalk trays—new pieces, ready for the new session. He carried them to a desk, sat down, spread them out on the desktop, and methodically ground them into a fine powder.

A white mound of chalk dust grew before him, consuming all the chalk. He blew on it, used his power to lift and sculpt it, creating a likeness of Rehanne's face, her eyes closed, her lips parted, the white dust creating a corpselike pallor.

He adjusted his creation, hollowing the cheeks, making the closed eyes sunken, the chin slack. No longer merely corpse*like,* the dead face hung before him, mocking him. Too stunned at what he had wrought to count the seconds, he stared in horror at the thing that refused to go away. Eyeless, it stared back in reproach. How long it endured, Gray couldn't estimate, but it did not dissolve on its own as all his other creations had done. Struck by Gray's fist, it exploded in a shower of chalk dust. He stood, sneezed, and shook the white powder from his clothes.

"Well, a fine mess you've made, Mr. Becq."

He whirled toward the door. Veronica stood in the doorway, hands on hips, her face stern.

She stepped into the room. "Did you think we don't have enough to do, getting ready for the new term? Did you think my new assistant needed an initiation?"

Past the pudgy maid he glimpsed a slim figure in a gingham dress and white apron. A bandanna hid her hair. She looked vaguely familiar, but he had no chance for a closer look.

Veronica advanced on him, shaking her finger. "No, sir, you'll not go around making messes for others to clean up. Consideration is one of the lessons Simonton School strives to teach, and you'd best be learning it. There's others in the world besides yourself, and many as have suffered and been treated unjustly, but they grow stronger for it instead of taking it out on everybody else." She drew a wet towel from her waistband and tossed it onto the desk. "You see that every bit of that mess is wiped up before you leave. We'll not clean up after you—now or anytime."

A great sense of shame rolled over him and he hung his head. He *had* been inconsiderate and thoughtless. Staring at the floor, he mumbled an apology. When at last he lifted his gaze, Veronica and her helper were gone.

He picked up the wet towel and got to work.

Lina stood, stretched, ambled to the window, drew aside the green curtains, and gazed out at the starry night. With tomorrow's convocation, the new school year—her last at Simonton School—would officially begin. She had little doubt that she'd be eligible for graduation at year's end. She'd already regained enough of her power to be confident of attaining third level. But she wanted much more than that. It galled her that her former roommate had reached the highest level. An Adept! Yet when they'd roomed together, she'd had to teach Tria to see through the illusion that disguised the school's true appearance.

Well, no doubt Tria saw a lot more these days. It was hard

not to be envious. At least she alone of all the students knew what Tria had become and where she was. She smiled and dropped the curtain back in place.

Restless, she prowled around the room. A spacious room, not far from luxurious, to her eyes. Tomorrow when Giselle arrived, her roommate would see the room far differently. To the second-year student the room would appear small and cramped, crowded with cheap and battered furniture. And Lina would not bother to enlighten her. Giselle had already reached second level and was, like Lina, striving for third. Learning to discern reality was a part of that striving. Lina didn't regret having helped Tria; Tria had, after all, helped her in return. She owed Giselle nothing: let her make her own discoveries.

It was pleasant to have the room to herself for this one night. Lack of privacy was the thing she hated most about the school. Of course, she'd grown accustomed to Tria, had enjoyed matching wits with her. But Giselle could not offer the same challenge. It puzzled Lina that they'd been assigned to room together; she could think of nothing she and Giselle had in common.

A glass of milk might relieve her restlessness. It would be fun to sneak down to the kitchen and raid the refrigerator. It was late, the lights would be off on the first floor, and the stairs were warded, but Lina could see in the dark, and her talisman would take her through the wards.

She opened her dresser drawer and reached into the corner for the braided gold circlet set with four gemstones.

It wasn't there.

She searched the drawer. Nothing.

She checked the other drawers, the vanity table, the chifforobe. The talisman was missing.

Not many knew about it. Kress did. She had lent it to him once, and he had found it useful. If he needed it again, he'd have no qualms about stealing it. No one was more likely to have taken it.

Lina snarled and flexed her fingers as though they were cat's claws. If she only had her full power, she'd deal with him immediately. But she, like Kress, could draw power, although she had not done so for many months. She'd restrain herself no longer. Kress needed to be taught a lesson; he'd grown too cocky. It might take two or three days, but she'd recover her talisman, and do it in a way that Kress would never forget.

4

THE MARK OF THE BEAST

Rehanne's mood matched the morning: sunny, warm, and golden. Her world had righted itself. She'd met Gray for breakfast and found his outlook so improved that he seemed his old cheerful self. They chatted and laughed and joked all through the meal. They met again later to walk to the opening convocation. The speeches were the same ones they heard every year, and they survived the boredom by exchanging whispered comments and meaningful looks. Just when they thought the last speech had ended and they would be dismissed, Headmistress stepped to the podium.

"While I am looking forward to a good academic year, as I'm sure are all of you, and I dislike having to inject a solemn note into this felicitous occasion, I have something I must caution you about."

Headmistress paused, and her stern look drew the attention of even the most distracted or uninterested. "I'm sure that many of you, when you arrived here, noted the presence of Chief Officer Ardrey, of the Millville Peace Officers," she continued. "I must warn you that he and many of the officers who serve under him are prejudiced against the gifted and against this school in particular. Fortunately, they do not have the manpower to post an officer here permanently. However, be assured that they will be alert for any excuse to cast the school in a bad light. You must exercise great caution when you have occasion to go into Millville and do nothing, absolutely nothing, to draw the attention of the peace officers."

Rehanne cast a glance back at Chantal, sitting two rows behind her and looking bored. She hoped the girl was listening. Last year she had joined with two second-year friends to pull a prank in Millville involving the use of power and bringing on themselves the wrath of the peace officers. The second-year students had been forbidden to come back this year because of that prank. Chantal had not received the same punishment only because as a first-year student she had been considered less guilty, influenced by the older girls.

Headmistress continued her lecture: "The staff and I will exert every effort to prevent anything happening at the school that would require the peace officers to return here. If each one of you will study carefully *The Student Rights and Responsibilities Manual* and follow scrupulously the rules set forth in it, we will have no problems.

"I cannot overstate the seriousness of this warning. Your conduct will reflect not only on Simonton School but on the entire Gifted Community of Castlemount Province. Please bear that in mind wherever you go and whatever you do throughout this school year."

Headmistress dismissed the gathered students, and they

poured out onto the patio and formed lines to receive their schedules. That closing warning cast a brief cloud over Rehanne's happy mood. Knowing that the tragic events of two years before had first brought the school to the unwelcome notice of the local authorities, she watched to see how Gray reacted to Headmistress's dour warning.

To her immense relief, he smiled and squeezed her hand. "It's okay," he teased, "I don't intend to exhibit my art in Millville."

Laughing, she left him and found the line for those whose names began with a letter in the last part of the alphabet, while Gray went to another line. When they had each received their schedules, they met by the fountain to compare them.

They would have two classes together: Alchemical Formulas and Healing Elixirs, taught by Master Hawke, and Case Histories in Ethics, with Master San Marté. In addition, Rehanne was assigned to Translation and Use of Arcane Languages, taught by Mistress Dova. The mage tongues were especially interesting to Rehanne; taught by her grandmother, she was fluent in the one most widely used for spells and knew phrases from another, more obscure and mysterious.

Overall, Rehanne was delighted with her schedule, though she wished someone other than Master Tumberlis could present the History of Spells and Charms. Old Tumbles tended to wander off the subject and had been known to fall asleep in the middle of his own droning lecture. But even so, with her talent for spell-casting she was bound to benefit from the course.

Gray, too, was pleased, and not only about the classes he and Rehanne shared. Discovering, Developing, and Expanding Talents, taught by Mistress Blake, should be a great help, but the big surprise was that he was assigned to a special course taught by Headmistress herself: The Community of the Gifted—A Special Study.

"Headmistress hardly ever teaches a class," Gray said, staring at the schedule card. "How do you think I got lucky enough to be put in this one?"

Rehanne gave him a sharp look, but his dazed expression assured her he was not being sarcastic. "She's always liked you."

He grinned. "Maybe she considers me her personal challenge."

Rehanne marveled at the change in Gray. His depression and anger yesterday must have been due to being tired after the two-day trip from Mercanton. She spotted Petra and Coral and waved until she caught Petra's eye. They made their way over, pushing through an excited tangle of first-year students.

Coral gave Gray a wary glance. Rehanne felt a smug satisfaction at seeing her friend relax.

"Our schedules are great!" Rehanne announced. "How are yours?"

"Good enough," Petra answered. "I have an advanced class with Aletheia. But I'm also in another dratted Ethics class."

"So are we." Rehanne laughed. "Case Histories?"

Petra nodded glumly.

"Well, the three of us will suffer together. Coral, you escaped it?"

"I got lucky. I have two classes with Mistress Blake and one with Master Hawke. For my fourth class I'm to work in the library and receive special instruction in library administration and methods of research from Mistress Dova." Coral held out her schedule card for Rehanne's inspection.

"Gray and I have that first class with Master Hawke, too," Rehanne said.

Gray grabbed Rehanne's arm, his bruising grip cutting short her enthusiastic comments. Coral's hand dropped to her side; her limp fingers released their hold on the card. Her face registered pain and anger.

"What's wrong?" Rehanne turned from Coral to Gray, addressing them both.

Gray pointed.

In the indicated direction, Rehanne saw Lina and Oryon strolling arm in arm around the rosebushes.

"They were together out here yesterday, too," he said, speaking through clenched teeth. "Are they starting it again?"

"No, Gray, they aren't." Petra's firm tone bordered on anger. "Don't see a conspiracy where none exists. What happened is over. Done with. Oryon is entirely different. You'd know that if you'd only talk with him."

"Yeah, I heard that all last year from Wilce. He could forgive. I can't."

"And it's making you miserable. It's eating you up inside. I dare you to go over right now and talk to Oryon and Lina."

"No."

"You're afraid." Coral's flat statement fell like a gauntlet.

Rehanne held her breath, her gaze fixed on Gray's face. Her friends were forcing the issue, but could there be a better time for it?

Gray released her arm and took a single step toward his two enemies. *Go, Gray,* she urged mentally.

He took another step, and another. He weaved through and around gaggles of first- and second-year students. Petra and Coral flanked Rehanne; she felt their unspoken support while her eyes followed his progress.

He had almost reached Lina and Oryon when Reece came bounding up to him from the opposite direction, stopped him, and spoke, gesticulating excitedly. Unable to hear the conversation, Rehanne could only watch and bite her nails in frustration as Reece kept Gray occupied while Oryon and Lina walked away, encountered Jerrol and Davy, and stood talking to them. Two other conspirators. Gray would never approach all four of them.

"So close," Petra mourned, echoing Rehanne's thought.

"We'll have to look for another chance," Coral said, patting Rehanne's arm.

As if forgetting what he'd intended, Gray accompanied Reece into the building. *Forgetting me, too,* Rehanne thought, blinking back tears.

Gray felt trapped, manipulated. He didn't want to speak to Oryon. Or to Lina. Yet Petra was right: his anger was poisoning his life. He didn't think he could talk it out, but maybe it was worth a try.

His steps slowed as he neared them. He had to force himself to keep moving.

Reece jumped in front of him. Gray drew back, startled; he hadn't seen him coming.

"Have you been back to the room since you left to go to breakfast?" Reece flung the question at him in a breathless flurry of words that Gray needed several seconds to sort out.

"No," he said. "Rehanne and I stayed downstairs talking until the convocation. What's wrong?"

"I went upstairs a few minutes ago. Someone's been in our room. The place is all torn up. Desks turned over, drawers pulled out and thrown on the floor, clothes all over the place. The armoire's been ransacked. I don't know if anything's missing or if it's just vandalism."

"And you thought I did it?"

"Well, I— No, I—I didn't know—"

"Never mind. I want to see it."

Reece spun around and led the way into the building and up the stairs. The living quarters were quiet, deserted. Everyone else was outside, chattering about schedules and enjoying the sunshine. Here it could as easily be night. The dim ceiling bulbs at either end of the corridor did little to dispel the shadows. Shadows that for a moment seemed to shift and twist like ghosts.

The illusion vanished when Reece flung open the door to their room, letting light spill into the hall. Sunlight streamed through the curtainless window, limning the wreckage in golden light.

Reece's excited description hadn't prepared Gray for the devastation. The wooden drawers lay splintered and broken. Bottles were smashed. The room reeked of spilled astringent and after-shave lotion. Clothes were not only scattered across the room; they were ripped and shredded as though a tiger had been loose in the room.

Or a panther.

Lina. Her classmates said she didn't shapechange anymore, but they could be wrong. She might have learned to be more secretive about it.

He walked into the room and picked up a mauled shirt, examined a set of long scratches on the broken desk chair, thrust his hand into parallel slits in his mattress, all the while becoming convinced that only the catgirl could have inflicted the damage.

"We'd better report this to Headmistress, hadn't we?" Reece had followed him into the room and was using his shoe to push the shards of a coffee mug into a pile.

"I suppose so," Gray said. "We'll have to hurry. Any minute now she'll be going to the dining hall for lunch."

"I'll see if she's in her office." Reece picked his way through the debris and left, his rapid footsteps beating a tattoo down the hall.

Gray hoped Reece wouldn't find her in. Reason told him Headmistress had to be informed, but a voice inside him said, *Find Lina and take care of this yourself.*

If he could. Lina might have lost much of her power, but she had more than he did. What could he do—create a sculpture and burst it in her face?

The shards of the mug and bits of glass from broken bottles rose into the air and formed the head of a horned animal, a goatlike creature, but no goat ever conveyed such an impression of evil. Its malignant leer mocked Gray. He willed it to fall, but it hung in place until Headmistress appeared at the door.

It turned slowly, faced her, and burst in a spray of glass slivers and jagged bits of china.

Headmistress raised her hand, the gem of her ring facing outward. None of the sharp projectiles struck her or Reece, who stood behind her; they fell harmlessly to the floor.

Gray was not so lucky. Needles of glass stabbed his face and hands. Incredible pain pierced one eye. Trickles of blood warmed his face.

Headmistress strode across the wreckage, glass crunching beneath her thick-soled shoes. "Hold still," she ordered, clasping his face between her hands.

"My eye," he screamed, letting his mouth fill with the salty taste of blood. He twisted in her grasp, trying to dodge the agony goring his eyeball.

"Hold still!" Headmistress repeated, tightening her grip. "Mr. O'Shannon, get over here and help me hold him."

Gray felt another pair of hands grip his shoulders. He fought. The beast's horn . . . impaling him . . . He had to get away from it.

"I'm here." A soft voice. A light touch. He quieted, stood still, hardly breathing.

Headmistress's fingers moved across his face. They reached his eye. "Easy now."

Something like a knife blade worked its way out of his eye. A red haze clouded his vision. His eye throbbed.

A light pressure beneath his eyeball eased the pain. He blinked several times. His vision cleared. Headmistress bent over him, moving her fingers across his face. Veronica stood beside her, one hand on Gray's arm.

"You can let him go, Mr. O'Shannon," Headmistress said. "Get a wet cloth from the washroom."

Hands released his shoulders. Reece stepped from behind him and sidled past Headmistress and Veronica.

When he was gone, Headmistress said, "That was your work, that beast?"

"I suppose, but I didn't mean to make it—or to break it." He rubbed his cheek. The cuts were healed, but the memory of them stung. "Nothing like that's ever happened before. My stuff has always been harmless. I don't understand what's happening. First this mess," he waved at the shambles throughout the room, "then the sculpture. I mean, there's no connection, but . . ."

"Don't be sure of that," Veronica said. She turned to Headmistress. "You'll not need me anymore, and it's time for lunch. Why don't you take Gray with you, and I'll get to work cleaning this mess."

"Good plan," Headmistress said. "Come along, Mr. Becq."

"Thanks, Veronica," Gray remembered to say as Headmistress led him from the room.

Reece met them at the doorway with the wet cloth, which he handed to Headmistress. She, in turn, handed it to Gray. "Clean the blood off your face and hands," she said. And to Reece, "The lunch bell has rung. Go ahead downstairs. We'll be down shortly. Veronica will clean your room. Do not speak of what has happened."

Reece disappeared down the steps, and Gray scrubbed at his face and hands. Headmistress inspected him and said, "Good. It's all off. How is your eye? Is there any problem with your vision?"

"I can't feel anything. The pain's gone." He closed the eye that had not been injured and tested his sight in the other. It seemed perfectly normal.

Headmistress nodded approvingly. "Excellent. Now, Mr. Becq, I must ask you, also, not to speak of what has happened. I will conduct an investigation. You are to do nothing about the room yourself, and you are to restrain yourself from creating any sculptures. That I must emphasize. Do not attempt to use your power. Is that clear?"

"Very," he said. "But I didn't mean to use it then. That thing formed itself."

"So. We must discuss this further. Report to my office after lunch. Something peculiar is happening, and we must discover what it is."

5

DISCUSSIONS

Gray followed Headmistress into the dining hall. He saw, and acted as though he hadn't seen, the empty chair next to Rehanne. She'd expect him to join her, but if he did, she'd also expect him to explain why he'd gone off with Reece. He'd tell her about the vandalized room; she could keep a confidence. But he'd have to tell her later, not in front of the others at the table—Petra, Coral, and Britnor. Even if Headmistress had not ordered him and Reece to tell no one, he would not have wanted the thing generally known.

He spotted an empty seat at a table near the door and claimed it, though the three fellows already seated there were first-year students. The third-year students rarely mingled with the first, and the young faces stared in awed surprise when Gray joined them.

"I don't bite," he said with a grin, "despite anything you may have heard to the contrary."

Their embarrassed silence confirmed his guess that they'd been warned about his black moods, probably told to avoid him. He recalled ruefully how two years ago, at the beginning of his second year, the new students had turned to him for encouragement and advice. No better time to try to rebuild his shattered reputation.

"I'm Gray Becq," he said. "This is my fourth year here, and I still haven't made third level. I guess you could say I'm an underachiever."

He'd meant it as a joke, but no one laughed. A skinny, pimple-faced lad swallowed nervously, his prominent Adam's apple bobbing up and down like a cork. "I'm Todrick, sir," he said. "And that's Dwayne." He pointed at his short, straw-haired, pink-skinned companion, who seemed too overcome to speak for himself.

Children, Gray thought. *They're no more than children.*

The third, a dark-complexioned youth with short black hair and large ears, leaned forward and said, "Your talent is art, isn't it? Mine is music. I'm Viad."

"Music?" Gray asked, interested. "You mean you use power to produce music?"

Viad nodded. "Like this," he said.

Soft as a whisper, a high, sweet melody like that of an

oboe played in Gray's head. The haunting sound of a violin joined it, then the pure notes of a trombone and the syncopated beat of a drum. The unusual blend produced music unlike anything Gray had ever heard before, chilling, a bit frightening, yet so compellingly beautiful that he felt sad and empty when it ended.

He glanced at Todrick and Dwayne to see whether they were as moved as he. Both were busy piling food onto their plates. "Is the food always this gross?" Dwayne asked around a mouthful of fish filet.

Ignoring the question, Gray turned back to Viad.

The dark eyes met his. "I sent it only to you." He confirmed Gray's guess.

"It was wonderful."

Viad shrugged. "But not very practical. Like your art."

"How did you know—" He broke off the meaningless question. They knew his reputation; they probably knew his whole history. He scowled.

Todrick thrust a bowl into his hands. "You aren't eating, sir."

Sir! They made him feel so old. The bowl held steaming rice. He scooped some onto his plate, accepted the platter of fish offered by Dwayne, and placed a filet on top of the rice. He didn't want the food, but eating gave him an excuse not to speak, and he wanted no more conversation, no talk of impractical, useless talents.

His table companions respected his sudden mood shift. They talked idly among themselves and made no effort to involve him. He left early and waited outside the dining hall, intending to catch Rehanne and take her aside for a private talk before he went to his appointment with Headmistress.

Lina strolled out alone. He couldn't pass up the opportunity; he swung into step beside her. "I want to talk to you," he said. "In private."

* * *

Puzzled and intrigued, Lina followed Gray into the classroom wing and waited while he tried doors until he found one unlocked and the room inside empty. This was not a location she would have chosen for a private chat. Instructors were getting ready for the first day of classes; the unlocked room might mean the instructor would return at any moment, carrying boxes of textbooks or other materials. Though the room was Master Hawke's, and he was, she knew, careless about locking doors.

Inside, Gray whirled to confront her, his face angry, his eyes wild. "You left your cat tracks all over the room," he said. "Do you think I'm stupid?"

Everyone knew how strange Gray had become. He must have gone over the edge. "Gray, I don't have any idea what you're talking about."

"The vandalism. Don't try to deny it," he raved on. "It had to be you. And I want to know why."

"What vandalism? Where? Why do you think I did it?" She edged away from him toward the closed door.

"The vandalism in my room, where else? Cut the innocent act. You were never innocent."

"I'm not putting on any act. I haven't done anything to you or to your room, and I don't understand why you think I would." She was growing angry as well as uneasy, but she tried to sound reasonable, to project calmness.

Her effort failed. He crashed a fist onto the nearest desk. "Who else can shapechange?" he shouted. "Who else would leave claw marks all over the furniture? Who else would rip my clothes to shreds with their teeth?"

"I don't know. But I haven't changed in a year—not since Tria . . ." She didn't finish. He knew about her loss of power.

She didn't think he could know how much she'd regained, and she didn't intend to enlighten him.

"Who else would have any reason to do it?" he persisted.

"What makes you think I have any reason?"

He snorted. "You were involved—I've seen you cozying up to Oryon. It isn't over. You won't let it be over."

"You're the one who won't let it be over, Gray—the only one. Everyone's sorry for what happened. Oryon isn't the same person, but you refuse to believe it."

"And this proves I'm right." He grasped the back of a chair as though ready to pick it up and hurl it at her.

"The only thing it proves is what a fool you are," she snapped, losing her hold on her temper. "You jump to conclusions based on something that happened two years ago and is no longer important to anybody but you."

"Then explain what happened to my room."

She kept an eye on his white-knuckled grip on the chair. "I have no idea what happened. I only know what you've told me, which isn't much. I gather someone got into your room and tore it up. You have a roommate, don't you? Were his things disturbed, too, or only yours? And when did all this take place?"

For the first time a trace of doubt flickered across his face. "It happened this morning. Sometime between breakfast and lunch. Reece found it." He frowned as though trying to remember. "His clothes . . . his bed . . . his desk. Yes, they were scratched and ripped up, too. Everything. The whole room. Like a cat—a panther—got loose in it."

"Between breakfast and lunch I talked to friends, went to the convocation, got my schedule, and stayed out on the patio until lunchtime, talking to Oryon. You saw us."

His anger flared again. "I saw you," he agreed. "Probably congratulating each other on what you'd accomplished. And I saw you with him yesterday on the patio. Plotting. Starting in again. Wanting power, always wanting power."

"If I wanted power, I wouldn't go looking for it from you."

He flinched. That, at least, had hit home. To reinforce the blow she focused on the chair he clutched. It shrank with a suddenness that unbalanced him, nearly toppling him onto the floor. He released his hold and flung out his arms to regain his balance. Lina used her power to lift the chair out of his reach and restore it to its original size.

Gray lunged toward her. "You! I'll—"

"What is happening here?" The sharp voice of Master Hawke came from directly behind her.

She sidestepped Gray's charge and darted behind the instructor, forcing Gray to a skidding halt. Master Hawke raised his heavy cane, held it in front of him as a shield.

"Miss Mueller, why is Mr. Becq pursuing you? He hasn't hurt you, has he?"

"No, sir. You came in just in time." Lina made her voice breathless and injected a note of grateful relief.

Gray snorted. "How could I hurt that she-cat?"

"Mr. Becq believes that I'm persecuting him, sir. He seems to have taken leave of his senses." She backed to the doorway. "I can't convince him that I mean him no harm. Perhaps you could talk to him."

"I shall certainly do so." Master Hawke continued to face Gray.

"I have an appointment with Headmistress, sir," Gray said hurriedly. "Could we have our discussion in her office?"

Lina didn't wait to hear Master Hawke's response. She ducked out of the doorway and sped down the corridor. Master Hawke regarded her kindly; she could convince him later that fear of Gray made her bolt. The last thing she wanted was an encounter with Headmistress.

She needed to find Oryon, to warn him of Gray's crazy suspicions. Maybe he'd have some ideas about who might have done the vandalism. Whoever had done the deed had awkward timing. No one could have known that she had intended to assume her panther form in the next day or so to teach Kress a lesson. Now if she carried out that plan and anyone learned of it, she'd be accused of the damage to Gray's room.

She'd have to change her plan, find another way to extract her talisman from Kress.

But I don't have to confront you as a panther, Mr. Klemmer. I'll pit my power against yours. I'm stronger than I was; a lot stronger than you think I am. You'll see soon enough.

The parlor was hot and stuffy, but Rehanne endured the discomfort because from her selected chair she had a good view of the stairs. Gray hadn't gone upstairs after lunch; she'd come out of the dining hall in time to see him disappear down the corridor to the classroom wing—in company with Lina! It occurred to her that he might have avoided her in the dining hall because of his failure to talk to Lina and Oryon earlier, and that he might be trying to fulfill that obligation before facing her. Rehanne decided to wait in the parlor and watch for Gray and Lina to return.

Shortly after she settled into her chair to keep her vigil, Headmistress went up to her office. Rehanne's anxiety grew when Headmistress came downstairs again, entered the parlor, and cast her long shadow over Rehanne's chair.

"Miss Zalos," she said, "have you seen Mr. Becq since lunch?"

"I—I think he's talking to someone. I'm waiting for him."

Headmistress stared down at her with a frown that made Rehanne feel like a small child caught at some transgression. "If he comes through here, please remind him that he was to report to my office after lunch. Tell him I'm waiting."

She turned and went back upstairs, leaving Rehanne both curious and apprehensive. *But she likes Gray,* Rehanne reminded herself. *She probably only wants to talk to him about the class she's teaching.*

Yet she could not evade the nagging feeling that it was something more, something serious. When Lina emerged alone from the classroom corridor at a near run and ascended the stairs two at a time, Rehanne's apprehension surged. A minute or so later Gray stomped out of the corridor with Master Hawke behind him, brandishing his cane like a guard brandishing a club. Rehanne jumped up, but the angry expressions on the two faces drove her back into her seat. She shrank against the cushions, not wanting Gray to catch her spying.

He never glanced in her direction but headed upstairs with Master Hawke following. Rehanne got up and stood where she could see them enter Headmistress's office.

Gray was in trouble! She could wait until he came out of the office, ask to see him alone, and let him tell her about it. But if he was in one of his dark moods, he might refuse to talk to her, to tell her anything. And if he was in serious trouble, she might not be allowed to see him. Yet he needed her help; she was sure of it.

She had a way to find out what was happening. It wasn't ethical; she could get into serious trouble if she was discovered. But her concern for Gray overrode her scruples.

She sped upstairs to her room, startling Chantal with her precipitate entrance. Ignoring her roommate, she yanked open a dresser drawer and found a candle and a box of matches. From another drawer she took a photograph of Gray and a scarf he'd given her on her birthday last year. And from the top of the dresser she grabbed a nail file. With these items in hand, she raced from the room, letting the door slam behind her.

One room on the women's floor was vacant this year. It was locked, but not warded, and the lock was easily picked with a nail file. Her hands shook as she manipulated the file. She'd already lost precious minutes. She might be too late to learn what she wanted to know.

The lock yielded and she went into the room, closing the door behind her. Hot as it was inside, she didn't take time to open the window. She removed the round mirror from the back of the door, set it on the floor, lit the candle, and dripped enough wax onto the mirror to hold the candle in place in its center. Crumpling the scarf, she set it in front of the candle and propped the photograph against it. Her eyes fixed on the black and white representation of Gray, she repeated in a mage language devised over a hundred years ago the chant that would invoke the spell and allow her to hear whatever Gray heard.

It would have worked better in a darkened room. The candle flame was scarcely visible in the afternoon sunlight streaming through the dusty window. The heat distracted her; sweat streaked her face and arms. But she persisted, and voices, faint and distant, spoke to her out of the flame of the candle.

She strained to hear, to distinguish the individual speakers and capture the thread of the conversation.

The first words she could clearly identify were Headmistress's: "... foolish and hasty act may have serious repercussions."

Gray's voice came through more clearly since he was the focus of the spell. "I didn't really scare her. She put on that act for Master Hawke's benefit. She knows I don't have the power to harm her."

"I understand that Master Hawke's perception of what transpired may be inaccurate. That is unimportant. Because of what he saw, I was forced to explain to him about the vandalism and its peculiar nature. I could not ask him to leave without first enlightening him. Although I told him as little as possible, it will have been enough to awaken his suspicions."

"He won't suspect Lina. She has him hoodwinked. He can't accept—"

Headmistress's voice cut across Gray's complaint. "No, *you* can't accept the possibility that Miss Mueller told the truth when she denied all knowledge of the incident."

"The evidence is clear." Gray's tone assumed its sullen, stubborn mode.

"I read the evidence differently." Headmistress's voice was uncharacteristically soft; Rehanne could scarcely catch the words. "Recall, please, the sculpture you said formed itself. Did you not recognize it?"

"No! I never saw anything like that before."

"Oh? I thought perhaps you had—while you . . . evil."

Rehanne lost several words, but she had little difficulty supplying their meaning. Headmistress must have referred to the time Gray had spent as a captive of the Dire Women. Gray's groan and low denial confirmed it.

"It was a demon spawned by the Dire Women who held you prisoner. I fear that . . ." Again Headmistress spoke so low Rehanne could not catch the words, though she leaned so close to the candle flame that its heat burned her ear.

"No!" Gray's shout jerked her back, away from the flame. "It couldn't . . . I didn't . . . You think I did it myself? How could I? I never went back to my room. I was with Rehanne from before breakfast until Reece came and told me what had happened."

Stunned, Rehanne tried desperately to hear Headmistress's answer, but the spell wavered, garbling the sound. Rehanne tried to recapture it, but her dismay had broken her concentration, and the spell faded.

Gray, she moaned. *Gray, why are you lying? What have you done?*

A sound behind her roused her from her worried thoughts. Quickly she blew out the candle and turned around. The door latch turned; the door slowly swung open.

6

MEETINGS

Gray sat in stunned silence, trying to comprehend what Headmistress was telling him. That a demon might be using him—using his art—to gain entrance to the school, to take revenge on those responsible for robbing the Dire Women of their prey. It wasn't possible—was it?

He could not dismiss the eerie way his last sculpture had created itself. Headmistress had suggested that he might have seen the demon while he had been under the control of the Dire Women. He remembered nothing of the sort, but his memory of that time was dim and clouded. Headmistress thought he could have repressed the memory until, under the stress of discovering the vandalism, it broke out, and his subconscious mind directed the sculpting.

That would not explain the way the sculpture had burst apart. None of his works had done that before. They simply surrendered to gravity as his power failed. The hideous goat head had exploded from within as though a malignant force had broken out of it.

"I've suspected for some time that you had unwittingly brought an evil back with you from that accursed dimension," Headmistress said, breaking the long silence. "I had hoped to be able to protect you until the thing manifested and could be exorcised. Unfortunately, it manifested in such a way that a simple exorcism will no longer be effective."

"Why?" His effort to understand was bringing on a nagging headache.

"When the sculpture burst, it set the demon free to roam at will and opened a way for others of its kind to follow. They may appear in many guises, and it may prove impossible to find and exorcise them all."

"But I'm free of the demon—it's left me?"

Headmistress sighed and clasped her hands together. "It may have left you, but I fear . . . the sliver of glass that pierced your eye could have let that demon—or another of its kind—reenter. I healed the damage to your eye, but I could not trace and expel the evil that might have spread from the wound."

Pain throbbed through his head like a caged beast. "But do you know—?"

"I suspect. It is a strong suspicion. But I am not certain. You will know better than I."

He didn't know. He stood, tried to pace, but the cramped office would not permit it. He circled behind his chair and leaned on the high wooden back. "If I *do* have this thing, one of these things, can't you get it out?"

She sighed. "I could, but doing so would not affect any others, and it or they might well return to you. No, we must find a way of ridding ourselves of the entire threat."

"How?" He gripped the chair and stared across the desk, trying to distinguish her expression in the dim light.

"I've already used a divination spell to learn the name of the demon you sculpted. It bears the hideous name of Gruefell. I shall endeavor to learn those of its companions as well. Knowing the names allows some measure of power over them. Then I plan to find a way to drive it back to the

Dire Realms. It is possible that, as you were the conduit for its coming here, you can be its means of exit. It may be possible to gather it and its brethren and channel them all back through you to the place they came from, after which we could close the gate."

He moaned and rested his head on his hands. She was saying that he had to let himself be the passage for a whole flock of demons. He could not! He'd already been through enough. Let someone else—

"No one else can do it, Gray," she said softly.

He needed to sit down. He was going to be sick. His head . . .

She was at his side, helping him into the chair. Her palm on his forehead eased the pain.

"I can't," he said. "I can't do it. You know how little power I have."

"I knew someone once who thought he had no power at all," she said softly. "You remind me of him. And like him, you have much more power than you think. But I will not force you to do this. It must be your own decision."

The sadness in her voice drew Gray out of his own misery, made him look up at her. Tears coursed down her cheeks. "Go," she said. "Do not speak of this. But if you decide to try my plan, come back to me."

She pulled him to his feet, steered him out of the office, and drew the door closed behind him. Dazed and shaken, he wandered to his room.

It was clean, all traces of the devastation vanished. The claw marks had disappeared from the furniture; his blanket, sheets, and mattress were whole again. He looked inside the chifforobe. His clothes, undamaged, hung neatly on hangers. His dresser drawers held tidy stacks of handkerchiefs, scarves, and underwear. Reece's things had likewise been restored. Only the bottled lotions and the mug were missing, their absence assuring him that the whole thing had been more than a vivid nightmare.

Rehanne stared at the opening door. She had nowhere to hide, nothing to do but wait and confront whoever it was.

The door swung wide, revealing the gaping doorway and the empty hall beyond it. Visible evidence to the contrary, the certainty settled over her that she was no longer alone. Chills crawled up and down her arms and back.

"Who's here?"

No one answered her whispered question. But she sensed someone—some presence—observing her. She jumped to her feet, poised to run, but her conviction that the unseen intruder was between her and the door paralyzed her limbs.

"Go!" She reinforced the spoken word with a strong mental command. A jolt shook her as her questing power encountered the unmistakable touch of another human mind.

She threw the full force of her coercive and suppressive talents into the instructions, *Leave this room! Forget that you came here. Forget that you saw me!*

The presence retreated. Rehanne relaxed. She was alone again.

It always made her feel guilty to use her talent for mental coercion and thought suppression. She considered spell-casting her major, more valuable talent. But she had misused it for this eavesdropping; someone had caught her at it, and she had felt forced to use coercion—all because she was troubled about Gray. And now she was more troubled than ever.

She gathered up her spell materials, cleaned the wax off the mirror, and replaced it on its hook on the back of the door. Quietly she eased into the hall and hurried to her own room.

Chantal sat at her desk scrawling lines on a piece of stationery. She didn't look up, and Rehanne, relieved not to be greeted with awkward questions, said nothing as she put away the candle, scarf, and photograph. That done, she left the room without exchanging a word with Chantal and headed downstairs in the hope of finding Gray.

He might still be in Headmistress's office. She hoped he was; she could watch the office door and not miss him when he came out. She couldn't let him know what she'd done, but she'd persuade him to tell her what he and Headmistress had talked about. If he resisted, she might, this once, resort to coercion. She had to know; otherwise, how could she help him?

Headmistress's door was closed. That told Rehanne nothing. She could only hope she hadn't missed Gray. From the parlor she wouldn't be able to see the office door, so she dusted a step halfway down and sat on it, scrunching against the wall to allow people room to pass. Not many did; most students were either in their rooms or outside enjoying their last free afternoon before the start of classes. So when a sobbing first-year student stumbled past her, Rehanne felt obliged to follow her down the stairs and offer consolation.

The girl went into the parlor and sank onto the sofa. Rehanne sat beside her and placed her arm around the shaking shoulders, dismissing the thought that she could not see the stairs. "What's wrong? Can I help?"

Brushing aside the long straight hair that had fallen in front of her face, the girl peered at Rehanne through red and swollen eyes.

"I'm Rehanne Zalos. I'm third-year," Rehanne said encouragingly. "If it's homesickness—"

A shake of her head sent the long hair tumbling back in front of her eyes. Rehanne waited while the girl regarded her uncertainly through the curtain of hair. *Get on with it,* she thought, trying not to let her impatience show. *You'll make me miss Gray.*

The young woman would not be hurried. Fresh streams of tears poured from her eyes. She dabbed at them with her hair, wiped her nose with the back of her hand, and, finally, said, "I'm Maridel," as though the name explained everything.

"And—?" Rehanne prompted.

The hair was again pressed into service as a towel. "I'm sorry," Maridel said, sniffling. "It's Moonbeam."

"Moonbeam?" Rehanne wondered if the girl were mad.

"My cat." The nonexplanation was followed by more sobs.

Rehanne looked despairingly toward the parlor door. She should never have allowed herself to be trapped like this. "What about your cat?" she asked.

"He's gone." Now the words poured out. "I brought him with me. I smuggled him into my room in my luggage. I have to have him, you see. I can't work my magic without him. And he's a good kitten, truly. He's quiet and doesn't mess on the floor or scratch the furniture or bother anybody. I keep his litter box under my bed and change it twice a day. Debra, my roommate, said it was all right, she wouldn't tell anybody, and she'd be real careful not to let Moonbeam out. But he's gone, and I can't find him anywhere."

By the seven levels! This poor, ignorant girl had really thought she could keep the presence of a cat a secret in a school for the magically gifted!

If the cat got out, it would not be bound by the illusion that gave the school its apparent structure. As a third-level student, Rehanne could catch occasional glimpses of the vast salons and long corridors stretching into other dimensions. The cat could find and explore them all. It might have chased a mouse into another universe.

She did not tell Maridel that. "You'll have to tell Headmistress about the cat and ask for her help in finding it," she said. "Come on. I'll take you to her office and help you explain." Thus provided with an excuse to knock at Headmistress's door, she could discover whether Gray was still in the office.

"Headmistress!" Maridel's horrified expression showed clearly what she thought of the suggestion.

But Rehanne was firm. "Don't think she doesn't already know about Moonbeam. She knows everything that goes on. You couldn't possibly have a cat here without her knowledge. So you're better off confessing it. Trust me, she can find it for you more easily than anyone else can."

Rehanne coaxed Maridel onto her feet and half led, half dragged her to the stairs and up them to Headmistress's office door.

Rehanne knocked while Maridel stood to one side looking terrified. The door opened, and Rehanne quickly glanced past Headmistress. Gray was not inside. She'd missed him.

"Headmistress, Maridel has a problem I thought she should discuss with you," Rehanne said, grabbing the girl's wrist so she couldn't flee. "Would it be convenient for her to see you?"

From her incredible height Headmistress peered down at Rehanne, her thin lips curved in an amused and knowing smile, her gaze exploring Rehanne's soul.

"I will be happy to see her, but I cannot help her find the cat. Had she not concealed the animal's presence, I would have provided a means of keeping it safe. Now its fate rests on her shoulders."

Those shoulders slumped, and Maridel tugged against Rehanne's grip, but Rehanne held tight. "Go in," she told the frightened girl. She steered her toward Headmistress, who stood aside to allow her to pass. Like a cornered animal, Maridel darted inside.

Summoning her courage, Rehanne asked quickly, "Headmistress, I also wanted to ask you if you've seen Gray. He said he had an appointment with you. I wonder if you know where he went afterward."

"I cannot tell you where he went when he left here," she

answered. "I would suggest you *not* try to find him. He needs to be alone, to think things over. You cannot make his decisions for him, Miss Zalos. Your concern is commendable but uninformed. You may be pitting yourself against forces far too strong for you."

"Well, if they're too strong for me, how can Gray hope to contend with them?" Rehanne argued, heedless of Headmistress's stern demeanor. "He's almost powerless."

"If he were powerless, he would not be here at Simonton School," Headmistress retorted. "You lack the talent for assessing levels of power. I would suggest you not attempt to solve problems the nature of which you do not understand. You did well in bringing Maridel Denham to me. You were right in recognizing that you could not deal with her problem. Recognize that Mr. Becq's problem, which is far more serious than Miss Denham's, is also best left in stronger and wiser hands than yours."

Headmistress stepped back into her office and shut the door, leaving Rehanne staring in stunned consternation at the closed door.

Lina waited in the shadowy library corridor where Oryon had agreed to meet her after the evening meal. The library was closed; it would open tomorrow when classes began. Tonight no one should have a reason to visit this area. But Lina arranged that anyone who did happen to wander into the dark hall would be seized with a feeling of dread and would flee from the haunted place, never noticing the two black-clad figures hidden in the gloom.

She had begun to adopt Oryon's custom of dressing entirely in black. Tonight she wore a calf-length black cotton skirt and a blouse of soft black silk that molded itself around her breasts. Black jet earrings dangled from her ears.

Oryon was late, and when he arrived she sensed his anger

before he spoke. "Something's wrong?" She placed her hand on his black-sleeved arm.

"I can't find my wand. It isn't where I left it. It's not in the room, and Troy swears he hasn't seen it."

"Like my talisman," she said. "Except that anyone with any talent can use the talisman, but who else could use your wand? Could Kress?"

"I don't think so. It's attuned to my power. Someone would have to be able to erase my pattern from it and imprint his own. I don't think Kress knows how to do that. I don't know anyone who does."

"Oryon, something very odd is going on." She slid her hand along his arm. "I haven't had a chance to tell you about Gray."

"What about Gray?" He stepped back, shaking off her hand, clearly in no mood to think about anything but the business for which they'd met. He probably hadn't noticed the silk blouse, the glittering earrings, the expensive perfume.

Dropping her coquettish pose, she described her encounter with Gray, trying to recall every detail and give Oryon an accurate rendering of the whole conversation. Only when she finished did she again move near him and slip her arms around his waist.

"He really did frighten me." She rested her head against Oryon's chest. "Not physically. I knew I could protect myself if he got violent. But I'm not used to dealing with a madman, and that's what he acted like. I was afraid that I might say or do something that would push him over the edge. I didn't want to be responsible—"

"Lina." He tipped her face toward his and shook his head. "Don't do this. You weren't afraid. Why don't you tell me what you want of me and be done with it?"

She pushed away from him with a rueful laugh. "You're

too stubborn, Oryon Brew. Why can't I ever catch you with your defenses down any more?"

He laughed, too. "Because I know you too well, Lina Mueller."

No point in being evasive. "Are you willing to help me do something about Kress?"

"I would be if I were as sure as you are that Kress is guilty."

"Who else could it be? Who else hates us the way he does?"

"Gray."

He was being deliberately maddening tonight. "Gray doesn't have the power."

"Kress doesn't have the imagination. Not to damage Gray's room and frame you for it. That's too indirect for him. I can see him stealing your talisman if he needed it badly for some reason. I could see him stealing my wand if he *hadn't* first stolen your talisman. But to steal from both of us, and in such a way that we'd be certain to suspect him—I don't think he'd have the nerve. He hasn't gotten all his power back either, you know."

"He can draw power."

"So can you."

"If I can find someone willing to let me. He won't have any trouble finding a first- or second-year girl he can charm into lending him power. That's probably exactly what he's already done. That silly Chantal—"

He laughed and ran a finger along her cheek. "And of course you have no charm at all, do you?"

"But I haven't—" she began indignantly.

"But you will if you can." He grasped her shoulders, dug his fingers into her flesh. "Listen to me, Lina. Don't act in haste—or in anger. We can find subtle ways of putting pressure on Kress. Ways that will show us whether he's guilty of anything worse than stupidity. Don't risk all you've gained in a rash act of misdirected revenge."

She squirmed free of his hold and rubbed her shoulders. She'd have bruises where his fingers had pressed. "What do you suggest?" She clipped the words, filled them with scorn.

He ignored the hostile tone. "I'm wondering what use someone could make of your talisman and my wand. And whether anything else has been stolen. Do we know anyone else who has any kind of magical aid?"

Lina thought. "Rehanne has some stuff she uses for spells. Candles and things like that. Oh, and Vanita has a fire jewel she centers on when she speaks with the dead."

"And Kelby has a specially carved stick he uses for water finding," Oryon said. "I'd like to know if it or Vanita's jewel or anything else is missing."

"I'll ask Vanita, and you can ask Kelby. I haven't heard anyone say they've lost anything. Except for Chantal. She's been bleating about losing a diamond earring—only one, mind you, but she's sure it was stolen. I suppose by a one-eared thief."

"Still, it's another missing item."

"Nothing mysterious about it: women lose earrings all the time. I've ruined dozens of pairs. One comes unfastened and falls off somewhere, and you don't notice it and never see it again."

Oryon halted her digression with a wave of his hand. "We need to find out if Gray or Reece have anything missing."

"You can talk to Gray. I'm staying away from him. I don't see how Rehanne puts up with him."

"I'd be the last person he'd tell anything. But I'll see what I can learn from Reece."

Lina was growing impatient. "Fine. When are we going to do what we came here for?"

He regarded her thoughtfully. "I wonder if we should. Maybe we have enough power for now."

"How can you say that? We haven't regained all we lost. I think we've reached third level, but Headmistress hasn't confirmed it."

"She wouldn't. I'm sure we're back at third level."

"And are you satisfied with that? Is that enough?"

Slowly he shook his head. "No. I've never been satisfied. I've always wanted more, no matter how much I had. That's what got me into trouble."

"But you're wiser. You won't make that same mistake again."

"Not that *same* mistake. But can I be sure I won't make another, even worse? How can you be sure you won't abuse your power again? This business of going after Kress—"

"That's what's bothering you? Look, I promise I won't do anything to Kress that he doesn't deserve. And I won't involve you." She reached out and caught his hands. "Come on, we gained so much when we did this last year. Why shouldn't we do it again?"

She fixed her gaze on his face, the dim light no barrier to her catlike vision. His frowning features reflected the struggle with his conscience. They softened as he yielded. "This once more," he said. "After this I think we'd better give it a rest for a while."

"If that's what you think best," she said meekly.

Fingers entwined, gazes locked, they stood facing each other. Lina summoned her power, cast it into the space between them, where, confined by their interlocked hands, it met and joined with the power he sent out. The combined powers swirled and mingled within that magic circle and grew, feeding on each other. The air between them crackled. Their hair stood on end; ripples of fire played up and down their arms.

"Now!" Lina said, and breathed deeply, as simultaneously they called back their power. Hers flowed into her like liquid flame, coursed through her, infusing her with energy, with a restless desire to test her strength.

"That was the best we've managed," she said with a triumphant grin.

Oryon's skin glowed; his eyes sparkled. His grin answered hers. "I'd forgotten how good it felt." He released her hands. "I'm going to search for my wand."

He melted into the darkness. Lina waited several minutes to be sure he was gone, then let her body flow into the lean, lithe panther form. She stretched and bounded off, padded paws making scarcely a sound as they streaked through the dark hall.

It would feel good to hunt again.

7

Night of Blood

Rehanne needed something to take her mind off Gray. She hadn't seen him all afternoon, and he hadn't come to the dining hall for supper. After supper she'd roamed around downstairs for a while, had gone to her room and made sure the clothes she'd wear to classes tomorrow were pressed and ready, her shoes polished, and her notebooks and pencil case set out on the desk. She'd hoped those preparations would make her more excited about beginning her new classes. But her anxiety about Gray crowded out the enthusiasm she should feel.

Chantal came in and looked startled to see Rehanne. "I thought you'd be somewhere with Gray," she said.

It was not what Rehanne wanted to hear. "I haven't seen him since noon," she said shortly.

"You haven't had a fight, have you?"

Rehanne wasn't fooled by the solicitous tone; her roommate was eager for gossip. "No, we haven't. We each had other things to do, that's all."

"Really? I just saw Gray in the parlor, and he wasn't doing anything but sitting there looking miserable. You sure he's not waiting for you?"

"We hadn't made any arrangements to meet," Rehanne said, frowning. She couldn't avoid the suspicion that Chantal wanted to get rid of her. She shouldn't go, shouldn't give the girl the satisfaction of seeing her ploy succeed.

But she did desperately want to see Gray. And if he was waiting downstairs, hoping to see her . . .

"I'll go check," she said, heading for the door. "He might have thought I said I'd meet him. He does get things mixed up sometimes."

She left with the resolve to take a quick look. If she found Gray, she'd speak to him only long enough to arrange to meet for breakfast. She wouldn't pry and she wouldn't disregard Headmistress's advice. She'd satisfy herself that he was all right, nothing more.

On her way downstairs she met Veronica coming up carrying a suitcase. "Ah, Miss Zalos," she said, blocking Rehanne's descent. "How lucky to find you. Giselle Dorr arrived on the evening bus and needs help getting settled. She'll be rooming with Miss Mueller, but Miss Mueller isn't in her room, and no one seems to know where she is.

"Miss Dorr has gone through a bad time. Her brother was killed in a riding accident, and she's had to stay on after the funeral and help her mother dispose of the boy's things.

She's hardly over the shock, and it won't be easy getting here so late and having to start classes first thing in the morning. If you could make her feel welcome and help her put away her things, I'm sure she'd be grateful to you."

Why me? Rehanne thought, and immediately reproved herself. *I shouldn't be seeing Gray anyway. This will keep my mind off him.* "I'll be glad to do what I can," she said, and turned back up the stairs.

Giselle was a second-year student. Rehanne had not known her well last year, but she recalled her appearance: slender and tan, with the sun-bleached hair and supple grace of someone who spends a great deal of time outside. She loved horses, Rehanne remembered, and talked a lot about riding. Her folks owned a ranch in Wide Sands Province in western Arucadi, somewhere near the city of Marquez. She had a way with animals; one of her talents was the ability to communicate with them. She had other talents as well, but Rehanne couldn't recall what they were.

Veronica pushed past her and entered the room. She carried the suitcase inside and announced, "I've brought someone to see you, Miss Dorr."

Giselle came forward, hesitated only a moment before throwing her arms around Rehanne and giving her a big hug. "Rehanne! I'm so glad you're here!"

Rehanne noted the deep shadows under the girl's eyes, the pallor beneath the tan.

"I'll leave you ladies," Veronica announced. "You'll have a lot of news to catch up on."

When Veronica was gone, Giselle said, "I'm so relieved to see you. I was dreading having to face Lina first thing. I didn't expect to be rooming with *her*. I thought I'd be with another second-year student."

"All four of us third-year women have second-year roommates," Rehanne said. "I don't know why. Some of the third-year fellows are rooming together, so it's not some new policy of Headmistress's."

Giselle looked around at the green curtains, the green satin bedspreads, the green-and-gold plush carpet. "Lina's got the room fixed up to suit herself. It's pretty, but I'm afraid I'll never feel at home here. I wish I could have come early and had a say in the decorating. But I had to help Mom—" She broke off and sat down on a bed, head bowed, hands in her lap.

Rehanne sat beside her. "Veronica told me about your brother. I'm sorry. Would it help to talk about it?"

"I think it might," Giselle answered in a low voice. "My brother Damon was two years younger than I. We were very close."

Rehanne listened as Giselle spoke haltingly of the adored brother, their rides together around the ranch, the mischief they'd gotten into as children, the trouble they'd often caused their parents.

Rehanne let her talk and then helped her unpack and arrange her things so that the room no longer looked exclusively Lina's. It was late when they finished, but Lina hadn't returned. Sensing that Giselle did not want to be left alone, Rehanne offered to stay until Lina came in.

"I can't imagine where she is," Rehanne said. "I wonder if she could have gotten caught downstairs after the stairs were warded."

"Not a good way to start the school year," Giselle said. She shuddered. "So much seems wrong. Is it just me? When I stepped off the bus and looked at the school, I saw it bathed in a dark brown aura. I could hardly force myself to walk inside."

Rehanne remembered that reading auras was another of Giselle's talents. "It's not you," she said. "The trouble's come back. You weren't here when it happened before, in my first year, but things have the same feel they had then." Glad to have a sympathetic listener, she told Giselle of her worry about Gray, though she omitted what she had learned from her eavesdropping spell. The late hour, the quiet, the bond of sadness made it easy to share confidences. She confessed her dislike for Chantal and her fear of using her coercive talent.

"But if you really need it, you must use it," Giselle counseled. "You have it for a reason, and—"

Screams tore through the night. A male voice, from a room on the floor below, cried out in pain and terror.

Giselle clutched Rehanne, clung to her, shaking. "That's the way my brother shouted when he fell—when the horse dragged him. I couldn't get to him. He kept screaming, and I couldn't help him. By the time I reached him, he was dead."

Rehanne held her tight. The screams faded, replaced by sounds of running feet, shouts, doors opening and closing.

"We have to find out what's happening," Giselle said, pulling free of Rehanne's embrace. "Maybe we can help."

They ran into the hall and found most of the other girls gathered in a knot at the head of the stairs. The wards blocked them from descending.

Another agonized scream rang out from below, followed by ominous silence. Finally, a male voice shouted, "Get a healer," and another called out, "Find Headmistress."

Giselle pushed her way to the front of the crowd, and Rehanne followed in her wake. "We've got to break the wards," Giselle gasped, hurling herself against the invisible net of power.

If she had time, if so much confusion weren't boiling around her, Rehanne could possibly have found a spell to break the wards. Lina had a talisman, Rehanne remembered. But that didn't help; Lina wasn't here. Who else . . . ?

A black-clad figure appeared at the foot of the stairs. "Anyone up there a healer?" he called.

Oryon. He used to be able to break wards. Maybe he could now.

"I can heal, a little," Giselle called down.

The claim surprised Rehanne; Giselle had never mentioned having the healing talent. She wasn't sure the distraught girl was telling the truth. But she shouted, "Break the wards, Oryon. Let us come down."

"I'll try." He pointed a finger at the stairs.

A hush fell over the knot of women. Rehanne kept silent with the rest, suppressing the question that fought to be shouted out: *Was it Gray who'd screamed?*

Rehanne's tight hold on Giselle's arm kept Giselle from tumbling down the steps when the wards suddenly dissolved. Rehanne kept her hold as Giselle vaulted down the stairs. She heard others start down after them, heard them stop when Headmistress appeared, pushing Oryon aside and glaring up at them. "Go back. All of you. Go to your rooms," she said.

Giselle didn't slow. Rehanne stayed with her as they bolted past Headmistress. Oryon fell into step beside them. "Third room on the right," he said. "It's Kress."

"Kress!" She released her hold on Giselle. "What happened?"

He didn't meet her eyes. "I don't know," he said. "Something's ripped him up."

"Ripped!" She went on to the indicated door. Giselle had already shoved through the crowd of fellows inside, but Rehanne was blocked by them until Oryon said, "Get out, everybody. Headmistress is on her way."

Most of them had been in bed. They were wearing pajamas, robes, or undershorts. They were unnaturally quiet and solemn, frightened. Rehanne saw Reece, Gray's roommate, but not Gray.

Headmistress came up behind Rehanne. "Miss Zalos, you have no right to be on this floor at this hour."

"I—I had to see," Rehanne said, standing firm as the boys slipped out around her.

"Very well, see." Headmistress pushed her into the room.

A retching sound drew her attention to the corner of the room, where Fenton, Kress's roommate, was being noisily sick.

"He's alive." Giselle's shaky comment drew Rehanne's attention to the bed.

Kress lay on a blood-soaked sheet, the second sheet covering his lower body not hiding his ripped-open stomach, the intestines snaking out of his gaping flesh. His breath came in ragged gasps. The stench of blood and feces filled the room. Giselle knelt beside the bed, her hand on his forehead. She looked up at Headmistress, eyes filled with tears. "I couldn't save my brother. I need to save this one, but I can't. My talent isn't strong enough. I feel him slipping away."

"No healer can save everyone, no matter how great their talent." Headmistress's voice was gentle. "I doubt that even mine is great enough to save him." She turned her head. "Mr. Brew, Miss Zalos, find Veronica. Quickly."

Oryon whirled around and raced from the room. Rehanne couldn't move, couldn't drag her gaze from the terrible wounds that were draining Kress's life from him. "Who—what did this?" she whispered.

"I don't know." Headmistress pronounced each word with deliberate emphasis.

She had to know. She knew everything. She had known about Maridel's cat. She—

"Since Mr. Brew went on the errand I gave you both, you might at least see to Mr. Rhoze."

Fenton! She'd forgotten about him. Rehanne looked around. He'd finished being sick and was leaning weakly against the wall. She hurried to him and pushed him into a chair. "You aren't hurt, are you?" she asked.

He shook his head.

"Were you here? Did you see what happened?"

"I was asleep. Woke up when he screamed. Couldn't see. Too dark. But those screams!" He put his trembling hands over his ears. "I still hear them."

"But you didn't see anything?" Rehanne persisted.

"I got up, tried to find the light. Something big jumped past me. Dark. Hot. Went out through the window."

"You must have seen it then."

He shook his head and groaned. "Happened too fast. Just a blur. Could have been a big cat. I don't know. I got the light on. Saw Kress." He retched again.

Rehanne steadied him, letting her power touch him, suppressing the horror.

Veronica hurried in, followed by her young assistant and by Oryon. Veronica and her assistant hurried to the bedside, but Oryon stopped beside Fenton. "Come on," he said. "You need to get out of here." He lifted Fenton to his feet, supported him, and guided him to the door.

Rehanne followed. "Why are the maids here?" she asked Oryon as they reached the hall. "They aren't healers, are they?"

"They're more than what they seem. You ought to know that by now." His sharp, impatient answer discouraged further questions.

She stood outside Kress's door and watched Oryon lead Fenton toward Davy and Jerrol, who were standing in a doorway two rooms away. They all disappeared into the room. Other boys loitered in the hall or in doorways, looking stunned, confused. She spotted Reece and hurried toward him. He had a dark blue bathrobe pulled around him; his hair was mussed as though he'd been sleeping.

"Where's Gray?" she asked. "Is he in your room?"

"I haven't seen him all evening," he said.

Fear clamped itself around her heart.

"Look, I'm sure he's all right. You should go upstairs."

Reece's nervous tone made her remember the late hour. She didn't belong on the boys' floor in the middle of the night. But she had to find Gray.

She nodded and walked to the stairs, eyes straight ahead except for a quick glance at Kress's room as she passed it. The door was shut.

She despised Kress; she remembered too well his part in Gray's abduction. She'd never understood why he'd been allowed to stay at the school. He hadn't changed as Oryon had. He was arrogant and self-centered, full of his own importance. But to be torn open—no, she wouldn't have wished that on him.

She reached the stairs, lifted one foot to the first step. The stairs were empty, yet she experienced the same sense of a presence as she had felt in the vacant room. Grasped by a sudden revulsion, she retreated, went downstairs instead.

Beyond the stairs, the first floor lay dark. She groped her way to the parlor door, stepped inside, and peered into the blackness. "Gray?"

"Rehanne?" The low voice answered her tentative call.

She rushed forward blindly, stumbled against an end table. "Gray, where are you?"

"Over here. In the big chair near the fireplace."

Guided by the sound of his voice, she shuffled through the darkness.

She bumped up against the chair, found his hand on the armrest, and clasped it. His hand was wet, his fingers slippery as they interlaced with hers.

She knelt beside the chair. "Where have you been? I've been so worried."

"I've been right here. Thinking." His dispirited monotone made her ache for him. "I guess I fell asleep. What time is it?"

"I don't know. Late. You didn't sleep through all the screaming, did you?"

"Screams?" His fingers tightened around hers. "The screams were real? I thought—I had a nightmare. I thought the screams were part of it."

She shook her head, though he wouldn't see the gesture in the dark. "It was Kress. Something got into his room while he and Fenton were sleeping and . . . and ripped him open. They're not sure they can save him."

She heard his sharp intake of breath. That was all. She willed him to say something, to reassure her, to drive away her doubt.

Doubt. His silence nurtured it, let it grow large. The overheard conversation replayed in her mind. She couldn't bear it. She had to get the thing out in the open where they could talk it through.

"Lina." Gray spoke the name into the stillness as though it answered everything.

Did it?

"Lina," he repeated. "Reece found our room vandalized today. Our clothes, our sheets and blankets ripped to shreds. Claw marks all over the furniture. I didn't get a chance to tell you. It was done this morning. Now this. Lina. In her panther form. It *has* to be."

"Why?"

He tore his hand free of hers and exploded to his feet. "*Why?* You know her—what she is—and you ask why?"

She stood, clutched his arm. "Calm down, Gray. Listen. You may be right. But I saw Kress. What was done—I don't think Lina would—"

"You don't think! You think Lina cares what she does when she's changed herself into a panther?"

"Shhh. Stop shouting. Calm yourself, please." As she spoke the words, she sent her power into his mind to spread a blanket of calm over his rage, to quell his—fear? Yes, her questing power felt it clearly, the terror that hid behind the violent temper. She sent reassurance, peace.

This was the third time today she'd used her talent—the one she'd sworn *not* to use. But she had to ease his pain, make him able to listen to reason. She increased the force that was dampening his emotions, pushed it deeper.

Her power boomeranged, slammed into her own mind with sledgehammer force, toppling her.

Thought returned. The thick upholstery of the parlor chair supported her back and head. Gray bent over her, his breath warm on her face as he called her name.

"Rehanne. Rehanne, what happened? Can you hear me? Rehanne?"

Her head hurt. Persuading her tongue to move, to form words brought pain. But she persisted. "I'm awake." She drew in a breath, tried again. "I'm sorry. I only meant to help."

"What do you mean? What are you talking about?"

He didn't know. He hadn't consciously felt her probe. He hadn't deliberately hurt her.

He couldn't. He didn't have the power. He hadn't felt her intrusion. Something else, something within him had hurled her out.

She took deep breaths. The pain eased. She reached out, placed her hand on his chest. "Gray, we have to talk."

"I'm listening."

"You were so angry. I used my power to suppress the angry thoughts. And something grabbed my power and slammed me with it."

"What do you mean, *something*?" Fear permeated his words.

"I don't know. Your power or—or something else."

He drew away from her. His voice shook. "Headmistress said I'd brought something—a demon—from the place the Dire Women kept me. She thinks it did the damage in my room. But it couldn't have. I never went back to the room after breakfast. You know that."

"Gray, I *don't* know it."

"But we were together all morning."

She struggled to her feet, not sure how he would react. But the truth had to be spoken. "We separated after breakfast. Don't you remember? I went back to my room. I thought you went to yours. We met at the foot of the stairs to go to the convocation."

"We stayed together." His tortured whisper made her wish she could see his face. "I remember . . ."

She found him, held him. He sagged against her. "We were apart about an hour, Gray. I'm sorry."

"What happened to that hour? Why can't I remember it?"

Hugging him to her, she said, "I wish I knew."

He broke free of her grasp, backed away. "You think I did . . . those things?"

"No, Gray, I don't think anything. It wouldn't have been you, anyway. It would have been the demon. But I don't know it was that. I don't know anything."

"Well, *I* know. I didn't do anything. And I can't make anyone believe it."

He blundered toward the stairs. She followed. "Gray," she pleaded.

He didn't stop. When he found the steps, he pounded up them and into the boys' hall. She started after him. A warding net stopped her. A single dim bulb provided enough light to let her watch him stomp to his room and disappear inside.

Sighing, she climbed the stairs to her floor. The hall was quiet, all doors closed. It must be terribly late.

She tiptoed down the hall. A crack of light shone from beneath Lina's door. Giselle must have returned. She could get news of Kress.

She tapped lightly on the door, waited, was about to turn away when it swung open.

"What is it?" Lina glared out at her. She was fully dressed in black skirt and clinging black blouse.

Rehanne felt foolish and a little afraid. "I was looking for Giselle. I thought—"

"She isn't here."

"I'm sorry I bothered you. I wanted to find out about Kress. I suppose you know what happened."

"I heard." The short reply held no concern, only impatience.

Rehanne stepped back with another mumbled apology. She glanced past Lina into the lighted room. Its green curtains blew in the breeze, letting her see what looked like a long smear of blood on the windowsill.

Lina shut the door, and Rehanne walked on to her own room. *Gray was right. I should have listened to him. It was Lina. It must have been.*

She put her hand on the knob and eased the door open, looking down as she did so.

Her fingers were stained with blood.

It might have come from something she'd touched in Kress's room. Or—she remembered the moisture she'd felt on Gray's hand. Could that have been blood?

She heard the squeak of bedsprings as she tiptoed into the dark room. Chantal's sleepy voice said, "Rehanne?"

"Yes. Sorry I woke you." But since she was awake, she surely wouldn't mind some light. Rehanne found the switch of her desk lamp.

Chantal sat up, blinking, her sheet wrapped around her

like a tent. Her eyes were puffy and red. "Do you know—is Kress alive?"

"I don't know." Rehanne didn't feel like talking.

Of course Chantal had learned about Kress; everyone knew. The news would have spread despite the warded steps. With her back to Chantal to discourage conversation, she quickly stripped off her clothes and slipped into her night-gown. She turned to Chantal to tell her she'd switch off the light when she came back from the washroom. On the floor by Chantal's bed a white handkerchief splotched with red caught her eye. Her startled stare drew Chantal's attention; she leaned over the side of the bed, saw the hanky, snatched it up, and thrust it under the sheet.

"It's mine," Chantal said. "I cried so hard when I heard about Kress, I gave myself a nosebleed."

Blood again. Blood was everywhere tonight.

8

MORNING-AFTER BLUES

Gray stumbled into the classroom and collapsed into a desk in the last row. He hadn't slept, hadn't washed, shaved, or changed clothes, hadn't eaten breakfast. He knew he presented a spectacle; he didn't care. Why he bothered going to class he didn't know, except that it was something to do, someplace to be other than in his room or brooding in the parlor. And Rehanne would be here.

He had nothing to say to her, didn't want to talk. He

wanted her to sit close to him, wanted to feel the comfort of her presence. He needed the calming effect she had on him. He didn't care that it was part of her talent, that she used her power to suppress his anxieties. They needed suppressing.

But today her presence wouldn't be comforting. She didn't believe in his innocence. He wasn't sure he believed it himself. He'd been so certain he'd spent the time between breakfast and convocation yesterday with her. If he hadn't, how had he spent it? Why couldn't he remember?

Was the beast destroying his mind?

Was there a beast?

He'd wrestled all night with these questions and found no answers, gained no peace.

Coral Snow came into the room. Her gaze immediately fastened on Gray and her delicate features registered panic. She chose a desk in the front, as far from him as possible, and the rigid set of her shoulders told Gray she felt his pain and was trying to shield herself. He should get out, out of the classroom, out of the school; go somewhere, anywhere. Except that he could think of no place where he wouldn't cause suffering and grief. And he lacked the energy to move.

Three second-year students came in together and paid no attention to Gray other than casting brief curious glances as they entered. They must know about Kress, but Gray saw nothing in their behavior to indicate they had heard rumors associating him with what had happened.

Jerrol hurried in and took a front row seat next to Coral. He swiveled in his chair, and his gaze darted over the other students and fell on Gray. The nervous jerk of his head, the frown that squeezed his brows into a single line reinforced Gray's impression of a ferret. He turned around and greeted Coral, ostentatiously ignoring Gray's presence.

His reaction might mean that he *did* know what Gray was

blamed for or merely that he was uneasy about being in close quarters with Gray after their first-day encounter.

Nevil Santomayor, another third-year student, was quiet and shy, and Gray hardly knew him. He was the only male third-year student who had not been involved in Oryon's plot two years ago, and because of that Gray would have liked to count him as a friend, but Nevil kept to himself and made few friends.

Master Hawke strode in, positioned himself in front of the class, and pounded his cane on the floor three times, the signal for class to begin.

Rehanne dashed in and slid into the chair next to Gray's. She couldn't say anything; Master Hawke had begun speaking. But her relief at seeing him in class was evident.

She looked tired and had probably not slept much more than he. He wondered whether she had news of Kress. He couldn't bring himself to feel any sympathy for Kress, but his own situation could become immeasurably worse if Kress died and he continued to be blamed for the attack.

He had to find a way to clear himself. If only he'd gone to his room last night instead of sitting alone in the parlor. Reece could have vouched for him. But he'd wanted to be alone, and he had been. No one had seen him until Rehanne had found him.

How long he had sat there he honestly didn't know. He'd told Rehanne he'd been sleeping. He thought he must have been, because he'd had a sort of dream (it had seemed real) in which he'd been lost and alone in a long gallery that displayed all the sculptures he'd ever made. All those fleeting bits of whimsy were preserved there, resting on marble pedestals along the walls. But as he reached each one and tried to examine it, it vanished. Until he'd come to the last one, the goat-beast. It had remained, grinning at him. Infuriated, he'd struck it with his fist, slicing his hand on a horn, but smashing the creature into tiny fragments that fled screaming into the distance. A door appeared where the pedestal had stood, and when he went through it, he found himself in the parlor and sat down in the dark. And heard Rehanne call his name.

It did not seem that the dream or vision or whatever it had been had lasted long. And he had no sense of passage of time between it and Rehanne's coming. Yet when he'd sat down in the parlor shortly after supper, the lamps had been lit, and he didn't remember their being turned off. Someone must have turned them off—Headmistress, perhaps, or Veronica. It was odd that he hadn't been wakened and ordered upstairs before the stairs were warded.

But the stairs hadn't been warded when he had climbed them after his talk with Rehanne. He'd gone up without thinking about the wards. They might have been removed after Kress's injury to allow the healers free passage, but it was possible that they'd not been set that evening.

A bell rang. With a jolt Gray realized that class had ended, and he had not heard a single word of Master Hawke's lecture. A textbook rested on his desk. So Master Hawke had distributed books and probably given an assignment. And he'd been aware of nothing. He picked up the slender brown volume and turned to Rehanne.

She was gone.

Unsteadily he rose and followed the other students from the room. What was happening to him? How had he missed seeing and hearing Rehanne leave when she was seated next to him?

She *had* been seated next to him, hadn't she? He hadn't imagined it—had he?

*   *   *

Hurt, anxious, confused, Rehanne hurried from the class-room wing and climbed the stairs to Headmistress's office. With Master Hawke's permission, she'd left class a few min-utes early, while he was distributing the textbooks. She wanted to reach Headmistress before the classes let out and others tried to see her. She had to talk to her, had to get ad-vice. Gray's behavior was bordering on madness. She had to know how to cope with it.

Last night had been unnerving enough—his insistence that they'd been together throughout the morning, his claim that he'd been sitting in the dark parlor all evening, the wetness that might have been blood on his hand. But she had at least been able to talk to him. This morning he'd sat through class with a vacant stare on his face, and when she'd tried to get his attention, he hadn't seemed to see or hear her.

But her knock at the office door was unanswered. Head-mistress might still be with Kress, though it was hard to be-lieve that he could have survived. Headmistress hadn't appeared at breakfast, but that wasn't unusual. At each meal usually only one faculty member attended to keep order and to ask the Power-Giver's blessing. This morning that honor had fallen to Mistress Dova. Rehanne had hoped to hear an announcement about the strange events of the night before and a report of Kress's death or survival, but Mistress Dova said nothing. Neither Lina nor Giselle appeared for break-fast, nor did Fenton. None of the other students had any in-formation, but all were curious and the rumor mill was in full operation.

Gray was bound to be involved in some of those rumors. She *had* to find Headmistress, had to get answers.

She walked hesitantly to the door of Kress's room, gath-ered her courage, and knocked.

The door swung open and she stood face to face with Veronica, hair in its customary disarray, dark eyes sharp and piercing in that round, doughy face. Smudges of dirt and what might have been blood marked the white apron that covered her gingham dress.

"Yes, miss?"

Rehanne always found Veronica intimidating, though she couldn't say why. Her voice choked as she tried to state her errand. "I, ah, was looking for Headmistress. She's not in her office, and I thought she might be here. And I . . . I wanted to know about Kress."

Veronica's expression was unreadable. She stepped back and let Rehanne see past her into the room. "Headmistress isn't here. I've been cleaning up."

All traces of the carnage had vanished. The beds were made up with fresh linens, the floor and walls had been scrubbed. White curtains hung across the window, though Rehanne had seen no curtains last night.

With a deep breath, Rehanne gathered courage to ask again, "And Kress?"

"I can't say, miss. You'll have to ask Headmistress."

"Well, do you know where she is?" Rehanne was growing desperate.

"No, miss. I'd guess she was resting. She was up all night, and she has a class to teach this afternoon. And don't you have a class to go to?"

"Yes, when break is over. I thought I could have a word with Headmistress first."

"Seems as not." She started to shut the door.

A scraping sound drew Rehanne's attention—something caught under the door. She and Veronica bent down at the same time. Their fingers touched as they both probed the narrow space between door and floor. Rehanne dislodged the object, flicked it toward her, and scooped it up.

It was a small crescent filigree earring, a diamond gleaming at its center.

"Chantal's missing earring!" She cradled it in the palm of her hand. "How did it get here?"

Veronica peered at it, frowning. "You'd best leave it with me," she said. "It needs to be shown to Headmistress."

"Why?" Rehanne closed her hand around the delicate adornment. "Chantal's been frantic about it. She'll be overjoyed to get it back."

Veronica shook her head. "You must say nothing to Chantal about it. It must be taken to Headmistress."

"All right. I'll take it to her. Tell me where she is."

With an exasperated snort Veronica stepped into the hall and closed and locked Kress's door. "Come along, then. But Headmistress won't like being disturbed, and she won't approve of you missing class."

She marched ahead of Rehanne, stiff-backed and angry. Rehanne didn't care. She'd grasped the opportunity, and she refused to let it go.

Past Headmistress's office, a narrow corridor gave access to the door to Headmistress's private apartment, and it was to that door that Veronica led her. Rehanne had never been here before. This small area was normally off-limits to students.

Veronica's knock was not answered at once. As they waited, Rehanne heard the distant bell, marking the end of break. She would miss her second class. Bad to miss the opening class of the year, but this errand was more important.

Headmistress opened the door. Rehanne was startled to see her in floor-length dressing gown and slippers, her hair unbound and falling loose about her shoulders. She looked so much more human, even vulnerable. Her eyes were puffy with sleep; wrinkles marked one cheek where it must have pressed against a pillow. She'd been sleeping and they'd awakened her. She'd be angry.

"Miss Zalos insisted on seeing you," Veronica stated with a sniff. "She's found something in the doorway of Mr. Klemmer's room and refused to give it up to me. When I told her you'd want to see it, she demanded to bring it to you herself. I told her you'd be resting."

The rush of heat in her cheeks told Rehanne she was blushing. Veronica seemed determined to present the matter in the worst possible light. "I'd been looking for you," Rehanne said quickly before Veronica could make other accusations. "I needed to talk to you about Gray. When I didn't find you in your office, I went to Kress's room. And I found this." She opened her hand and displayed the earring. "It's Chantal's. She's been terribly upset about losing it. She thinks someone stole it."

Headmistress's thin fingers plucked the earring from Rehanne's palm and examined it closely. Her large orange gemstone sparkled as her ringed hand moved. Her lips were drawn in a tight thin line. She neither spoke nor looked at Rehanne.

"It was caught under the door," Veronica explained. "That's how I missed it when I cleaned."

Headmistress raised it to her face, sniffed it, and wrinkled her nose as though some foul odor clung to the crescent. She dropped it into the pocket of her robe and brushed off her hand, her lips pursed in an expression of distaste.

Her gaze avoided Rehanne and rested on Veronica. "This injects a new complication into our puzzle. I think we must learn whether this is indeed the earring that was lost rather than its nonstraying mate."

Veronica nodded and turned away. Rehanne heard her ascend the stairs to the third floor.

"You will not speak of this to Miss Navarese." A coldness in the firm tone alerted Rehanne that the statement was not merely an order but a binding. Headmistress had used power to assure that Rehanne *could* not speak of finding the earring, nor of Veronica's mission to search for its mate. "What was it you wished to say about Mr. Becq that could not have waited a couple more hours?"

Rehanne felt small and foolish, but she was determined not to back down. In a rush of words she told Headmistress about finding Gray in the darkened parlor, about their conversation, about his certainty that they'd been together all that morning though they had not, about his conviction that Lina had been responsible both for the damage to his and Reece's room and the wounding of Kress. She concluded her tale with the account of how peculiar Gray had acted in their first class. And she waited for Headmistress's reaction.

"Thank you for telling me these things," the tall woman said in the same cold tone. "You will speak of them to no one else. You have missed your second class. If you hurry, you will have time to see Master Tumberlis and apologize for your truancy before reporting to your third class."

She stepped back into her apartment, hesitated, leaned forward, and said, "One more thing, Miss Zalos. I would be remiss if I neglected to warn you that you may be in serious danger. I will take what steps I can to protect you, but I advise you to remain alert and to resist involving yourself in Mr. Becq's problems."

After three morning classes, Lina was more than ready for lunch. She'd been in a bad mood to begin with, having to get up for an early morning class. She loathed having classes during all three of the morning periods, and she was extremely displeased with her schedule: two classes with Mistress Dova and one with Mistress Blake in the morning, then another with Mistress Blake in the afternoon. She hated having only women instructors. She was irked at not having a class with Master Hawke, her favorite teacher. Mistress

Dova was so prim and proper; Mistress Blake wasn't bad, but she was strict and clever, and Lina could never outwit her.

She stalked into the dining room and looked around for an empty seat. A first-year student approached her, a frightened look on the portion of the face visible through the long straight hair that hung in front of it. She gave the impression of peering through a haystack. Lina tried to deflect her with a threatening scowl, but the girl was not deterred.

"I'm Maridel Denham," she said. "Someone said I should talk to you."

Lina crossed her arms and glared.

The girl did not back away. "I've lost my kitten, Moonbeam. A second-year student told me you might know how to find him."

"Why? Do I look like someone who collects stray cats?"

"Oh, no, but this person told me you understood cats."

"Who might this terribly helpful person be?" Lina's long nails tapped her arms with a message of irritation that the pest seemed too dense to receive.

"I'm not sure I should tell you." Maridel brushed her hair back from her eyes—a futile gesture; it fell back across her face when she released it.

"You had better if you expect me to tell *you* anything."

"Oh. Well, in that case—yesterday at supper I talked to Chantal Navarese, and she told me to see you, and I've been looking for you since then."

Lina's hiss of rage would have warned off any prudent person.

Maridel imprudently persisted. "Have you seen my kitten? Can you tell me how to find him?"

"No."

"But you said you could tell me something." She sounded on the verge of tears.

"I'll tell you not to be so stupid as to listen to Chantal. The little snake was playing a joke on you. She won't think it's funny after I finish with her. Now if you don't mind, I'd like to find a seat and eat lunch."

But Maridel didn't move. "Please, I didn't mean to get Chantal in trouble. And I've *got* to get my kitten back."

"In that case, you definitely do *not* want me to find it for you." Lina pushed the startled girl out of her way.

She spotted Oryon, but no empty seat was left at his table. Petra, Rehanne, and Coral were eating together at a table that did have an empty seat, but if Lina joined them in her present mood, she'd give Coral a fit. She slid into a chair next to Chantal. Might as well have entertainment with her meal.

Chantal looked alarmed, but Master Hawke's call to rise for the invocation prevented her saying anything. Two other second-year students were at the table: Vanita Trask and Ferene K'Sere. When the invocation ended and everyone took their seats, Lina nodded pleasantly at her tablemates and bestowed a sweet smile on Chantal.

"You look pale, Chantal." Lina invested her voice with concern. "Are you ill?"

"I'm worried, terribly worried about Kress." Chantal bit her lower lip as though to stop it from trembling. "No one knows how he is. Headmistress must, but no one's seen her at all today."

"Well, no news is good news, they say." With that cheery rejoinder, Lina picked up the platter of meat from the center of the table. "Isn't anyone eating? I'm starved."

With the serving spoon, she lifted a beef roll onto her plate. How did the others see the food? Ferene ate eagerly, but Chantal refused the platter, and Vanita wrinkled her nose in disgust as she gingerly took a small serving. Lina guessed that they had not yet learned to see through the illusion designed to test students' perception. To them the savory meat roll might seem a bit of hard, dried beef with the flavor of shoe leather; the fresh-cooked garden vegetables might appear as a dish of rotten cabbage and hard little potatoes.

She took a beef roll from the platter, balanced it on the spoon, and thrust it toward Chantal. "You must eat, Chantal. You'll feel better." She used her power to dispel the illusion, letting her quarry see the plump roll and smell the rich, meaty gravy. "Mmmm, isn't that good?"

The girl's eyes lit up with delighted surprise. Lina placed the roll on the plate, and Chantal picked up her fork.

Lina's power created a new illusion carefully directed at Chantal alone. As Chantal plunged her fork into it, the roll became a fluffy cat's tail, one end a bloody stump, the tip end wagging beneath the fork. Chantal let out a horrified gasp, and her fork clattered to the plate.

"Oh, how wonderful!" Lina enthused. "I can tell Maridel I've found part of her missing kitten." From the dish of vegetables she scooped out a large piece of cauliflower and placed it on Chantal's plate. For Chantal's benefit alone the piece acquired the shape of a cat's head, complete with ears, whiskers, and a black button nose. A pimiento clinging to the side formed a lolling red tongue. "Why, here's another piece."

Chantal shoved her chair back, leaped up, and ran from the dining hall. Lina shook her head sadly. "I guess I shouldn't have urged her to eat. I thought it would help, but of course I knew how infatuated she was with Kress."

Vanita was staring in openmouthed bewilderment. But Ferene glared at Lina. "Why do you enjoy being cruel?" She got up and hurried after Chantal.

Lina gave Vanita a mystified shrug. But she was worried. Ferene should not have seen the illusion Lina had directed at Chantal alone. Lina tried to remember what Ferene's talents were, but if she'd ever known, the recollection escaped her.

Master Hawke approached their table. Lina was glad he was the presiding faculty member at today's lunch.

"Miss Mueller, what happened to Miss Navarese?"

"She became ill because of her grief for Kress," Lina explained earnestly. "She was telling us she hasn't been able to learn whether he is alive or dead, and she became so upset she had to rush out. Ferene's gone after her to comfort her. I'm sure she'll be all right, sir."

"I see." The explanation seemed to satisfy him. He returned to the head table without other comment.

Lina hadn't tricked him into imparting any information about Kress, but she breathed a silent sigh of satisfaction. Pulling off that bit of vengeance lightened her mood, and she devoured her lunch with great relish.

As she was leaving the dining hall, Oryon caught up with her and grabbed her by the wrist. "Let's talk," he said. "Privately."

9

Tête-à-Têtes

He wasted no words. "That was stupid, calling attention to yourself that way with whatever you did to Chantal."

No point in denying she'd done anything. She could sometimes fool Oryon, but never for long. "She deserved it."

"Probably. But aren't you in enough trouble already?"

She thrust out her chin. "Why am I in trouble?"

"You shapechanged."

"So?"

"Kress. Did you do it?"

"Of course not."

"You said you wanted to teach him a lesson."

"I didn't say I planned to kill him."

"Is he dead?"

"I don't know. You just implied that he was."

"Stop sparring with me, Lina. Whether you did it or not, people will *think* you did."

"I can't help what people think. Who made you my keeper?"

"Nobody, thank the Power-Giver. But you need one, after this latest stunt. This is no time to draw attention to yourself."

She burst into laughter. "I see what it is," she said. "You're afraid suspicion will fall on *you*. People have seen us together. They know Kress hates you. You aren't worried about me at all, Oryon. You know that anyone who blames me will also blame you."

He glowered at her. "That's not—"

"Of course it is. And how do I know *you* didn't do it?"

"Don't be ridiculous!"

"But I'm not being ridiculous. I'm thinking of your recent history, and others must be doing the same. Who is more capable of such an act?"

He opened his mouth, shut it again, turned his back, and walked away from her.

She'd hit a nerve, had probably gone much too far. She didn't want to antagonize Oryon, not permanently. She needed him for the exchange of energies that was restoring the power they'd lost. She thought they'd both already reached their former level. But she did not intend to stop at that.

No, she'd be foolish to allow Oryon to stay angry with her. Later, she'd apologize and assure him that she did not really suspect him of injuring or killing Kress.

*   *   *

When Rehanne reached her third class, the one on arcane languages that she'd so looked forward to, Petra was already in the room. Rehanne greeted her friend and took a seat beside her, pleased that Petra was assigned to the class. They could study together.

Nevil Santomayor hurried in, took a seat behind Rehanne, and murmured a shy greeting to her and Petra. It was time for class to start, and Rehanne thought perhaps the three of them would comprise the entire class; third-year classes tended to be very small.

Then, to her disappointment, Oryon walked in, followed moments later by Lina. Though Rehanne told herself that she did *not* share Gray's antipathy for them, being with both of them in this small class made her uncomfortable.

Nevil gave Lina a glance and quickly shifted his gaze away. He gathered up his notebook and pencils and moved to a front seat on the far side of Petra, away from Lina and Oryon.

"What's the matter, Nevil?" Lina asked. "Afraid I'll bite? Or scratch?" Grinning, she curved her hands like claws and scratched the air.

Nevil paled. "No, I—I . . ."

"Don't!" Petra rebuked her. "You should know that's not funny, especially after last night."

Lina arched her eyebrows. "Oh, was there something special about last night?"

"Playing innocent only makes you look guilty," Petra snapped.

"Who's playing?" Lina snarled back. "I'm guilty of nothing."

"You're guilty of being rude, and there's no need for it," Petra scolded, her voice rising.

Lina's eyes narrowed to catlike slits. She rose partway

from her chair, and only the timely arrival of Mistress Dova averted a fight.

Mistress Dova gave Petra and Lina a sharp look. "Since I've arrived a bit late, I had expected the class to be seated and quiet," she said. "Mr. Brew, would you please distribute these textbooks?"

Oryon went forward and picked up one of two stacks of books from Mistress Dova's desk. He placed one of the slender brown volumes on each desk, meeting no one's eyes as he did so.

"These also," Mistress Dova said, indicating the other stack of books.

Lina smirked as he took up the second stack. These were heavier books, dictionaries as it turned out, and he dumped one off the stack at each desk, then took his seat, his face dark and angry.

The strained atmosphere prevailed throughout the class. Rehanne was glad that Coral was not in the class; she would have been devastated by the tension, most of it emanating from Oryon and Lina.

Mistress Dova ignored the ill feeling, though she was undoubtedly aware of it. She handed out printed outlines of the material to be covered in the class, discussed the course requirements, and lectured on the reasons for and nature of the ancient mage tongues. She asked no questions and gave no opportunity for the students to raise any. Already familiar enough with the material of the lecture, Rehanne let her mind wander, worrying as usual about Gray.

Her last class of the day was Case Histories in Ethics. She was eager to see whether Gray would show up for it and selected a seat toward the back of the room, where she could watch for him.

Master San Marté came in and had already greeted the class when Gray slouched in and dropped into a seat. There was no chance to talk with him; Rehanne could only smile encouragement and signal her desire to talk after class. He looked terrible, worse than he had in the morning class. His eyes were dull and unfocused; he gave the impression of someone walking in his sleep.

Master San Marté distributed textbooks: thick, heavy volumes of double-columned small print. The prissy little man simpered on and on about their value, the "wealth of instruction" they contained. Rehanne tuned him out, wishing for the gift of altering time so she could speed up the hour. Dutifully she copied into her notebook the assignment for tomorrow, but took no other notes. Gray, she observed, never picked up his pen or opened a notebook.

The class consisted mostly of third-year students, but Giselle and Chantal were also assigned to it. Fortunately, Chantal had calmed considerably since her hasty exodus from the dining hall. Giselle was not present. Rehanne had not seen her all day and therefore had not had a chance to ask her about Kress.

Fenton sat near Rehanne, his face pale beneath a spattering of freckles, his characteristic good humor vanished. He might have received word of Kress's condition. She scribbled the question in a note, tore it from her notebook while Master San Marté expostulated loudly about the nobility of the historians and ethicists who had faithfully recorded the ethical problems compiled in the text. When Master San Marté adjusted his toupee and peered at the book to read a passage from the introduction, she reached across an empty desk and placed the note in front of Fenton.

He shrugged, hands spread open. So he didn't know either. The note must have revived his memory of the horror. He shuddered and leaned forward, elbows on his desk, head in his hands. Rehanne felt guilty for having upset him. She also felt something else: an emotional response imposed from without.

Chantal must have observed the passing of the note and guessed its purpose. It revived her grief and rage; the emotions drove at Rehanne, and in her mind the refrain echoed: *Lina, Lina, Lina!*

She felt ready to explode, to scream out the anger, the accusation. Nor was she the only one affected; the whole class was growing restless, tapping pencils, swinging feet, opening and closing books, casting frequent glances at the clock. Fenton shook his head as though involved in an interior argument. Master San Marté's nervous mannerisms increased: he adjusted and readjusted his toupee, smoothed his mustache, tugged at his cravat, rose up on tiptoes, swayed, pranced back and forth until Rehanne thought she'd go mad.

At last the bell released the class, and the students erupted from the room as though a demon were chasing them.

Maybe one was.

Rehanne suppressed the thought and hurried to catch up to Gray, who'd dashed out without waiting for her. She shoved past Chantal and Britnor only to be stopped by Fenton.

"Rehanne," he said, stepping into her path. "I want to talk to you."

"Can it wait?" Gray was disappearing into the crowd of students from the other classes.

"It's important. Something I remembered. I don't think—"

"I'm sorry. I have to see Gray. I'll find you before supper, okay?" She barreled off without giving him a chance to answer, drove through the clump of students at the head of the corridor, broke into a run, and caught up with Gray at the foot of the stairs.

"Gray," she panted, out of breath. "Why didn't you wait for me?"

His blank look could have been bestowed on a stranger. "Gray?"

He blinked; his gaze focused. "Sorry. What'd you say?"

"Never mind. Can we go somewhere and talk privately?"

"I have that seminar with Headmistress after break. Can't be late."

"We'll watch the time." She led him toward the library. It was open but deserted except for the second-year student at the desk. They sat at a table in the far corner and kept their voices low.

"I wanted to apologize for doubting you last night," Rehanne said. "I think we were both upset and—"

"And I was acting weird," he finished for her. "I'm sorry, too."

She placed her hand over his. "I was scared. I'd come straight from Kress's room. I wasn't thinking clearly."

"I haven't been thinking clearly for a long time." He wrapped his fingers around hers.

"When I went upstairs I saw a light in Lina's room. I thought it might be Giselle, so I knocked on the door. It was Lina. She was dressed, hadn't been to bed, and, Gray—I saw a bloody pawprint on her windowsill. So you were right. She had to have been the one."

"You'll have to tell Headmistress." Excitement animated his voice. "We've got to convince her."

"I'm not sure she'll listen to me." As she said it, she glanced at Gray's hand, remembering that it had been wet with what could have been blood. Dirt encrusted under his fingernails had a reddish cast.

Doubt again. When only a moment ago she'd been so sure.

"I think you had blood on your hand last night," she whispered, glancing at the student at the desk to be certain she couldn't hear. "What happened?"

He released her hand. "So you aren't sure after all." His voice was flat, the excitement gone.

"Yes, I *am*. But I—"

"No. You aren't," he interrupted. "It's all right. I'm not sure either. I *want* it to have been Lina. But that's too easy, isn't it? Because the truth is that I *did* have blood on my hand. I saw it when I got to my room, and I don't *know* how I got it. I don't know where I was and what I did last night. I don't know where I was and what I did yesterday morning. I have to find out. Until I do . . ."

She reached for his hand, squeezed it. "I'll help you. Somebody must have seen you during those times."

"Thanks." He got to his feet. "I want you to stay out of it. I don't want to put you in danger."

"I'm not afraid."

"You should be. I have to go to class. Be careful. Please." He touched her cheek lightly and left.

If Gray himself doubted that Lina had vandalized his room and attacked Kress, it could only mean that he'd come to accept Headmistress's theory that an evil creature had possessed him. Was it because of the memory lapses, or had something else happened, something he hadn't told her?

Rehanne remembered how Fenton had tried to tell her something. "It's important," he'd said.

She should have listened. Whatever he'd remembered might help Gray—or it might condemn him. She had to know.

Because suddenly she *was* afraid. Terribly afraid.

10

CONSORTING WITH THE ENEMY

Gray walked into the seminar room and stopped short. Oryon was seated at the oval table along with Headmistress. No one else was in the room.

"Come in, Mr. Becq, and have a seat," Headmistress directed.

Though the table was large enough to accommodate six people, only four chairs were arranged around it. Gray advanced slowly into the room, his gaze fixed on Oryon. He hadn't expected to be the only student in this special study, but he could not endure the thought of being paired with Oryon in a two-student class.

He came to the chair beside Headmistress, leaving the remaining empty chair between him and Oryon. He placed his hands on the back of the chair but did not sit down. "Is this—is anyone else in the class?"

"I always keep my seminar groups extremely small, Mr. Becq. You and Mr. Brew will be the only members."

"I can't . . . I don't . . ." Gray hunted for words to voice his objection. More than objection—revulsion.

"I understand your reluctance, Mr. Becq," Headmistress said. "I had good reason, however, to select the two of you for this special study on the Community of the Gifted. If you will please take a seat, I will explain."

Gray pulled out the chair, lowered himself into it, and sat

stiffly, ill at ease and resentful at having been thrust into this confrontation.

Headmistress rolled a long yellow pencil, newly sharpened, back and forth in her fingers as she spoke. "You well know the importance Simonton School places on the formation of a true community among the gifted. We consider it imperative that the gifted cooperate with one another and support one another rather than competing and forming rivalries that result in dangerous, even deadly displays of power. The unfortunate incident of two years ago provided a vivid illustration of the destructiveness of misused power."

Gray cut a glance to Oryon. The dark one's face was impassive; the gaze fixed on Headmistress, unreadable.

"We will not speak again of that incident," Headmistress continued, reclaiming Gray's attention. "It is past. We will speak of the present, of the need for reconciliation and cooperation. Of the structure of the Community and how that structure can be strengthened through free exchanges of power. We will not deal in theory but in practice." From directing her remarks to Gray, she turned her gaze to Oryon.

"I considered assigning Miss Mueller to this seminar as well, but I feared that Mr. Becq would find it too hard at first to work with both of you."

Hard! At first! Gray shifted in his chair, fighting the urge to get up and stalk out.

"Mr. Brew, the experiments you and Miss Mueller have been engaging in to rebuild your power are an example on a small scale of the kind of cooperation I envision for the entire Community. You have discovered that power increases when it is shared. If it does so when only two share it, imagine what might be wrought by a Community acting in total accord to share power equally among themselves."

Gray swung around to glare at Oryon. "So that's what you two have been up to. I knew you—"

"Mr. Becq! Heed me!"

Power spoke in Headmistress's command, silencing him, forcing him to turn away from Oryon and look at her. Though rage seethed within him, he could not tune out her words.

"I did not say I approved or condoned the experiments. They hold greater capacity for misuse when restricted to two people for their own private purposes than when practiced by a large number for the mutual benefit of all. And before the practice could be indulged by the Community, safeguards would have to be established to protect the nongifted. In this seminar we shall discuss the possibility of power exchanges and determine what restrictions must be placed on their use."

She paused and studied the point of her pencil for several minutes before proceeding. "I have said this seminar was to be practical, not theoretical. The two of you will learn ways to cooperate and exchange power. Our discussions of Community cooperation will be based on what you discover in your own exchanges."

Gray's resentment was a red-hot brand within him. If she thought he could be forced into helping Oryon gain more power . . . "I don't have power to share," he said, his voice sullen.

"You have a curious and unusual talent that certainly requires considerable power," Headmistress said. "You have never realized the extent of your power because it is all focused into a single talent, which until recently you have tended to underestimate. I must speak frankly, though you will not wish to hear what I say."

She dropped the pencil onto the table, clasped her hands

together, and leaned forward, speaking directly to Gray. "I have warned you of the evil thing you may carry within you. I believe that it has goaded you into using your talent so that it can feed on your power. I also believe that Mr. Brew has both the talent and the strength to help you protect yourself."

Gray jumped to his feet. "I don't want help from him," he yelled.

"Sit down, Mr. Becq." Headmistress's level-voiced command forced him down, though he strained against it.

She had no right. Where were the ethics she ranted about? He writhed in the chair but could not break the strands of power that bound him to it.

"I did not select Mr. Brew solely to antagonize you, as you seem to believe. Nor did I do so merely because I desire to see peace between the two of you, though I do desire that. I selected Mr. Brew for the practical reason that his experiences of two years ago render him more resistant to the demon than anyone else who might try to help you. Anyone!"

Meaning Rehanne, Gray thought bitterly. *She's telling me I have to accept Oryon's help or endanger Rehanne. She's caught me in a neat trap. But I'll find a way out, if I have to take the final way. I won't take help from Oryon.*

"Gray, I'll work with you if you'll let me," Oryon said quietly. "I don't blame you for hating the idea. But I'd like a chance to make amends."

Gray sat in stony silence, mouth clamped shut, eyes fixed on the opposite wall. Headmistress could force him to remain here, but she could not bend his will.

Headmistress stood. "I had feared that words alone would not sway you, Mr. Becq. I must show you something. It may be more persuasive than my words have been."

Gray resisted but found himself lifted to his feet and forced to follow her. Oryon walked beside him like an evil shadow in his black clothing. If he'd really changed, he wouldn't persist in wearing black.

Headmistress led them through the classroom door. Beyond it, instead of the familiar corridor, they faced a long stairway. Gray ascended it because he had to, but his reluctance diminished as his curiosity increased. He had never before seen any of the mysterious other-dimensional rooms and halls and stairs that were said to intersect with the school's primary reality.

A covert glance at Oryon showed no surprise or wonderment in his expression. It almost seemed that he had been here before and was familiar with these secret ways.

These halls and stairs were not lit by electricity, but by tapers in sconces. The tapers burst into flame as they approached, flickered out after they passed.

They proceeded down a long hallway and paused before a door that Headmistress unlocked with a silver key. Beyond it a circular staircase wound up and up. Gray was winded by the time they reached its top and the narrow corridor that led to a single door.

Headmistress did not use a key to open this door, but spoke a word of power. The door swung open at her command. They entered the chamber, about the size of a student dormitory room. Its only furniture was the narrow, high bed in its center.

On the bed Kress lay, arms at his sides, flesh waxen and pale. A corpse?

"It took three healers, working together, sharing power, to heal his body," Headmistress said, answering Gray's unspoken question. "Unfortunately, he has an affliction beyond our healing."

A sheet covered most of his body, its slight rise and fall confirming that he lived. Wanting a closer look, Gray edged toward the bed. A warding net halted him.

"You must beware," Headmistress said. "Stand back. Mr. Brew, you may attempt to dispel the wards."

Oryon moved forward, and Gray stepped away from him. "I find this easier with a wand. Mine has been stolen." He pointed a finger at the bed and muttered something beneath his breath. After a few moments, he squeezed his eyes shut. Drops of sweat beaded on his forehead. Finally he said, "It's double-warded. I've broken through the first layer, but I can't breach the second."

Headmistress nodded and spoke a second word of power. The word thundered through the room; flames danced over the bed. "Come quickly, before he wakens." She moved to Kress's bedside.

Gray followed, heedless of Oryon's presence beside him.

Headmistress reached out with her ringed hand, lifted one of Kress's eyelids, exposing an eye of flame. The other lid lifted. The fiery, hate-filled eyes of a demon glared at them. Kress's mouth opened, but the roar of rage that issued from his throat was never human. He sat up, lunged toward them.

"Back!" Headmistress thrust Gray behind her and spoke another word. She and Oryon leaped out of the way. The power Headmistress had unleashed wove around the demon, which raged against it. Currents of power stood Gray's hair on end. His ears buzzed. The room shook and seemed to flicker in and out of existence. Terrifying images, scenes of carnage and death, superimposed themselves, leading Gray to think for a moment that he was back in the hideous realm of the Dire Women. He screamed.

The room righted itself. Kress lay back on the bed, motionless, eyes closed as though sleeping peacefully.

"The wards are back in place," Headmistress announced. "That demon is contained." She turned to Gray. "You see what it can do. I do not know whether Mr. Klemmer can be freed. So long as he is possessed, he will remain here, securely imprisoned. But we must prevent others from becoming similarly infected. I have done what I can. It is not enough. I am hoping that you, Gray Becq, and you, Oryon Brew, working together, can stop the demons from possessing others as this one has possessed Mr. Klemmer."

Gray took a deep breath and, difficult as it was in Oryon's presence, asked the question he had to have answered. "Is that the demon that came through me? Did it infect Kress because of me?"

Oryon gave him a curious look.

"I am not certain that it is the same demon," Headmistress answered. "I do fear that it gained entrance to the school through you, and that it attacked Kress because of your antipathy toward him."

"If that's the case, why didn't it attack Oryon? Or Lina?"

"Perhaps because they have defenses Kress lacks. Or perhaps—Veronica told me that on your arrival you had a brief altercation with Kress and Jerrol. It may have reacted to that."

Gray had forgotten that incident on the stairs. "That was more Jerrol than Kress," he said. "Yet Jerrol wasn't attacked."

"I don't pretend to understand the situation thoroughly," Headmistress said. "What is important is to deal with what we do know, which is that this demon is contained but not conquered, and other demons may be skulking about. We must end that threat. And, Mr. Becq, that will require your cooperation. There must be no enmity for the demons to exploit."

While Gray mulled over that assessment, Headmistress led him and Oryon back to the seminar room and dismissed them. When they left the room, they exited into the usual corridor, and Gray knew he would not be able to rediscover the way to the room where Kress lay imprisoned.

"How about it, Gray?" Oryon's question broke into his thoughts. "Are you willing to work with me?"

"I don't know. Give me time to think about it."

"We may not have much time."

But Gray hurried away without answering. The thought that the demon he had witnessed in Kress had come from him was nauseating. And the need to work with Oryon repelled Gray. He had to find some other recourse. If he could talk it over with Rehanne . . .

He couldn't. He had to stay away from Rehanne. If anything happened to her . . . but nothing would. If he had to work with Oryon to ensure her safety, he'd do it. But he wouldn't like it.

11

Lost!

In search of a quiet place to think, Gray turned into the hall leading to the library. A few other students might stop in to read until suppertime, but it wouldn't be the busy place it would become later in the term. He could sit at a table alone and plan what to do. Decide, possibly, on the surest form of suicide.

In his depression, the effort of lifting his feet as he walked required more energy than he could summon. He shuffled along, shoulders slumped, gaze fixed on the floor. He missed the library door; he must have plodded past it without seeing it. He only realized how far he'd come when he bumped into the door at the end of the hall. That door leading outside the building was always kept locked.

He pushed on the door, expecting nothing to happen. It

creaked open. He peered outside, gazing at the garden with its neat rows of vegetables ready for harvest. He had a sudden urge to walk among those rows and breathe in the fresh scent of growing things, the smell of the rich soil that nurtured them. But if he went out this door, it could lock behind him. To make sure it didn't, he bent down and wedged his notebook between door and jamb.

He wouldn't stay out long, only long enough to clear his mind. Walking at a faster pace, he pushed his way into the tall stalks of corn and strolled between the rows, enjoying the feel of the leaves brushing his arms and face, the soft whisper of the corn tassels.

He was starting to relax when voices nearby interrupted his idyll. Two people, male and female, coming toward him. He didn't want to see anyone, didn't want to be seen. He spun around and retraced his steps at a near run, burst out of the corn, and hurried to the door.

It was shut; someone had removed the notebook. He grasped the latch and yanked. The door shuddered, creaked open. He slipped into the hall.

He was in luck; the hall was still deserted. No one witnessed his use of the forbidden door. In fact, the hall was so dark, he doubted that anyone *could* have seen him. The ceiling bulb must have burned out. He groped for his notebook on the hall floor, but didn't find it. No big loss if it was gone; he hadn't taken any notes, had written nothing in it except his name. He went on to the library.

It, too, was dark and deserted, though some light filtered through the coating of dust on the windows. He frowned; the windows hadn't looked like that when he and Rehanne had been here earlier.

The tables, too, wore coats of dust. Through the cobwebs that curtained the bookshelves he saw worm trails etched on the moldering spines of books. The smell of old paper and rotting leather permeated the room. He went to a shelf, pulled out a book, and opened it. The cover crumbled; the yellowed pages broke into brittle fragments in his hands.

He walked to the rear of the library, peered into the workroom, found it dark and abandoned to the busy spiders. Brushing strands of web from his face, he hurried through the library back into the corridor and checked as he came to them the dining hall, parlor, and classrooms. All had the same long-deserted look as the library. Nowhere did he find any sign of other occupants. The dust on the floors seemed to have accumulated undisturbed for years.

He climbed the stairs. The banister shivered beneath his touch; the steps were treacherous with rotted wood.

The room doors were open, revealing rusted bed frames and an occasional weathered and broken desk or dresser. No water flowed from the washroom's rusted taps. The porcelain fixtures were cracked and chipped.

He went up to the women's floor and found the same derelict condition as the lower floors.

This had to be an illusion, but who had created it and for what purpose he could not imagine, unless— Could it be a trick of Headmistress's to force him into cooperating with Oryon?

Illusion or not, it seemed real and terribly desolate and lonely. He returned to the first floor, negotiating the stairs with great care, tried the double doors of the main entrance, and found them securely locked. He went next to the patio doors. They, too, were locked and refused to budge when he slammed himself against them.

He moved on to the door that led from the classroom section to the garden. Having no better luck with it, he returned to the library corridor and the door through which he'd entered this nightmare. By retracing his steps through that door out to the garden and back, he might be able to reverse this unnerving spell.

The door confounded his hopes by being locked like the others. No amount of banging, pounding, pulling, prying, kicking, and battering would open it. The effort only gave him bruised and bleeding knuckles, sore toes, and an aching hip where he'd uselessly but painfully thrown himself against the door.

Near panic, he made another tour of the building in search of some clue, something he had overlooked that could explain his terrifying predicament and point to a way of escape. He found nothing but a new worry. A thorough search of the kitchen failed to turn up anything edible. If he couldn't find a way out of this illusion, he'd starve. And while he'd considered suicide, he wouldn't have chosen starvation as the method.

When he could drag himself no longer through his futile rounds, he sank to the dusty floor of the parlor, cushioned his head on his arm, and slept.

In his dreams the demon loomed over him, laughing and jeering.

He awoke with the sound of the demonic laughter ringing in his ears. Cramped and sore, he sat up, stretched, and looked around. His situation hadn't changed; sleep hadn't dissolved the illusion. But his troubled sleep must have lasted all night. The red-gold light of early morning strained through the grimy panes.

Unable to think of anything else to do, he set off on another tour of the building, trying again each outside door, picking his way up the treacherous stairs. Careful as he was, his foot crashed through a rotten board and the jagged edges of the board tore a gash in his leg as he pulled it out. He had nothing to use to stanch the flow of blood, could only let it trickle onto his shoe and leave bloody footprints as he limped through the remainder of his inspection.

The loneliness and desolation became unbearable. If he used a broken chair to smash a window and crawl outside, where would he find himself? He didn't know, but he had to try. To continue to do nothing could only lead to madness. As bad as things were in the school, they were better than here. Life, people, friendships acquired new value. If he got out of this, he'd put away thoughts of suicide, follow Headmistress's advice about how to defeat the demon, even work with Oryon if he must.

Back in the parlor, he broke apart a ruined chair, selected the most solid-looking piece of wood, and slammed it against the window.

The wood splintered. The glass remained whole.

He tried with other chairs, other windows in other rooms. The windows refused to break.

Sealed in! He sank to the floor in despair. Cuts and scratches covered his hands, splinters pierced his fingers and palms. He buried his head in his arms and wept.

A sound roused him from the depths of his wretchedness: the loud meow of a cat.

Rehanne left the library to look for Fenton, found he had a class with Mistress Blake, and returned to her room, deciding to rest a bit, go downstairs before time for the class to end, and meet him at the classroom door.

She slipped off her shoes and lay down on her bed. Tired as she was, she dared not let herself drift off to sleep or she wouldn't wake in time to meet Fenton. She'd only close her eyes for a few minutes . . .

The clang of the dinner bell brought Rehanne to startled wakefulness. She jumped out of bed and checked the clock, not believing she had slept so long. The clock confirmed the bell: it was dinnertime, and she had missed her chance to meet Fenton after his last class. She'd have to see him after dinner. She smoothed her clothes, pulled a comb through her tangled hair, and hurried to the dining hall.

She looked in vain for Gray. This was the third meal he'd missed. She resolved to sneak some food out for him.

She couldn't spot Fenton, either, and it was unusual for him to miss a meal. Though today he was far from his usual self. She hoped she'd be able to find him after dinner, but finding Gray and making sure he ate was more important.

Giselle was seated at a table with Lina and Vanita and one empty place. Rehanne headed for it, eager to talk to Giselle, whom she hadn't seen all day. Maybe at last she'd find out about Kress.

Giselle, pale with deep circles under her eyes, nodded at Rehanne but did not speak. When they took their seats following the invocation, Rehanne spoke to her. "You look like you haven't slept at all. How long were you with Kress?" She hoped Giselle in answering would volunteer the information she *hadn't* asked for.

"I was up all night, but I got a little sleep earlier today. Headmistress excused me from classes."

Giselle picked up a platter of ham and served herself as she spoke. She cut off a large bite and put it into her mouth before taking servings of vegetables and bread. Rehanne suspected she was trying to forestall questions about Kress and held back on asking until a more opportune time presented itself.

Lina, who seemed more subdued than usual, was talking quietly to Vanita. Rehanne hadn't paid attention to the conversation. But when she heard Vanita say something about Chantal's missing earring, her interest was piqued.

"That was the first, as far as I know," Lina replied to whatever Vanita had said.

"I knew about that. Chantal asked everybody about it. But I didn't know anything else had disappeared, so when I couldn't find my fire gem, I never connected it with the lost earring."

"I doubt that there *is* a connection with the earring," Lina said around a mouthful of food. "The silly girl probably just misplaced it. It's possible that her yelling about it and claiming it was stolen gave somebody the idea of stealing the other things. The earring's not an aid to magic like all the others." She turned to Rehanne, apparently noticing her interest in the conversation. "Is anything of yours missing? Anything you use for spells?"

Rehanne shook her head, startled by the question. "I don't think so. I don't have anything special—only candles and stuff that you could find anywhere. But what else is missing?"

"My ward-breaking talisman," Lina answered. "Oryon's wand. And the fire jewel Vanita uses to communicate with the dead." She nodded at her table companion.

"I missed it last night." Vanita pushed her food around her plate, not eating. "That was the first time I'd opened the box I keep it in since I got here, so I don't know when it disappeared. I searched my room for it, and then I reported the loss to Headmistress. It's odd that she didn't tell me about the other thefts."

"I haven't said anything to her about my talisman, and I doubt that Oryon's reported his missing wand," Lina said.

"Maridel's lost a kitten, and I know she went to Headmistress about that," Rehanne offered. "She said she can't work her magic without it."

Lina sat forward, suddenly intent. "The cat's a familiar? I didn't know that."

"Have you seen it?" Rehanne asked.

"No. She asked me about it. I supposed it had wandered

off; I didn't associate it with the thefts." She leaned back, eyes closed, forehead furrowed in thought.

"You aren't missing anything, are you, Giselle?" Vanita asked.

Giselle had continued to eat without entering the conversation. She shook her head and took a second helping of vegetables, then busied herself eating as though to indicate she wanted to be left alone.

Why is she acting so strange? Rehanne wondered. *After being so friendly last night, why does she seem not to want anything to do with me today? Is it only that she's tired, or is it something she's hiding?*

Lina opened her eyes. "Vanita," she said, "no one without your talent could use your fire jewel, could they?"

"No. I don't think someone else *with* the talent could use it, either. It's tuned to my vibrations."

"Anybody could use my talisman, but Oryon's wand is like your jewel. And no one can channel through someone else's familiar. So why bother to steal something that won't do the thief any good? Unless," she mused, "the thief didn't take the things to use them but to stop *us* from using them."

"But Oryon can use his power without his wand," Rehanne said.

"How do you know that?" Lina's voice was sharp, the gaze she turned on Rehanne filled with suspicion.

"I saw him do it last night." Remembering that Lina had not been there, Rehanne explained how Oryon had broken the wards on the stairs so that Giselle could help Kress. But the memory revived her mistrust of Lina, and she wondered whether she should be joining the conversation. Giselle was probably wise to have stayed out of it.

"So he showed everyone how much power he had," Lina said, her frown indicating her opinion of Oryon's imprudence. "But the thief might not have known until then that he could do anything without the wand." She pushed her plate away and jumped to her feet. Without bothering to excuse herself, she left their table and crossed to the one where Oryon sat with Britnor and Reece. The unclaimed place at that table had probably been reserved for Fenton.

Lina bent and whispered into Oryon's ear, and he rose and accompanied her from the dining hall, both of them ignoring the rule that no one at a table should leave until all those at the table had finished. They probably knew they wouldn't be called back: Master Tumberlis presided alone at the head table, and his extreme nearsightedness would prevent his noting the transgression.

Rehanne picked up a dinner roll, split it open, folded two slices of ham into it, wrapped it in her napkin, and slipped it into her pocket. If Lina and Oryon could leave early, so could she. "Excuse me," she said, and got up to begin her search for Gray.

She stopped by the table where Lina had stopped and asked Reece, "Do you know where Gray is? Is he in your room?"

"He wasn't when I came downstairs. I haven't seen him all day. We don't have any classes together."

"Have any of you seen him? Or Fenton?"

"Fenton went up to his room after our last class." Britnor sounded eager to be helpful. "I stopped by to walk down with him when the dinner bell rang, and he wasn't there. I thought he must have come down early. I don't know where he might be. We saved him a seat."

She thanked them and left. First she searched the downstairs area, the parlor and library, then the classroom area and the quadrangle. The assembly hall was locked, the faculty hall parlor empty. She returned to the main building. Though the work detail roster posted by the dining hall doors told her neither Gray nor Fenton was assigned to the kitchen crew, she checked the kitchen anyway, without find-ing them. Her check of the basement laundry room was equally futile. She climbed the stairs to the men's floor and went up and down the hall knocking on doors. The only third-year student in his room was Nevil Santomayor, who seemed terribly embarrassed by her visit and had no infor-mation for her. None of the first- and second-year fellows could help her either. She paused at the door to Head-mistress's office. She'd been ordered to stay away from Gray, but she could ask about Fenton. It was possible that the two were together.

But she didn't knock. Headmistress would see through her subterfuge and deliver another lecture. And if she did know where Gray or Fenton was, she would not likely give Re-hanne the information.

Rehanne headed upstairs to question the girls as she had the boys. Someone must have seen one or the other. They couldn't have vanished into another dimension.

Lina paced relentlessly until she drove Giselle from their room. Good. The only cure for this restlessness was to shapechange, but she couldn't do that in Giselle's presence.

Oryon was responsible for her mood. When she'd told him of Vanita's missing fire jewel, he hadn't reacted with the interest she expected. He merely shrugged and turned away, and when she'd called him back, he'd been distant and haughty, like the old Oryon.

His coldness prevented her from apologizing for her ear-lier accusation. If he was too angry with her to be civil, she'd let him stew. She'd been willing to admit that she was wrong, but she wouldn't grovel. Not for anyone.

Her mind gave the command, her muscles tensed, then re-laxed as her limbs flowed into the panther form. She jumped to the sill of the open window, crouched, and stared out into the night, her keen eyes gauging the distance to the garden below. She aimed for soft dirt and sprang.

The spongy loam and leafy plants provided a safe landing place; she was jarred but not hurt. She sat a few moments grooming herself until she recovered from the force of the jump.

She glided along the rows of lettuce, alert, sniffing for her prey. Plump rabbits roamed the garden nibbling on lettuce and cabbage, and she was hungry for a kill. A shift in the wind brought her distended nostrils the sharp scent of blood.

Cautiously, ears twitching, muscles poised for action, she followed the scent. Her nose led her into the tall corn. She might have welcomed the cover, but the sense of danger was greater here. Crouching, belly to the ground, she crept slowly, smoothly, rustling scarcely a leaf as she passed.

Corn stalks crackled, snapped. Something rose up out of the darkness ahead of her. Something too dark for cat's eyes to see. A stink of evil rolled from it, and she yowled and whirled and streaked away through the garden and into the pastures and fields beyond. As fleet as she, the thing raced after her until she leaped across a narrow stream. On the far side of the shallow water she slowed, sensing that her pursuer had abandoned the chase.

She set off on a wide loop that would bring her back to the stream far from her original crossing place. If it was safe, she could jump over and follow a circuitous route back to the school.

Before she reached the stream, the scent of rabbit distracted her from her plan. Recalling her hunger, she loped off toward the promise of food.

Later, muzzle bloodied from her feast, satisfaction having

driven away all vestiges of alarm, she sprinted back to the school the most direct way. Long ago she'd discovered a reasonably safe route back to her room. She circled the buildings until she faced the stone wall that enclosed the courtyard. It was an easy leap to the top of the wall. Another leap took her to the roof of the single-story Assembly Hall. She sped across the roof and made a high spring to the roof of the two-story Faculty Residence Hall. From that vantage point she could view the window of the women's washroom and, when no light shone inside, a final powerful spring would carry her through that window. In the washroom she would change back to human form and stroll to her room.

Except that this time as she leaped from the sill of the washroom window to the floor, the light came on. At the light switch, Ferene K'Sere gave a startled jump and stifled a scream with a hand clamped to her mouth.

"Lina? You must be. Ugh! You're all bloody. What have you been into?"

The panther growled and crouched as if to spring, though she only wanted to scare Ferene away. But instead of moving, Ferene stretched both hands in front of her. "Hold!" she ordered. "Daneu V'Liet!"

The words meant nothing to Lina; to the panther they meant only that a scare was not enough. The panther sprang but halted in midair, frozen in place by an unexpected act of power. She twisted and turned but did not fall. Some kind of invisible net held her suspended, trapped.

Unable to free herself, Lina tried to change to human form to reason with Ferene. She could not. Nor could she see Ferene or the washroom or anything else. She was caught in a white haze that blocked both vision and sound. Even her own howls and snarls were smothered into silence.

She could not endure this terrible nothingness.

12

CRIME AND CONFUSION

Gray didn't appear at breakfast; he hadn't slept in his room last night, and no one Rehanne questioned had seen him. Frantic, she was determined to see Headmistress and report him missing. But she was assigned to kitchen duty for the hour between breakfast and the first class. She had to get away for a last search and a visit to Headmistress's office.

She reported to the kitchen as soon as she could leave her table, began work early, and when the other students on that work detail appeared, asked them to excuse her for a few minutes. Most were first-year students more than willing to help a third-year. She left second-year student Troy Cavender in charge and hurried out.

Where might Gray have hidden? Would he have left the school? She checked the library, glanced toward the door at the end of the corridor. A thin sliver of light breached the usual darkness. The door must not be fully closed. Rehanne rushed to it and saw something wedged between door and frame.

She pushed the door open far enough to allow her to retrieve the object and propped it open with her foot while she examined her find. The small black notebook was inscribed with Gray's name. He must have gone out this door and left it in place to be sure he could get back in. So he hadn't left with the intention of not returning. But he hadn't returned.

She swung the door open wide and peered out. A group of students was working in the garden, as always at this hour. Gray was not assigned to that detail, she knew, but perhaps she should leave the notebook wedged in the door and make a quick trip to the garden to ask if anyone had seen Gray.

She stooped to replace the notebook but was jerked upright by a loud scream. The garden workers were running toward the rows of corn. Pocketing the notebook, she ran toward the field, letting the door slam shut behind her.

When she reached the stand of corn, she heard cries and the snaps and crunches of stalks being broken and trampled.

"He's dead!" someone shouted. "His throat's torn open."

"No!" Rehanne pushed through the corn. She stumbled into the knot of students and tried to elbow through. "I want to see him," she sobbed. "Let me see Gray."

But arms caught her, held her back. "You don't want to see him," a male voice said. "It's horrible."

Petra slipped an arm around Rehanne's waist. "It isn't Gray," she said. "It's Fenton."

Not Gray! Rehanne froze, relief giving way to a terrible certainty. Fenton had remembered something. He was dead. Gray's notebook in the door, Gray missing—they could mean that Gray had done this dreadful thing.

But the notebook hid in her pocket. It could be the only clue that linked Gray with the murder. If she revealed it, she would be responsible for condemning Gray. But if Gray had killed once, maybe twice—she didn't know whether Kress was alive or dead—he might kill again. She couldn't permit that.

Of course, it wasn't really Gray doing the killing. It was the beast within him, the cruel thing he'd brought back from the Dire Realms. He couldn't be held responsible for its actions. But the thing would have to be exorcised. She'd have to confess to Headmistress what she knew, show her the notebook, and hope that Headmistress could find a way to deliver Gray from the evil that was destroying him. Headmistress had been sent for and was on her way. Rehanne did not want to have to accuse Gray in front of other students. She'd speak to Headmistress in private, not out here so near Fenton's mutilated body.

She broke away from the arms that held her and dashed back to the building, entering by the door into the classroom wing, since the door into the library wing would have locked behind her. She ran back to the kitchen, and, somehow, hid her anxiety and finished her work with the crew, telling them only that she hadn't found Gray and hadn't seen Headmistress.

At the end of the hour she walked slowly to her first class. Master Hawke met the students at the door. "Class is canceled," he said. "Report instead to the Assembly Hall in thirty minutes for a specially called meeting of the student body."

By the time thirty minutes passed and the students and faculty gathered in the Assembly Hall, the news had spread, and Rehanne knew through both overheard whispers and straightforward conversations that everyone was aware that Fenton had been murdered and that Gray was missing. And Lina. No one had seen Lina since late last evening.

So I'm back to the same dilemma, Rehanne mused. *Gray or Lina?*

Headmistress's address offered no answer. She announced bluntly that Fenton Rhoze had been found murdered in the cornfield, that the provincial authorities would conduct an investigation with which all students were asked to cooperate fully, that she and the faculty would conduct their own inquiry as well, and anyone with any information, no matter how insignificant it might seem, was to report to her after the assembly. Classes were canceled for two days. Students were not to leave the campus for any reason. A solemn service would be held tomorrow to honor Fenton. Students were strictly enjoined from using any form of power for any reason. Students were also warned to refrain from gossip and rumormongering. The work detail assigned to the garden was excused from its duties until the resumption of classes, and no one was to go into the garden until then. Finally, any student who had lost any personal belonging should report that loss to her.

After that injunction, Headmistress dismissed the students to spend the remainder of the day mourning for Fenton.

Four or five students made their way toward Headmistress as the others left the Assembly Hall. They must have information. Gray's notebook felt heavy in Rehanne's skirt pocket. She should join the informants. She started in that direction but hesitated when she saw Chantal in the group. Did her roommate merely intend to report the missing earring, or did she have other information?

Curious, she approached the group clustered around Headmistress and positioned herself behind Chantal while taking note of the others waiting: Reece, Britnor, and a first-year student whom Rehanne had heard addressed as Dwayne. But Ferene K'Sere had reached Headmistress first and the rest waited while Ferene took her aside to whisper in her ear. Rehanne noted that Chantal strained to hear Ferene's communication, but she herself could hear nothing, and she doubted that Chantal could.

When Ferene finished, Headmistress turned to the others. "I must accompany Miss K'Sere to take care of a matter. I shall not be long. Please, the rest of you go directly to my office and wait for me at the door."

She and Ferene hurried off. The others exchanged puzzled looks and trooped after them across the quadrangle and into the classroom wing. Rehanne, busy with her own thoughts and fears, didn't notice until they reached the stairs that Chantal was no longer with them. Rehanne hadn't seen her veer off anywhere, but she was gone, in direct violation of Headmistress's order. The foolish girl was asking for trouble.

Headmistress and Ferene preceded them up the stairs to the second floor, then continued to the third while the waiting students grouped in front of Headmistress's office and shifted about in embarrassment, avoiding one another's eyes.

Reece cleared his throat, stuck his hands in his pockets, and looked at Rehanne, a red flush suffusing his face. "I, uh, I have to tell her, you know, that Gray wasn't in the room last night. She probably already knows it, but she'll expect me to report it. I'm not trying to get Gray in trouble."

"I know," Rehanne said. "I'm planning to tell her myself how I've hunted for Gray last night and this morning. After all, suppose . . ." A sob caught in her throat, and she shuddered. "Suppose something's happened to Gray, too."

Reece nodded, but without meeting her eyes. It was clear that he suspected Gray and probably intended to tell Headmistress so.

"I've got to tell her I may have been the last person to see poor Fenton alive," Britnor said. Perhaps he wanted to spare Reece more embarrassment; perhaps he simply needed to talk. "I mean, besides the killer. We walked upstairs together after our last class, and I left him at his room. He was gone when I went by on the way to supper. I haven't heard anybody say they saw him after that."

"I did." The boyish voice squeaked with nervousness. The chubby first-year student stood at the edge of the stairs, on the fringe of the group. Rehanne had forgotten his presence. She joined the others in turning to stare at him.

Dwayne's normally pink skin turned rosier. "I—I was in the library reading the first assignment for Beginning Ethics while I waited for the supper bell. I happened to look up and see Fenton walk by. He wasn't alone. He—" He gasped and jerked, as if yanked from behind, teetered on the edge of the stair, and toppled backward. Too late, the others jumped to grab him. Bouncing and tumbling, head crashing against the risers, he fell all the way to the bottom of the stairs.

Everyone froze in horrified shock until Rehanne let out an involuntary scream. Amidst more shouting, Britnor and Reece clattered down the steps and bent over the crumpled body. "Get a healer!" Reece bellowed.

"I think it's too late," Britnor said in a hollow voice. "I think his neck's broken."

"Well, at least you can't blame me for *that* death."

At the cold, hard voice Rehanne spun around and saw Lina standing between Headmistress and Ferene like a prisoner escorted by guards.

Headmistress released her grip on Lina's arm and hurried down the steps to kneel beside Dwayne. Other students were gathering, drawn by the screams. Giselle came flying out from the parlor, threw herself down by Dwayne, and thrust her hands between Headmistress's to touch his face and neck.

Headmistress shook her head. "You can do nothing, Miss Dorr."

"No!" Giselle screamed. "No! Not again! He can't die! I won't let him. I won't have another death! I won't!"

She threw herself on top of Dwayne, her face covering his, her hands pressed on his chest. Britnor and Reece squeezed out of the way and backed up the stairs to the landing, forcing Rehanne to step back beside Lina and Ferene. She saw that Ferene still clasped Lina's arm and that the cat-girl radiated anger.

"This was an accident," Ferene said. "What happened to poor Fenton wasn't."

Rehanne's gaze shifted from Ferene and Lina back to the figures on the stairs. Headmistress was bending over Giselle, her hands on the would-be healer's head. Calming her, she thought. Consoling her for being unable to raise the dead.

Something had caused Dwayne to lose his balance and fall backward at the critical moment before he could speak the name of Fenton's companion. An accident? Rehanne didn't think so. She'd had a brief impression of a presence on the stair behind Dwayne as he fell. The same chilling presence she'd sensed in the empty room and later on the stairs after the attack on Kress.

And if that unseen presence had killed Dwayne and attacked Kress, Lina wasn't guilty of those crimes. Surely the same criminal had murdered Fenton. Two murderers couldn't be loose in the school.

Gray couldn't be guilty either.

Where *was* Gray?

Lina cared nothing for the fat boy who lay broken on the stairs. She did not believe the death had been an accident, but she didn't bother to contradict Ferene. The less attention called to her humiliating plight, the better. She regretted that she had spoken at all.

Ferene was only a second-year student, yet the ease with which she'd captured Lina suggested that she must be at least fourth level and might be higher. Lina didn't know what force had held her prisoner. She only knew that the entrapment had seemed to last forever. Being deprived of all sensory input had so unnerved her that when she was abruptly tumbled into the world of color and sound and changed back to human form, she found herself on hands

and knees, gibbering. Headmistress's touch had calmed her
and allowed her to rise and attempt to reclaim her dignity.

And then she had heard Ferene accuse her of murdering
Fenton by ripping open his throat while in her panther form,
offering as proof that the panther's face had been smeared
with blood when she came through the washroom window.
Headmistress had added that pawprints were found near
Fenton's corpse.

She'd been given no chance to deny the charges. Headmistress and Ferene had grabbed her arms and marched her
off toward Headmistress's office. She'd tried to resist and
break free, but their power held her in check. She could only
grind her teeth in rage as they paraded her down the hall like
a common criminal.

When Headmistress ran to the fallen student, Lina still
could not break Ferene's grip. She stood unmoving, not
wanting the other students to realize her helplessness.

Lina spotted Oryon in the crowd at the foot of the stairs.
She tried to catch his eye. If she could somehow communicate her need, he had the power to free her. He did see her,
and his gaze lingered a moment on her face. But mind-
speaking was not among her talents. She frowned in Ferene's direction and glanced significantly at the hand
clamped around her arm, but Oryon gave no sign of understanding the message.

If only her power would come back. She wasn't sure
whether she'd merely depleted it by her struggles to escape
the prison Ferene had enclosed her in, or whether Ferene
was somehow suppressing it. The young woman had to be
using considerable power to maintain the hold Lina could
not break. Maybe she could draw enough of that power. She
relaxed, concentrated, tried to open a channel from her captor to her. Ferene shot her an angry look and tightened her

grip on Lina's arm. The channel refused to open. Lina couldn't repress a grudging admiration for the girl's astonishing ability, but it made her no less eager to free herself.

She doubted that anyone else was using power, but she cast about anyway. A probing tendril sent back an unexpected jolt. It had tapped into a strong talent. Lina tested to be sure that the source was not Headmistress or Giselle. No matter how desperate, Lina was not foolish enough to attempt to draw power from Headmistress. And she could not be so cruel as to draw from Giselle while she attempted healing.

The flow came from among those at the foot of the stairs. Not Oryon; she'd recognize his touch. Then who? And what was the person doing? She saw no manifestation of power, yet the strong flow indicated a reckless expenditure of talent.

Lina breathed deeply, drawing in the power, reveling in the infusion of strength.

A thing dark and poisonous swept over her, a sensation as of spiders crawling over her flesh. She squeezed off the channel. Shuddering, she fought to control the nausea that twisted her stomach, filled her mouth with bile.

She glanced at Ferene to see whether she, too, felt that evil flow. Ferene was frowning, and her hand was icy, but her gaze was fixed on Headmistress and Giselle.

Lina followed the gaze and saw Headmistress lift Giselle off the fat boy's body and help her stand. Lina's mind flashed back suddenly to another accident, years ago, on the stairs in her home in Stansbury, when her little brother had fallen and died. She closed her eyes.

She opened them at the sound of footsteps on the stairs, saw Veronica reach Headmistress, take charge of Giselle, and lead her off through the crowd below.

Headmistress recruited Oryon and Kelby Carter to lift Dwayne's body and carry it into the parlor. She ordered everyone else to his or her room, but Ferene stayed stubbornly where she was, and Lina had no choice but to stand beside her to be stared at by each person who ascended the stairs.

Chantal shot her a venomous glance as she passed. Lina hadn't seen her among the gawkers and wondered briefly where she had come from.

Rehanne didn't join her roommate, but stayed on the landing with Lina and Ferene. She, at least, paid no attention to Lina but stared down at the parlor door, her face drawn and anxious. When Headmistress came out and climbed the stairs, Rehanne stepped in front of Ferene, intercepted Headmistress, and said, "Please, I must speak to you right away."

Headmistress nodded and glanced wearily at Ferene. "I'll see Miss Zalos first, but I won't be long."

She and Rehanne entered the office, and Lina prepared to endure another wait, guessing that Rehanne wanted to whine about Gray. But it must have been more than that. The office door opened again, Headmistress leaned out and said, "I shall be delayed. Miss K'Sere, release Miss Mueller, and both of you return to your rooms. Miss Mueller, you will find your shapechanging ability taken from you until these crimes are resolved."

Lina clenched her fists and bit back a protest. It would be useless. Headmistress shot back into her office, not waiting to see whether Ferene obeyed her. For several minutes it seemed she wasn't going to. She didn't speak, just held on to Lina and glared at her. Finally she gave a disgusted snort and cast Lina's arm loose as if ridding herself of a nasty bit of garbage. Lina let her get well ahead of her before she, too, ascended the stairs and hurried to her room.

Giselle's absence gave her freedom to experiment. She tried to shapechange, but Headmistress had not misled her. She retained her human form. She tested her other talents.

She could lift books off her desk and float them across the room, shrink and expand her desk chair, create and dispel the illusion that her bed pillow was a large, dark stone.

So Headmistress hadn't taken those abilities, only the shape-changing. Surely she would have taken them all if she really believed Lina guilty of killing Fenton. Unless she knew how depleted Lina's power was—but she'd expect it to increase. Headmistress wouldn't wait long before calling her back to face Ferene's charge.

She could build her power up quickly if she could find Oryon and persuade him to perform another exchange. She left her room and headed for the stairs.

Rehanne stepped off the stairs as Lina reached them. Lina intended to hurry past her, but Rehanne blocked her way. "I have to talk to you," she said.

"I'm busy," Lina snapped.

But Rehanne wouldn't let her pass. "It's important," she insisted. "I need your help."

The appeal aroused Lina's curiosity. She nodded and led the way back to her room.

The loud meow was so unexpected and jarring in the stillness that Gray had to hear it several more times before he was sure he was not hallucinating. He jumped to his feet and hunted for the source of the sound.

After making certain that no cat hid in the parlor, he followed the sound into the corridor that led to the classroom wing. Not much light penetrated here. He strained to see in the gloom and caught a glimpse of what might have been a furry tail disappearing into an adjoining corridor. He broke into a run, rounded the corner, and raced panting through the hall, his pounding feet stirring up clouds of dust, making it even more difficult to see.

Another meow told him he was following the right trail.

He paused where the corridor forked. A swish of silver tail a short distance ahead led him up the right fork.

Fork? There were no forking corridors in the school. Intersecting, yes, but that had been a fork he'd passed. He didn't stop to puzzle it out but hurried in search of his feline guide.

Another meow. A twist of the passageway.

The school's halls were straight; they didn't twist.

The light was better here. Rainbow-hued light streamed through narrow windows of stained glass. The school's windows were all plain—clear (albeit usually dirty) glass.

Never mind. This glass was clean, the hall free of dust, and ahead of him paraded a silver cat, its fluffy tail hoisted high like a banner.

"Puss, puss. Here, puss," Gray called.

The cat ignored him and pranced on. Gray followed.

With a purposeful air it led him into a magnificent chamber hung with crystal chandeliers and lined with floor-to-ceiling mirrors in heavy gold frames. Gray gaped at his reflection, appalled at the gaunt, dirty, whiskered, wild eyed apparition that stared back at him, out of place amid the elegance of the room. Shamed, he tore his gaze away and searched for the cat, saw it priss through a door at the far end of the chamber.

He skidded across the white marble floor and into what appeared to be a throne room. His feet sank into a red plush carpet. Exquisite tapestries lined the walls. Hundreds of candles glittered in jeweled chandeliers hung from a high domed ceiling. Opposite him on a dais was a golden chair with red velvet cushions. The cat jumped up on the chair, circled, and sat on its haunches, regarding Gray as a king might regard a petitioner in his court.

"Cat, what have you brought me to?" Gray asked, his voice echoing strangely in the large empty chamber.

He didn't expect an answer. He didn't get one. But the cat

stared at him as though it expected something of him. Not having a clue what that might be, he broke away from the cat's unwavering gaze and wandered around the room.

Straight-backed chairs of polished mahogany with cushioned seats were arranged along the walls. He stepped between two of them to examine a tapestry.

The work was of superior quality. The pastoral scene depicted a shepherdess leading a flock of sheep down a verdant mountain slope toward a distant village. To one side, watching shepherdess and sheep, a satyr perched on a large rock and played reed pipes. So perfectly executed was every detail that Gray thought he could hear the high, haunting melody.

He backed up and wandered to the next tapestry. This one was a forest scene showing a stag drinking from a stream while the same satyr sat on the limb of a tree and played his pipes.

Again Gray imagined the notes. He thought of Viad, the first-year student with the ability to fill a selected person's mind with eerie music. But Viad was not here, and the music was only a product of Gray's imagination, overstimulated by the opulent and mysterious surroundings.

He moved on to another tapestry, found the piping satyr in it, too, though in a wintry setting with children skating on a frozen lake.

Under the cat's watchful eye Gray examined every tapestry, found the satyr in each, though never as the central figure and sometimes so far in the background that Gray had to study the work carefully to spot him.

The horned and bearded satyr made Gray think of the goat-demon, but he rejected the association. In every tapestry the satyr had a merry face, a jaunty pose, and seemed a symbol of joy or tranquility, not evil.

Having made the circuit of the room, Gray stood again in front of the enthroned cat. "So what does it all mean?" he asked.

As if in answer, the cat jumped down from the throne and strolled toward the door. Gray followed it back into the chamber of mirrors. The cat paused before one mirror and flicked its tail toward the glass.

He looked at his reflection in the mirror, saw the same scruffy, unshaven figure. But around him the reflected room was not empty but filled with people, gorgeously clad, moving about, nodding, bowing, and curtsying to one another as if mingling at a state reception. Behind him, grinning over his shoulder, was the satyr with his pipes.

Gray whirled, stared at the empty chamber, flung out his arms, and grasped at the space where the reflected satyr had stood. His fingers clutched only air.

He turned back to the mirror and saw again the populated room. Of all the occupants, the satyr alone seemed aware of his presence. Meeting and holding his gaze, the goat-footed figure put the pipes to his mouth and played. The mirrored folk gathered around the satyr, listening to music Gray could hear only in his imagination. The satyr bowed and everyone applauded. But all the while he had played, his eyes had been fixed on Gray, and Gray was certain that the concert had been for him, not for the audience in the mirror.

Again Gray turned and verified that the chamber was empty.

The cat meowed and strutted away, leading Gray from the hall of mirrors, down a corridor, through a narrow doorway into a dark passage. He could no longer see his guide. He considered turning back into the light, when he felt the cat press against him. Purring loudly, it rubbed his legs and seemed to nudge him forward.

Gray bent and scratched the cat's ears. "Guess I'd better trust you, fellow. You seem to know your way around." He moved forward into blackness.

Several steps brought him up against what felt like a brick wall. "Now what?"

No answering meow or purr. No soft padding of cat's feet. Nothing.

He probed the wall in front of him, felt an edge, an opening. He measured it, pushed himself through it.

And found himself in the school parlor. The real one.

He was standing by the fireplace. At the door, their backs to him, stood Oryon and another student whom after a few moments he recognized as Kelby Carter.

In the middle of the room a body lay stretched out on the floor. The features were familiar. The baby-faced first-year fellow he'd met at the table with Viad. What was his name—oh, yes. Dwayne.

He stepped closer, stared down at the round face, its ruddiness replaced with the pallor of death.

He must have made some sound. Oryon and Kelby spun around. "Where did you come from?" Oryon demanded.

"I don't know." It sounded stupid, but he had no explanation for where he had been or how he had come here.

Oryon's eyes narrowed; his brows arched. Kelby stared in bewilderment. And something else. Fear.

"You look awful," Oryon said with no hint of sympathy. "Headmistress just left here. She'll want to see you and hear what happened to you. We're supposed to stay on guard and keep everybody out of the parlor until the peace officers get here. But I think she'd want me to take you up to her."

Gray shook his head. "Kelby can go tell her I'm here. That'll give me a chance to talk to you before I see her."

Oryon looked surprised but nodded. "Go on, Kelby. Hurry."

Kelby darted from the room as if he welcomed the chance to escape.

Oryon waited for the clatter of feet on the stairway. "He's gone," he said. "What did you want to say?"

Gray swallowed and forced out the words. "Only that I've decided to work with you. I don't have any choice."

"Did you do this?" Oryon cocked his head toward Dwayne's corpse.

"Did I—Of course not!" Gray spluttered, stunned. "I don't even know how he died."

"What about Fenton?" Oryon asked. "Somebody tore his neck open. Was it you?"

"Fenton? I—No!" Gray collapsed into a chair. "I think you'd better tell me what's been happening here."

13

PAN-DEMON-IUM

Oryon had time to give Gray no more than a quick summary of the morning's events before Headmistress came downstairs. At the same time, the provincial authorities arrived in a long black limousine. Headmistress looked more annoyed and flustered than Gray had ever seen her.

"I'd hoped they wouldn't get here until after lunch," she said, peering out the window. "I wonder whether they've brought someone gifted with them as I asked. If they haven't, they'll never understand what's been happening here."

Will even a gifted understand? Gray wondered. *Does Headmistress understand?*

He knew *he* didn't. Confused and shaken by what Oryon had told him, he could only sit and stare dazedly at Headmistress.

"Veronica will admit them and hold them off for a few minutes, but then I must go and speak to them," Headmistress continued. "You gentlemen go upstairs. Gray, if you hurry, you'll have time to clean up before lunch. I'll stall the investigators as long as I can. You'll be better able to deal with them after you've eaten."

She thinks I did it. The realization rolled over Gray with terrible force. *She's trying to protect me, but not because she believes in my innocence.*

Of course, she thought it was the demon acting in him, so she didn't blame him. She wanted to help him. She'd called him Gray, not Mr. Becq. But she thought he'd committed the crimes.

But he'd had no memory loss this time. What had happened to him hadn't been a dream; it had been real. He'd probably never get anyone to believe his story, but at least *he* knew he'd had nothing to do with either Fenton's death or Dwayne's.

"Come on, Gray." Oryon roused him, helped him to his feet. "Let's get upstairs before the peace officers see us."

Gray wanted to refuse Oryon's help, but his knees nearly gave way when he stood, and he would have fallen but for Oryon's supporting hand. At least no one was around to witness his humiliation. Kelby hadn't come back downstairs, and Gray remembered Oryon saying that Headmistress had ordered all students to stay in their rooms except to go to the dining hall.

His shakiness had subsided enough by the time he reached his room that he was able to shower and shave without assistance, though he could have called on Reece if he had to. His roommate was surprised to see him. Gray offered no explanation of where he'd been. "It's a long story," he said. "I don't have the strength to tell it now."

By the time he had cleaned up it was too late to go to lunch, but Oryon found him and told him not to worry. "I've arranged for food to be brought up here." The dark one grinned. "It took some doing. But it will give us a chance to talk."

Gray finished dressing and headed for Oryon's room. The hall was quiet; everyone else was in the dining hall for lunch—or so he thought until he opened Oryon's door and saw not only Oryon but also Rehanne and Lina. Startled and dismayed, he started to back out of the room, but Rehanne rushed forward and threw her arms around his neck.

"Gray, I've been so worried about you. When Oryon told me you were here, I had to see you. Where have you been?"

His arms tightened around her; he held her close against him without answering. She shouldn't be here. He didn't want her involved in this mess. But the comfort of her presence overwhelmed him. He buried his face in her hair, breathing in its clean, warm scent, feeling its softness against his cheek, his lips.

"Touching reunion, but we don't have time for it." Lina's voice, tinged with sarcasm, intruded on the moment, dashed it with bitterness.

Gray pulled free of Rehanne's embrace and turned to Oryon. "What's she doing here?" he asked with a flick of his head toward Lina.

"I invited her," Oryon said. "Rehanne was with her, so . . ."

Gray swung back to Rehanne. "You were with *her*? Why?"

Rehanne blushed. "I—I had a conference with Headmistress." She hurried past that statement as though it had been a confession she hadn't wanted to make. "She advised me to talk to Lina. She said if we pooled our knowledge, we might discover that we each had pieces of the puzzle that we could put together to form a picture. She also said," she hesitated, took a deep breath, "that Fenton and Dwayne were killed because of something they knew that no one else knew. So if we all have the same information, we'll be protecting ourselves. The killer would have to murder all four of us to suppress it. He wouldn't find that easy to do."

"Or she," Gray said darkly, glaring at Lina. "And if he or she is one of us, that would only leave three to kill. Maybe only two." His suspicious gaze swung back and forth between Oryon and Lina.

"I haven't murdered anybody," Lina snapped. "Have you?"

"We're wasting time with this sparring," Oryon said, cutting off Gray's angry retort. "If one of us is the killer, he isn't likely to admit it. But if we share information and one of us lies, he—or she—may trap himself—or herself. And if we can't figure something out before the peace officers interrogate us, one or more of us might wind up in a cell in the Millville jail."

Rehanne linked her arm in his. "Please, Gray, come and sit down. Oryon has lunch."

He let her lead him to the two desks, which had been pushed together to form a table and were spread with plates of cold roast beef, cheese, bread, tomato slices, and pickles. A pitcher of iced tea stood among four glasses.

"Rehanne said you'd be hungry," Oryon said, pouring the tea. "We can talk while we eat."

He should be hungry, but the sight of the food and the thought of eating with his enemies turned his stomach. He stood uncertainly behind the chair and didn't reach for the glass Oryon held out to him.

"Oh, gods! This is useless." Lina flounced toward the door.

Oryon set down the pitcher with a force that sent tea sloshing over the sides. "Come back here!"

Oryon's command halted her, but she didn't turn around. She stood stiff-backed, immobile.

"I knew I shouldn't have come," Gray muttered.

Rehanne hovered at his side, looking ready to burst into tears.

"Can't we act civilized for one hour?" Oryon demanded.

Lina spun around. "You're a fine one to talk about acting civilized," she said, her eyes like green fire. "And how do we know you aren't the murderer? You're the only one I know who could have pulled that poor boy down the stairs and broken his neck. Who else has the talent of invisibility?"

Rehanne gasped.

Gray slammed his fist against the back of the chair. "That's the first sensible thing she's said."

"It seems Headmistress overestimated us," Oryon said in an icy tone. "We can't cooperate, even to save ourselves."

"So you admit it's yourself you're trying to save," Lina said with a snarl.

"Me, and you," Oryon pointed at Lina, swung his finger toward Gray. "And him, and—"

"Oh, stop it! This is ridiculous," Rehanne shouted, tears spilling down her cheeks. "This isn't what we came here for."

"What did we—"

A knock interrupted Lina's question. No one went to the door, but it opened anyway.

Kress walked into the room.

He smiled.

No one moved. No one seemed to breathe.

"Well! I've been wondering where everyone was. Is this reception for me? How kind of you. I hadn't expected a party." He moved toward the table.

Lina shrank aside as he passed her. Instinctively Gray stepped close to Rehanne, put an arm around her.

Kress's eyes glittered. His voice had a cold, hard edge, like a spell knife. He snatched up bread, slapped a piece of meat on it, and crammed the whole thing into his mouth. He picked up a glass, gulped down the tea, dropped the glass, letting it shatter on the floor, and crammed more meat into his mouth, this time not bothering with bread.

Gray nudged Rehanne, nodded toward the door, and eased slowly away from Kress while he was distracted by the food. Rehanne moved with him, not questioning though she must have wondered. Oryon had backed to the rear of the room and edged over to the window. Maybe he intended to dive out if necessary.

Kress continued to gorge himself, and Gray began to think they might make it out to the hall, where they could run for help. Rehanne was trembling against him. She must have realized what Kress had become. He had to get her to safety.

He and Rehanne passed in front of Lina. She clutched their arms. "What's the matter with him?"

"Possessed," Gray hissed, trying to force Lina to back with them to the door.

"And you're going to duck out and leave Oryon alone with him?"

At her indignant whisper Kress raised his head and grinned at them. A piece of cheese dangled from the corner of his mouth. Crumbs studded his whiskered chin. He dropped the second glass he'd emptied and moved toward them, the shards crunching under his feet.

"We've got to use our power against him," Lina whispered, standing her ground.

What power? Gray asked himself. Maybe Lina and Oryon together could do something to stop the murderous thing. He couldn't, and he didn't think Rehanne could. He tore free of Lina's grasp, swung Rehanne behind him, and pushed her toward the door. "Run!" he told her. "Get Headmistress."

Praise the Power-Giver, she obeyed. Gray heard her race down the deserted hall.

"Fool!" Lina shouted. "We need all the power we can get. Use yours!"

With a maniacal screech Kress lunged at them, teeth bared. His hands pummeled them, tore at them; his teeth sank into Gray's shoulder.

Oryon hurled himself onto Kress's back, caught him in a headlock. Kress released Gray and Lina and grappled with Oryon.

Use your power, Lina had said. But as far as Gray could tell, Oryon was fighting only with his normal physical strength. Kress threw him to the floor, sat on him, and wrapped his hands around Oryon's throat.

"Help me, Gray!" Lina shouted. A chair lifted into the air, hurled itself at Kress, broke over his head with no apparent effect. Books and a heavy lamp crashed against his skull. Lina was doing her part, but Kress shook aside her artillery as if it were a cloud of gnats.

Gray used his talent to draw up the broken and crushed glass, form it into the face of the satyr in the tapestries, and position it in front of Kress's face. It was the only thing he could think of.

With a roar of rage, Kress released Oryon and swatted at the sculpture. Slivers of glass fountained upward. Gray regathered and reformed them, this time into the head of the cat. Kress backed away from it.

Holding his neck, Oryon staggered to his feet. "Lina, ward!" he croaked.

Lina jumped to Oryon's side and clasped his hand. Gray felt currents of power stream from them. He concentrated on holding the cat sculpture together to keep Kress distracted while they worked.

His power wasn't strong enough. The sculpture crumbled. Kress growled and sprang at him. His shoulder rammed into Gray's chest. He fell backward, and Kress fell on top of him, pressing him to the floor, squeezing the air from his lungs. A blow exploded against his head. He descended into a terrifying blackness.

Rehanne raced to Headmistress's office. She pounded on the door. No one answered.

She must be at lunch. Or conferring with the peace officers. She dashed down the stairs.

The parlor was empty. Dwayne's body had been removed. Rehanne wheeled around, ran toward the dining hall.

Veronica stepped out of the shadows and blocked her way. "What is it, miss? More trouble?"

Rehanne nodded, panting for breath. "Kress. He's attacking Gray. And Lina. And Oryon. He's—"

But Veronica had already gathered her skirt in her hands and broken into a run for the stairs.

Rehanne hesitated, wondering whether she should continue looking for Headmistress or follow Veronica. She knew that Veronica's role of maid concealed some other more important function, and that Veronica wielded considerable power. But with Gray's life at stake, would Veronica's talents be enough? She couldn't take a chance. The dining hall was only a few steps away, close enough so that she could hear the clatter of silverware, the murmur of conversation. Lunch was still in progress. She rushed forward.

Veronica's young assistant stepped into her path. "No, Rehanne," she said. "Headmistress isn't in the dining hall. She's talking with the peace officers in the Faculty Residence Hall. You can't disturb them."

"It's an emergency," Rehanne said impatiently. When the assistant didn't move, Rehanne tried to shove her aside.

The slender body could have been a boulder. Rehanne was larger and heavier, but her thrust had no effect.

"Go back," the maid said. "I'll go with you."

Who did this upstart think she was? Rehanne moved to go around her.

The young woman slid over, blocking her. She placed her hands on Rehanne's shoulders. "Rehanne."

The voice. Rehanne knew it. She stared as the unremarkable features changed, assumed a familiar configuration. "Tria!"

Her friend placed her finger to her lips. "Shhh! No one else knows. Except Lina. She always sees through illusion. Now come on, hurry." She pushed Rehanne toward the stairs. This time Rehanne went.

So many questions she wanted to ask, but this wasn't the time. She ran, and Tria ran with her, up the stairs, along the corridor, through the open door to Oryon's room.

Veronica stood in the room, hands on her hips, gazing around at the spatters of blood and splinters of glass that covered the floor. Gray, Kress, Oryon, and Lina were absent.

"Where are they?" Rehanne gasped.

"Gone," was Veronica's unsatisfactory answer.

"Gone where?"

She turned toward them and exchanged glances with Tria. "I don't know," she said. "That's what we'll have to find out."

14

TEA PARTY

Rehanne gazed despairingly at the blood and broken glass scattered and spattered all over the floor of Oryon's room, trying to imagine what might have happened after she left. She shouldn't have gone. She should have stayed at Gray's side.

Her eyes lingered on the remains of the lunch Oryon had provided. If they hadn't fought, if they'd talked and cooperated like civilized people, they might have been able to defeat Kress.

Maybe the others *had* defeated him.

No. If they had, they'd be here. She could not view the blood and the glass and think that all was well.

Tria caught her wrist, pointed to blood spots near the door. "Let's check the hall," she said. "They may have left a trail we can follow."

They left Veronica standing in the middle of the room, doing nothing that Rehanne could see. Rehanne regretted letting Tria talk her out of reporting to Headmistress. She'd only wasted valuable time, time that might mean the difference between life and death to Gray.

In the hall a bloody trail led past Kress's room and on toward the washroom. Rehanne's hope revived. Tria stopped her at the washroom door. "I'll go in alone," she said.

She slipped into near invisibility, opened the washroom door, and stepped inside. A few moments later she was back.

"Not there," she said. "There's no blood on the floor. I don't think they got this far."

"Where could they be? In a room?" Rehanne squinted, trying to pick up the trail that seemed to end in midcorridor.

"We can check them." Tria jiggled a ring of keys at her waist. "I don't think it will do any good."

"Kress may have gone to his room," Rehanne suggested, pointing to the closed door.

"We'll look." Tria unlocked the door and peered inside. Rehanne looked over her shoulder. The room was empty and clean. No trace of blood marred the floor.

When they turned away, Veronica appeared beside them. "A great deal of power's been unleashed," she said. "Too much, and not coordinated. I can't tell what they've done; the signs are mixed. No point in staying here, though. They're not anywhere we can get to through any of *these* doors.

"Come along, both of you. We'll go to my apartment for a spot of tea."

"Tea!" Rehanne couldn't believe her ears.

"Tea clears the mind and sharpens the wits," Veronica said cheerfully.

The indignant refusal that rose to Rehanne's lips was stifled by Tria's hasty explanation. "She has things in her rooms that will help us locate them. It may take some time, but she'll get right to work on it. Don't worry, she isn't just giving a tea party."

Rehanne had no stomach for tea, but she followed Tria and Veronica downstairs.

Students were leaving the dining hall, coming upstairs. Lunch was over. She got several curious looks as she trailed along after the two "maids." She was relieved when they reached the relative safety of the Faculty Residence Hall.

"Miss Zalos." Headmistress's call from the residence parlor brought her to a halt. She had forgotten that Tria had said Headmistress was there with the peace officers.

Headmistress hurried from the parlor, three men in the green and silver uniforms of Castlemount authorities following her. "I'm glad I've found you," Headmistress said. "These officers would like to question you."

Rehanne's heart sank. *Not now!*

Veronica stepped to her side while Tria hurried on. "Since you missed lunch, may I suggest that the gentlemen join us for tea in my sitting room? It will be private and no one will interrupt."

"Excellent, Veronica," Headmistress said. She turned to the men. "We can find no better or more private spot for your use in interviewing students."

One man frowned and another scratched his chin, but the third nodded, and all three fell into line behind Headmistress and Rehanne, while Veronica led the parade.

Rehanne chafed at this development, unable to endure the delay, thinking only of what could be happening to Gray and the rest while they wasted time.

The presence of the peace officers deterred her from blurting out the problem to Headmistress. She didn't know how they might react to her strange tale or what conclusions they might derive from it. So she let herself be drawn along to Veronica's apartment on the first floor of the Faculty Residence Hall and there be ushered into a wingback chair. Tria wheeled out a tea cart and placed a cup of tea in her hand. Veronica served a platter of cookies. No one seemed in a hurry. Everyone was relaxed and congenial. Rehanne thought she would go mad.

"This gentleman is Chief Officer Telpor Ardrey," Headmistress said, indicating the tallest of the three, a middle-aged man with a long, hooked nose and eyes that darted restlessly, never seeming to look directly at anything or anyone. "He directs the Millville Peace Officers and has taken complete charge of the investigation. We are, of course, extending him every courtesy and complying with his every request."

Something in Headmistress's voice contradicted her words and warned Rehanne to exercise caution.

The man cleared his throat. "I understand you have information about the crimes," he said, his gaze focusing on a point near Rehanne's left ear. "Please tell us everything you know. My assistant, Adjutant Lewis Canby, will take down your testimony."

The man he indicated took out a small notepad and a pencil, resting the notepad on his knee with the pencil poised to write.

Rehanne found her hand trembling so that her teacup rattled in its saucer. Surely she dare not really tell these men about Gray, about the notebook in the door, about the mysterious presence on the stair.

She glanced at Headmistress, hoping for some signal, but the woman sat sipping her tea, stony-faced, silent. Veronica and Tria had left the room. She was on her own.

The third man, she noticed, was watching her intently. He was younger than the other two, and had a long face with heavily pockmarked skin. Something peculiar about his eyes drew her attention. It took her a few moments to realize what it was: he had no eyelashes. His steady stare reminded her of a snake. She shuddered.

Ardrey must have noticed her scrutiny. "Your Headmistress requested that at least one member of the investigative team be gifted," he said to the arm of her chair. "Mr. Shardan, there, has the gift of discernment. He will know whether you speak truth, and if you withhold information, he will know that, too. Please begin."

Rehanne took a deep breath. "My name is Rehanne Zalos. I'm a third-year student. I—"

The clatter of the tea cart interrupted her. Tria pushed the cart around while Veronica refilled everyone's cups and offered more cookies. The peace officers looked annoyed but offered no objections.

When everyone had been served, Tria wheeled the cart away, but Veronica remained standing in the center of the room. "Sirs," she said, "it is our custom to present a bit of entertainment with a formal tea. We have for your pleasure a most talented musician."

She beckoned, and a young man, a first-year student, entered and bowed.

Ardrey glared at the tea cart. "See here, woman. We don't have . . ."

His voice trailed off into silence. His eyes glazed, his jaw dropped open.

The secretary's pencil dropped from his fingers. The notepad fell to the floor unnoticed.

The gifted man's serpent eyes closed. The lashless lids gave his face an eerie, empty look.

Headmistress smiled.

Veronica grasped Rehanne's arm and pulled her to her feet. "Hurry," she said. "I'm not sure how long Viad can keep his music going."

"I don't hear any music," Rehanne whispered, puzzled.

"They do."

Veronica pushed her out of the room and through a short hall into a small kitchen where Tria waited. "There's a stiff penalty for interfering with an official investigation," Veronica continued. "We need to work fast, to get you back and get Viad away before they realize what hit them. Quick, tell me everything you know—or think you know. I'll judge how much of it is safe to tell the peace officers."

"But the one who's gifted—he'll know if I leave anything out."

"Pah! He's no great talent. I'll take care of that. He won't know anything we don't want him to know."

Rehanne looked doubtfully at Tria.

"Don't worry," Tria assured her. "Veronica can handle him."

"What about Gray? And the others? How will we find them?"

"I'm working on that. The information you give me will help. So get busy. Start from the beginning and tell me everything."

Tria pushed a kitchen stool toward Rehanne. She sat on it, and Veronica hoisted herself onto a second stool. Rehanne started with Gray's arrival at the school and how Chantal's lost earring caused her to miss meeting him. It was a long story, and she fretted inwardly about the time being lost.

Tria remained standing. Glancing at her, Rehanne was startled by Tria's unfocused eyes, her rigid stance, the look of intense concentration on her face. Her gaze traveled from Tria to the kitchen clock, on a shelf on the opposite wall. The clock had stopped; its hands didn't move as her story progressed. Either Tria was suspending time, or the clock was broken, and Rehanne was sure she knew which.

Reassured, she redoubled her effort to recall every detail, no matter how small, that might relate to Kress's injury and the deaths of Fenton and Dwayne.

Veronica listened intently. She did not interrupt, but from time to time she closed her eyes and her hands made odd motions as though weaving the strands of Rehanne's tale into some larger tapestry.

She was finishing her story with the account of Kress's abrupt arrival and his mad behavior, when Veronica hopped off her stool and extended her hands. Rehanne stopped speaking.

"Go on, go on," Veronica ordered impatiently, not looking at Rehanne but fixing her gaze on something only she could see.

Mystified, Rehanne completed the tale.

"Ah, yes," Veronica said. "I think I have her."

Whatever it was that Gray had been doing, it had provided more power than Lina would have guessed. She had always ridiculed Gray's single talent. But his sculptures had blocked the demon's power. When Kress knocked him unconscious, the immediate cessation of power flow rocked her and must have weakened Oryon as well.

Kress, seated on Gray's chest, threw back his head and howled. He dragged Gray from the room, leaving a trail of blood in his wake. Oryon dashed after him, and Lina followed.

Kress stopped in midcorridor, lifted Gray, and slung him over his shoulder. Gray's eyes blinked open. He moaned and struggled against Kress's hold.

Oryon caught up with them and grabbed Gray's shoulders, trying to pull Gray away from Kress. If only she could shapechange. In her panther form she could launch an effective attack on Kress.

She caught up with them as Kress, snarling, loosed Gray and attacked Oryon. Gray tumbled from Kress's shoulder. She grabbed him, kept him from falling. Together they clutched at Kress.

A wave of dizziness passed over her, breaking her hold. The building seemed to rock. Kress tore free and bolted down the corridor. Recovering her equilibrium, she set off after him.

And stopped in bewilderment.

The corridor had changed. Kress was disappearing down a long dim tunnel that looked carved from rock. She stared around her and saw Oryon and Gray gazing with faces as startled as hers must be. Wherever they were, it wasn't the school.

Oryon was the first to recover. "We've got to catch him," he shouted and ran after Kress.

"Come on," she called to Gray and dashed after Oryon. She heard Gray gasping and wheezing behind her, remembered that he was hurt, realized that he couldn't keep up. But she kept going, not wanting to lose Oryon. He and Kress were already out of sight, vanished into the increasing darkness of the passageway.

She ran on until the loss of light forced her to slow. In the blackness she had no idea where she was or where she was going. "Oryon!" she shouted. "Gray!"

No one answered. She groped about, trying to find a wall to guide her. "Gray! Oryon!" She kept calling the names as she stumbled blindly, encountering nothing to help her orient herself.

Her night vision was excellent. She should be able to see *something*. But the darkness defeated her.

She reached out with her power, testing, pouring all her strength into her ability to strip away illusion. It was a talent that usually came easily to her, yet it seemed that the blackness was absorbing her power, draining it and giving nothing in return. Not wanting to be left powerless, she halted that effort and shouted again for Oryon and Gray.

Finally, in desperation, she shouted, "Kress! Kress, are you here?"

No one answered, but she thought the darkness around her seemed a little less dense. She peered into it, trying to distinguish some feature. Was that spot to her left darker than the area to her right? She moved toward the area that seemed lighter.

She walked a considerable distance, moving slowly, her hands extended to keep from crashing into a wall or other unseen obstacle, not sure she was not imagining the slight increase in light because she wanted it to be there.

Darker shadows did seem to float through the gloom in front of her.

"Oryon? Gray? Kress?" she called, not loudly this time but in a small, frightened voice. "Anyone? Is anyone here?"

Something—a hand?—clamped around her wrist. She gave a startled scream and jerked her hand toward her. Whatever was holding her pulled harder. She was yanked forward and to the side.

Light sprang up around her, blinding her. She blinked rapidly until her vision cleared.

She was standing in a small kitchen. Veronica held her wrist, Rehanne sat on a stool nearby, and Tria leaned against the wall in some sort of trance.

"Lina!" Rehanne jumped off the stool. "Where have you been?"

Tria's eyes focused. She pushed away from the wall and smiled at Lina. "I thought you'd be the easiest to find. Your mind lays a strong trail."

"Welcome, Miss Mueller," Veronica said. "You're just in time for a spot of tea."

15

BARRIERS AND BLOCKADES

I don't know where I was," Lina said. "I don't know how I got there or how I got back here. I lost Oryon and Gray and Kress. Oryon was chasing Kress, and I was trying to follow them, but it was too dark to see. Gray was somewhere behind me. I shouted for all of them and no one answered. We have to find Oryon. If he's with Kress, he's in terrible danger."

"So is Gray," Rehanne added. She wanted more details, but the kitchen clock was working again.

"We'll try to find them," Veronica said. "The first thing, though, is to get rid of those peace officers. Miss Zalos, you go in and tell your story—all you remember."

"You mean, tell them exactly what I told you?"

Veronica chuckled. "I've rearranged your recollection a bit. Only temporarily, mind you. Tell them everything you think of. Things we'd rather they didn't know, you won't think of. Come along. Viad's concert must be close to an end."

Rehanne supposed she should feel grateful to Veronica, but instead she felt resentful that Veronica had prowled about in her mind without her awareness.

As she took her seat in the wingback chair, Viad backed slowly from the room, and Veronica exited with him. Seconds after they left, Chief Officer Ardrey and his two minions stirred, blinked, and looked expectantly at Rehanne, seemingly unaware of the interruption.

"Come, come, Miss, ah, Zalos, is it? We're wasting time," Ardrey said, speaking to some point above her head. "We want to hear all you know of these crimes."

Here I go again. Rehanne repeated the story she had told Veronica. It was easier this second time and went faster. While she spoke, Adjutant Canby wrote furiously, filling page after page in his notebook.

Ardrey interrupted several times to ask questions: "Why didn't you stop and hear what Fenton wanted to tell you?"

She was still explaining that she had been trying to catch up with Gray when he fired the next question: "Do you have any idea what he might have wanted?"

She had barely gotten out the words, "I suppose he remembered something," when he shot out, "What kind of thing could he have remembered?" followed closely by, "Did he tell you anything at all in Kress's room? Anything that might be a clue to the attacker?"

Her denial brought a change of subject: "What about Dwayne? He said he'd seen Fenton with someone. Who might Fenton have been with?"

Each answer she gave triggered a new question: "Who were Fenton's friends? Did he have a girlfriend? Why don't you think Dwayne fell down the stairs accidentally? Are you in the habit of sensing 'mysterious presences'? Why are you here at this school?"

She tried to answer each question fully, but the last question angered her. It had nothing to do with the investigation. She bit her tongue to keep from snapping a rude retort and forced herself to answer it patiently. "I wanted to improve my skills as a spell-caster. I'd learned a lot about spells from my grandmother, but I knew there were other things she couldn't teach me."

"So that's your talent—spell-casting? You use it much?" He was glaring at the wall behind her.

"I use it occasionally. We're only allowed to use our power under the supervision of a faculty member."

"So you didn't try any spells to find your roommate's lost earring or any of the other missing items?"

"No." Rehanne hesitated, surprised by the realization that she could have used a spell to find Chantal's earring, but had never thought of it. Finally she said, "Chantal didn't ask me to. I would have had to get permission."

"These spells—they always work? You always get results from them?"

"They don't always work the way I intend them to." Rehanne hated these questions. "I always get some kind of results."

"They backfire now and then, do they?" He smiled, but the smile turned into a sneer. "Ever hurt anybody?"

"No!" This time she let her anger show. "I'm very careful. I never cast evil spells, only good."

"I see. Perhaps I'll ask your headmistress to allow you to demonstrate one of these 'good' spells. But for the present I think we have all we need from you." He glanced at the gifted assistant.

"Satisfactory," the man said.

Ardrey nodded. "Thank you for your cooperation, Miss Zalos."

That was it. She was dismissed. She looked to Headmistress for guidance. "Veronica will see you out, Miss Zalos," was all she said.

Veronica came, led Rehanne to the door, and stepped into the hall with her. "Tria and Lina are waiting for us in Mistress Dova's classroom," she said. "We can talk privately there."

More talk! They'd talked enough already.

* * *

Lina perched on the edge of a seat in Mistress Dova's classroom. "So. I'm no longer the only one who knows you're here. Does it bother you?"

Tria shook her head. "It's better that few people know, but I trust Rehanne. I suppose she's a bit hurt that I didn't tell her before, but I've acted on Veronica's instructions. If people know I'm here, they'll certainly figure out that I'm not working as a maid."

"Which means that they'd also figure out about Veronica. Do you think all the third-year students haven't already figured out by now that she's a lot more than a maid?"

Tria laughed. "Not all are as perceptive as you, Lina."

"That's true," Lina said, chuckling. "I remember how long it took you even to see the food as it really is."

Veronica walked into the room with Rehanne right behind her.

"What's funny?" Rehanne asked, scowling. "You're sitting here chatting like old friends while Gray and Oryon are lost and may be ripped up by a demon!"

"We *are* old friends," Lina said, standing. "And what's the harm in filling in the time by chatting? We were waiting for you."

"Well, we're here, though I'm not sure why."

"Because there are things you must understand," Veronica said. "Now please, sit down." She indicated the desks and sat in one herself, wedging herself into the narrow seat.

Hands on hips, Lina remained standing. "When is Headmistress going to restore my ability to shapechange?"

"That's a question you'll have to ask her," Veronica answered. "I can't help you."

"You won't, you mean."

Veronica shook her head. "I can't undo what Headmistress has done. I doubt that you need the ability as much as you think."

"Of course I need it! I should have had it when Kress attacked us. How long has he been possessed, anyway?"

"Since the night he was attacked," Veronica said. "That's why we kept him out of sight, locked in a place he shouldn't have been able to get out of."

"It's good to know you aren't infallible," Lina said, enjoying the rare opportunity to goad Veronica.

But Veronica refused to be baited. "I've never claimed infallibility," she said mildly. "Now, please, sit down, and I'll explain what we're dealing with. But first, let me restore the memories I took from Miss Zalos."

A startled look came over Rehanne's face. "Gray's notebook," she said. "I forgot to tell them about finding Gray's notebook in the door. And the earring. Chantal's earring that I found under Kress's door."

"You found the earring? In Kress's room?" Lina had eased into a chair, but she sprang to her feet again. "When was this? Why didn't you tell me?"

"Headmistress forbade me to speak of it. It's not important. We have to find Gray."

"How do you know it's not important?" Lina demanded.

"Miss Mueller, please sit down and remain seated," Veronica said. "And Miss Zalos, you can do nothing to find Gray, but Gray is capable of finding himself."

"But he can't!" To Lina's disgust, Rehanne looked ready to burst into tears. "Gray's only talent is creating sculptures. You know that."

"He *thinks* it's the only thing he can do," Veronica corrected her, shifting her bulk in the desk. "We've always known he had more power than could be expressed in those transient creations, lovely though they were. We couldn't discover another talent, but we knew he had to have one.

"Headmistress once knew someone for whom the sudden discovery of a hidden talent had fatal consequences. She did not want that to happen to Gray."

"And it could?" Rehanne asked, biting her nails, a habit Lina detested.

"It has not. Gray's other talent seems to have come out of hiding. He has been using it without being aware of it. Your stories made me suspect it." She nodded at both Rehanne and Lina. "And Tria was able to confirm it."

"What is it?"

"Tria will explain."

Tria smoothed her plain gingham work dress. "You know I have the gift of folding time," she said in a quiet voice, as if it embarrassed her to speak of her unusual talent.

Rehanne nodded. "You did it a while ago in Veronica's kitchen while I told my story."

"It's not such a great thing, really," she said. "Some people have the ability to shift from one place to another—Davy does, for example."

"You can, too," Lina put in.

Tria frowned as if to warn her former roommate against further interruptions. "Space-shifting is really folding the spatial dimensions so that you transfer from one location in space to another. Time is only another dimension. When I fold time, I transfer from one time to another.

"That kind of dimensional transferring is different from what Aletheia teaches in her interdimensional travel class. Aletheia can travel between the dimensions and by doing so gain access to other universes. Petra has learned to do that."

And so have you. This time Lina didn't speak the thought aloud.

Rehanne's teeth tore savagely at her nails.

While Lina glared at Rehanne, willing her to stop, Tria came at last to her point. "Gray has an ability that somehow allows him to travel between time and to access other times."

"Other times?" Lina shifted her gaze to Tria.

"It's hard to explain," Tria said, rubbing her chin. "When you space-shift you move from place to place in our world. Usually from place to place in the same building. When I time-shift, I go from time to time in the same time line— back an hour or two, then forward again. But just as interdimensional travel leads to places not in our world or even our universe, intertemporal travel leads to a different time line than ours where time moves differently and where the traveler can witness events that never happened in our time line but could have. He's not in a different world. He's in an alternate version of this world."

"Gray can do this?" Rehanne interjected. "I don't believe it!"

"When I shifted time I felt a disturbance shaking the time line—a disturbance I wasn't responsible for," Tria said. "I opened my mind to Veronica, let her feel it, too. She guessed what it was. Finding Lina proved it."

Tria turned to gaze directly at Lina. "Gray took you all between times, and when you separated from the others, you became stranded between time lines. That's why Veronica could locate you. You were the disturbance I felt. Gray, Oryon, and Kress weren't there. They'd entered some other time line."

She turned back to Rehanne. "I'm sorry. I know this will be painful to hear. But we have no way of finding them. It isn't possible to trace them, to find out where they are. Gray has access not only to all the alternate time lines of this plane of existence, but to those in all planes of this dimension. The possibilities are infinite. He will have to find his own way back."

"And Oryon?" Lina demanded. "What will he do? He doesn't have the talent."

Tria bowed her head. "I'm afraid it's all up to Gray. He took them wherever they are, and only he can bring them back."

Rehanne jumped to her feet and confronted Tria. "No! We can't abandon them. What would have happened if we'd abandoned Gray in the other trouble?"

"This is different," Tria said wearily.

"How is it different?" Rehanne persisted. "It's an extension of what happened then. The demon that's controlling Kress is a creature of the Dire Women we were battling then."

"The difference," Tria said, meeting Rehanne's gaze, "is that Gray and Oryon aren't captives in the Dire Realms. They aren't where we can find them, but they *are* free, and they have the resources they need to defeat the demon and return here."

"You don't know any of that," Rehanne screamed at her.

"I know that Oryon and Gray aren't together." Lina stood beside Rehanne. "What's going to make Gray, who hates both Oryon and Kress, go looking for them? He won't care if they're not rescued."

"Do *you* care?" Tria's piercing stare skewered her former roommate.

"About Kress, no. He and his demon can stay lost forever. But Oryon . . ." She shrugged and finished somewhat grudgingly, "He's been useful lately."

"Ladies, please sit down again and listen to me," Veronica interrupted. "Arguing like silly bubbleheads won't solve anything."

Rehanne returned to her seat like a chastened schoolgirl.

Veronica's using coercion on her, Lina realized. *No point in giving her a reason to use it on me.*

She sat and listened, but it was Rehanne to whom Veronica spoke.

"Rehanne, you're young to be a mother, but that's what you've been trying to be to Gray." The maid did not adopt a lecturing tone as Headmistress would have. Her manner was straightforward, even friendly, but anger and hurt registered in Rehanne's eyes. "You've been trying to protect Gray. He doesn't need that. He needs to find his own strength and put it to good use. He has the chance to do it. He might fail, but I wouldn't bet on it."

The Adept turned from Rehanne to Lina. *Uh-oh. My turn,* Lina thought, steeling herself.

"Lina, you've been using Oryon. I'm surprised he allowed it." Veronica's tone was less friendly, more stern. "But it worked both ways, didn't it? You let him use you, too, knowing what he had been and what he could become again, given too much power too quickly. I can't say what will happen to him or what he does or doesn't have the power to do, but whatever it is, you won't have to share the responsibility for it. Bring him back here and keep on the course you'd set, and you'd share the blame for the results. Maybe you already do."

The implication that she might have goaded Oryon into murder struck Lina like a burning arrow. Her anger kindled, she reached again for the panther caged within her. Unable to release it, she could only lash an invisible tail and bare her teeth as Veronica went on.

"Gray, Oryon, even Kress will find their own way back or they won't return. You can't help them, and you must accept it. You have something else to do. Those peace officers aren't going to solve our mystery and catch the murderer. The longer they stay here snooping around, the more they'll muddy the trail. That gifted fellow's a dunce, not over second level. We have to let them walk around acting important.

The school could lose its license if we don't cooperate. But Gray and Oryon are better off out of their reach. Headmistress is right, you know. We can't count on the provincial authorities to deal fairly with the gifted.

"You two, that's your job: Put a stop to this killing. Get busy and find the guilty one. Make it safe for the young gentlemen to come back, and maybe they'll get here."

"But—but—it was the demon," Rehanne spluttered. "And it's gone. It's in Kress."

Veronica shook her head. "There're more demons than one by now," she said. "The one in Kress was contained—sealed—when Fenton and Dwayne were killed. It wasn't responsible. Kress wasn't. Demons can only come here if someone brings them or summons them from the Dire Realms. Headmistress thinks the demons came through Gray, but I consider that unlikely. Someone else is trafficking in demons, and you must find out who that someone is."

Lina leaned forward, intent, her anger dissolved with the prospect of action. "How? And how many demons are there? How many killers are we looking for?"

"How many would be bold enough and cruel enough to summon demons?" Veronica said. "I suspect that you are looking for one person, and a single person could not—would not have dared to—bring more than one or two demons. That person is the real killer—someone who enjoys giving the demons work to do."

"Why are you setting us to looking for him?" Rehanne asked. "Headmistress warned us not to get involved."

"She'll change her mind," Veronica said shortly.

You mean you'll change it for her, Lina thought.

Veronica continued, "You're clever, you've been tested before, you've already been searching, though you may not have known it was a killer you were searching for, and I think you've turned up important clues. You're third-year and at least third level. Together you command a lot of power. Whoever is guilty is highly talented. It took someone with extraordinary power to free Kress. And it wasn't demon power that was used. The power net he was held in was specially warded against demons."

"Ferene!" Lina jumped to her feet. "She has power. Almost as much as you, Tria. Let's go talk to her."

"Be careful," Veronica warned. "I have to get back to Headmistress, but Tria can go with you. Remember, no one else is to know who she is."

Lina nodded impatiently and headed for the door. She stopped suddenly and spun around. "I do need my ability to shapechange."

"You have other talents," Veronica said. "I've already told you that what Headmistress took only she can restore."

Lina didn't believe her. Lip curled in disgust, she stalked from the room, with Tria and Rehanne following.

On the third floor they knocked at the door to Ferene's room. Her roommate, Sindia Carroll, answered. Clearly puzzled by the delegation, she opened the door wide to let them see that Ferene wasn't in the room. "I haven't seen her since before lunch," she said.

While Tria waited by the stairs, Lina and Rehanne stopped by Rehanne's room first to question Chantal. Lina waited at the door while Rehanne went inside, where Chantal was standing in front of the dresser, pulling things out of her drawer and dropping them onto the floor. "Now my other earring is gone," she said before Rehanne could ask her question. "Have you seen it?"

"No, I haven't. One earring wouldn't do you much good anyway. Do you know where Ferene is?"

Chantal dropped the slip she was holding, bent to pick it up. "Why do you want to know about Ferene?" she asked.

"I have to ask her something. It's important."

"Headmistress told us all to stay in our rooms, and that's what I've done. If Ferene hasn't stayed in hers, I have no idea where she could be." Chantal turned dismissively and went back to pawing through the drawer.

I should be doing the questioning; Rehanne's too mild, Lina thought. She projected the illusion of a large, hairy spider into the drawer Chantal was searching. Chantal gave a shriek and slammed the door shut.

Grinning, Lina stepped into the hall, out of sight.

"Why scare her like that?" Rehanne asked, joining her. "What did that accomplish?"

"Made me feel better," Lina said, and headed for her own room.

It was a brief stop: Giselle wasn't there. They went to the other rooms asking if anyone knew where Ferene might be, but their visits were all unproductive. The other girls were in their rooms, but none knew Ferene's whereabouts. They reported their failure to Tria.

"Would she be downstairs, in spite of Headmistress's order?" Rehanne asked. "Could Headmistress have sent for her?"

"I don't think so," Tria said.

"What about the empty room?" Lina pointed at the door near the head of the stairs. "Should we look in it?"

"Might as well." Tria lifted the key ring on her belt and selected a key, fitted it into the lock, turned it, and swung the door open.

A shadow on the floor drew Lina's attention. Her gaze traveled slowly upward from the shadow to what cast it.

Ferene's body hung from the light fixture in the center of the room.

"Too late again," Lina said bitterly. "She won't tell us anything."

16

TIME-OUT

Gray couldn't catch up with Lina; he didn't have the strength. He hadn't eaten in far too long, he was aching from Kress's blows, and he bled from cuts all over his back where the glass on the floor had stabbed into him when he fell. To the physical injuries was added the mental confusion caused by being jerked from the school hallway to this unknown and dismal place, a place as close to nowhere as anything he'd ever seen.

His steps slowed, stopped. He looked around. The surface on which he stood was solid, dull gray, and so featureless it was impossible to tell whether it was stone, metal, or something else. He bent and ran a finger over it, but touch told him no more than sight. It felt cool with a slight roughness but no distinguishing texture.

That featureless floor provided his only link to reality. He saw no walls, no ceiling, only empty space around and above him. Whether that space stretched to infinity or enclosed him in an invisible bubble, he could not say. His outstretched arms encountered no obstacle; he could walk in any direction and nothing changed.

He no longer had any idea in which direction the others had gone, how he could find them, or whether he wanted to.

He should consider himself well rid of them. Except that it was lonely here. In the abandoned school he'd had recognizable surroundings, objects he could touch, rooms and hallways and stairs and doors. Here he had nothing, no one but himself.

"We'll see how much I like my own company," he said, in an attempt at grim humor.

It didn't take him long to decide he didn't like it at all. He'd welcome any company, even Oryon's. Or Kress's.

Demon and all? he asked himself wryly.

He began to wonder whether Kress's attack had left him mortally wounded and his belief that the others had come here with him had been no more than a dying dream. He would have expected more of a transition between life and death, but what did he know?

He poked and prodded at himself. His body felt solid. A pinch hurt. He stretched his arm behind him to feel the wounds on his back and yelped with pain; his fingers came back stained with blood. He *must* be alive.

Well, if he was alive, he had better find a way out of this place. When he'd thought of his life as empty, he hadn't known what emptiness was. And when he'd avoided people, he hadn't known what it was to be completely alone. He'd thought he'd learned when he was lost in the deserted school building. The isolation had made him resolve to work with Oryon.

If only he'd kept that resolve. He might have, but for Lina. The catgirl had angered him and made him forget his promise.

But he had cooperated with both of them when Kress attacked. And where had it gotten him? Here!

How had Kress gotten free?

Someone had to know how to find the hidden room he'd been kept in. Headmistress had shown him and Oryon, but he didn't think any of the other students knew. And that someone had to have the power to break Headmistress's double wards.

He could think of only one person who met those criteria. Oryon.

Kress had come to Oryon's room. Why? How had he known where to find them unless the dark one had told him?

His suspicion of Oryon grew to a near certainty. Oryon was responsible, must be responsible, for Kress's condition, for Kress and the demon being free, for Kress's attack on Gray, for his being alone in this place. Oryon had started it all two years ago; he was behind all the evil that had befallen Gray.

Gray's fists clenched. *Let me out of here,* he thought. *Let me find Oryon.*

He pictured the familiar face with the mocking eyes, the shock of black hair dipping over the forehead, the prominent chin, uplifted, arrogant. He looked around, wanting something from which to sculpt the face, give it reality. Nothing. If he could give form to the nothingness, shape it into his enemy . . .

His teeth ground together. Sweat dripped down his face. His whole body trembled from the effort. In front of him a shadow deepened, turned solid.

Oryon stumbled out of the void. His hair was wild, blood poured from a gash over one eye, one arm hung limp at his side. "Gray!" he gasped. "Thank the Power-Giver!"

He pitched forward and fell senseless at Gray's feet.

Rehanne stared in horrified fascination at Ferene's purple face, the protruding tongue, the bulging eyes, the rope that cut deep into the neck. Tria pulled her away, pushed her and Lina from the room, and shut and locked the door.

"I'll go report this," she said. "I'll tell the peace officers I found her when I opened the room to clean. You two go to Lina's room and lock yourselves in. Don't let anyone in, and don't come out unless Headmistress sends for you. In that case, either Veronica or I will come for you. Don't open to anyone else."

"Not even the peace officers?" Rehanne asked.

"Especially not the peace officers."

"How long do we have to hide?" Lina asked. "And why? We haven't done anything."

"You're in danger, and there've been enough deaths. Go! Use the time to think things through. Talk over everything you know. See if together you can reason anything out."

"You'll join us soon, won't you?" Rehanne felt safer, more confident with Tria present.

"No. This is your problem, not mine. I'll help when I can, but don't count on me." She turned and ran down the stairs.

"Come on," Lina said, and led the way to her room.

Rehanne's stomach churned as what she'd seen struck with belated force. When Lina opened the door, Rehanne hurried past her and collapsed onto Giselle's bed, shaking. "So many deaths! So much evil!" She couldn't control her sobs. "How do they expect us to stop it? What can we do against a force that no one can see, that strikes in secret, that—"

"Feeling sorry for yourself won't solve anything." Lina's rebuke was like a shower of cold water. "If you don't want any more deaths, sit up, dry your eyes, and help me figure out what we can do."

Rehanne sat up, but her tears continued to flow. This third death coming on top of Gray's disappearance was too much to bear. "It's useless," she said. "What can we do against demons? Why is it up to us?"

Lina spun toward her, raised a hand, and slapped her hard across the cheek. "Stop sniveling!" she shouted. "You think you can do Gray any good by sitting around whining?"

Rehanne rubbed her stinging cheek and glared at Lina.

The catgirl flounced to her desk, opened a drawer, and took out pencil and paper. She sat down at the desk.

"Pull yourself together and think," she ordered. "We'll start with the missing items. Let's make a list of everything we know is lost, whose it is, and when they missed it. We'll start with my talisman." Lina's pencil sped across the paper. "I missed it the first night I was here. I'd arrived early that morning and unpacked before lunch. I put it in my top dresser drawer. When I looked for it late that night, it was gone. I'd been out of the room most of the afternoon, but I always lock my door. And of course, Giselle hadn't arrived. I thought Kress must have stolen it, since he was one of the few people who knew about it, but I don't know . . ." She tapped her pencil against her chin. "What was next? Oryon's wand?"

"What about Chantal's earring?" Rehanne said. "That was the first thing that disappeared."

"It's not a magical device," Lina objected, frowning. "But, all right, I'll put it on the list. She lost it—when?"

"That first day, before Gray arrived," Rehanne said. The scene played back in her mind. "Chantal said she'd worn the earrings to lunch—to dazzle Kress, I think. She took them off and put them both in the tray on her dresser, she says. Later, when she went to put them on, one was missing."

"I don't see what the earring has to do with anything," Lina groused as she jotted notes on her paper.

"It might, though. And now she's lost the second earring. I wonder whether the one I found under Kress's door was the first one she lost or the other one."

"Hmmm." Lina's pencil scratched across the paper. "Maybe there's a connection after all."

"I remember something else," Rehanne said thoughtfully. "I went into the library looking for Gray, and Petra was there. I told her about not meeting Gray's bus because of looking for Chantal's earring. I told her how upset Chantal was about it because the earrings belonged to her mother and were a valuable family heirloom. Petra didn't believe that story. She said Chantal's family was so poor that her mother wouldn't have inherited anything like that."

Lina stopped writing and focused her full attention on Rehanne. "We need to have a talk with Chantal," she said. "I'd like to know where she did get the earrings, and why she lied about it."

"Petra could be wrong."

"I doubt it. She's sharp, and she's not a gossip. And Chantal *is* a liar. Maybe the earrings do have some magical purpose, and Chantal doesn't want anyone to know." She went back to writing. "All right. I have that down. So we go to Oryon's wand."

"No, wait. I've remembered something else." Rehanne leaned forward, her excitement growing. "When I was in the library talking to Petra and Coral, Britnor was working in the back room. He came out all upset about a missing book. It was some kind of spell book, I think. I'm trying to remember what he said the title was. Something about transformations. I don't know if they found the book, but the library hadn't opened yet and no books had been checked out, so it should have been there."

"That means we need to talk to Britnor, too." Lina reached for a second sheet of notepaper. "I'd better start a list. It looks like we're going to be busy when we can leave this room."

They added to Lina's list the items they were already both aware of: Oryon's wand, Maridel's kitten, Vanita's jewel. Again Lina asked as she had at the lunch table whether the items might have been stolen to prevent their use by their owners.

"That wouldn't be true of the book," Rehanne mused. "If

it really is missing, it must have been one of the first things taken, and it must have been taken by someone who wanted to use the spells."

"So we're probably looking for someone who has the spell-casting talent," Lina said. "It's a common talent, though, so that won't help much. I suppose it would let us eliminate a few people."

"Maybe," Rehanne suggested as the idea popped into her head, "we need to find out who's used some kind of transformation spell."

"We need to know more about the book and what spells are in it." Lina made another notation.

"I wish we could find the book and the other things," Rehanne said. She jumped to her feet as a realization hit her. "If we could find Vanita's jewel, she could use it to contact Fenton and Dwayne and Ferene. She could find out what happened and who killed them."

Lina slapped the desk. "Yes! That might be why the jewel was taken. To keep Vanita from doing that. We've got to find it." She stood and went to the door, put her hand on the knob.

"But the jewel was taken before anyone was killed," Rehanne said. "Anyway, we can't leave. Remember what Tria said."

"We've got too much to do to stay here."

"I don't think we've covered everything," Rehanne said. "Maybe we ought to make a list of questions we need to find answers to. For example, 'Who vandalized Gray's room and why?'"

Lina's hand fell away from the knob. "And, 'Who has the gift of invisibility?' All right. You make this list." She returned to her desk and thrust paper and pencil into Rehanne's hand.

"Who set Kress free?" Rehanne added while she jotted down the first two questions.

"I think I can guess the answer to that one," Lina said, standing at Rehanne's shoulder. "I think it was Ferene. She had amazing power, and I think someone talked her into using it. Then either that person killed her, or she killed herself when she realized what she'd done."

Rehanne stared. The theory made sense.

"A more important question is, 'Who injured Kress?'" Lina continued. "And what did Fenton remember? Who did Dwayne see walking past the library with Fenton?"

"Why did Gray have blood on his hand the night Kress was attacked?" Rehanne stopped writing and gazed accusingly at Lina. "And you. You shapechanged that night. When I came by here looking for Giselle I saw blood on your windowsill."

Lina looked startled. She backed slowly to her bed and sat down. "I'd forgotten that," she said thoughtfully. "I *did* change to a panther that night. But that smear of blood wasn't from me. I didn't come back through the window. Even as a panther I can't jump up to a third-story window. I'd meant to ask Giselle about it, but with the excitement over Kress, I forgot."

Rehanne frowned, not sure whether to believe Lina. "Your room is right above Kress's," she pointed out.

Lina got up, walked back and forth in the narrow space between the two beds. "I know," she said. "But I didn't go near Kress's room. And that wasn't a panther print. I don't know what it was—it was too badly smeared. I thought maybe Giselle had hurt herself and—" She whirled toward Rehanne. "Where *is* Giselle?"

"I don't know. I haven't seen her since Veronica led her away after she tried to heal Dwayne."

Lina nodded grimly. "Veronica led her away. But she must have comforted her and let her go. We were in Veronica's apartment, and Giselle wasn't there."

"Veronica might have hidden her somewhere."

"Why should she? It's more likely that she calmed her down and told her to go to her room." Lina strode to the door. "We've got to find her."

"Do you think—?"

"She was with Kress during the healing, and Kress is in the middle of this whole mystery. She had her face against Dwayne's, trying to bring him back. He might have whispered something to her as he died. Or the killer may think he might have. The ones who've been killed all had some special knowledge. I think Giselle is in danger. She may already be dead." She jerked the door open. "We can't wait here any longer. We've got to find out."

17

OUT OF TIME

Lina had no idea where to begin looking for Giselle. The logical course would be to find Veronica and ask her where she'd left Giselle and how long ago. But she'd be ordered back to her room unless she could convince Veronica of the danger to Giselle.

She cast a wary glance toward the room where they'd found Ferene. The door was closed and she saw or heard nothing. Motioning Rehanne to follow, she headed for the stairs.

She descended slowly, alert for sounds below. The halls were eerily quiet for midafternoon. She peered down at the landing and made certain that the door to Headmistress's office was shut and the hall beyond it was empty. With another signal to Rehanne, she went on to the first floor.

Rehanne caught up with her, tapped her on the shoulder, and nodded toward the parlor with a questioning look. Lina shook her head, sure that Giselle would not be in the parlor. She turned into the hallway that led to the classroom wing.

A door opened. Chief Officer Ardrey stepped out from a classroom. "Who are you?" he barked. "What are you doing here?"

"I—I was looking for Headmistress. I had something to report."

"Something to do with the murders?"

"I hope not, sir." Lina thought fast. "My roommate is missing, and I thought I should report it."

The other two men stepped into the hall, closing behind them the door of the room they'd occupied. Lina guessed that Ferene's body was inside.

"What about you? Miss Zalos, is it? Why are you here?"

"She came with me," Lina answered quickly. "I was afraid to come downstairs alone."

"Who is your roommate?"

"Giselle Dorr."

One man jotted something down in a notebook. The third edged closer to Lina. He'd be the gifted one. She'd have to be careful.

"When'd you see her last?"

Lina decided to risk a lie. She didn't want to admit to being present at Dwayne's death scene. "I haven't seen her since breakfast."

"And what is your name?"

"Lina Mueller."

"She's the shape-shifter," the one with the notebook said. "You wanted to talk to her."

Ardrey nodded, gazed at the ceiling. "Miss Zalos, return to your room," he said. "Miss Mueller may be detained for some time."

Rehanne gave Lina a helpless look and retreated, no doubt intending to obey orders. *It'll never occur to her to sneak around and get Tria or Veronica,* Lina thought. *I'll have to get out of this mess on my own.*

"Any reason you suddenly became worried about your roommate?" the tall man asked.

"Aren't two murders reason enough?"

"Don't answer with a question," Ardrey snarled.

With an exasperated toss of her head, Lina said, "I didn't think she should be out of our room."

"But you thought it was all right to go out looking for her and to take a friend with you."

It wasn't a question, so Lina didn't answer.

"Where were you planning to look?"

"Everywhere."

"Where were you going when I stopped you?"

"To the patio. I thought she might have wanted some fresh air."

"What is it you change to? Some kind of cat?"

"A panther." Lina saw no point in denying it. They would already have the information in their notes.

"How about a demonstration?"

She wished she could. "Headmistress has forbidden me," she said virtuously.

The gifted man smiled at that, a hard, cruel smile.

Ardrey lunged forward, grasped her wrists. His secretary dropped the notebook and produced from his pocket a short chain with a shackle at the end. He snapped the shackle around her wrist.

"What are you doing?"

"Bringing our investigation to a successful conclusion."

Ardrey smirked. "You are charged with committing the murder of Fenton Rhoze while in panther form."

"What about the others?" Lina spat out the furious question. Too late, she realized her mistake.

"Others?" Ardrey seized on the slip. "You know of the third death, do you?"

"I know about that first-year fellow—Dwayne What's-his-name. And Kress Klemmer. Everybody thinks he must be dead."

Ardrey exchanged a quick glance with his gifted assistant, while the adjutant reclaimed his notebook and scribbled something in it.

Ardrey pushed up his uniform sleeve and clicked the end of the wrist chain into a lock on a steel band around his arm. "We must have a long talk, Miss Mueller," he said. "But only when you are safe in a cell in Millville."

With a rustling of her skirt Headmistress strode toward them from the direction of the stairs. "Officer Ardrey," she said. "Why have you shackled one of my students?"

"I believe her to be dangerous. Our investigation shows her to be the most logical suspect."

"Scapegoat, you mean!" Headmistress stepped in front of Ardrey. Lina had never seen her look so angry. "I cannot permit this travesty of justice."

"Step aside, madam. You know the penalty for interfering with peace officers," Ardrey said. "She'll be judged in the provincial court. This school will lose its license if you fail to cooperate."

Reluctantly Headmistress stood aside. She met Lina's gaze, held it until Ardrey dragged Lina past her and toward the entranceway. The gaze held warning and something else. Lina felt a resurgence of power. She wouldn't test it yet, but she was sure Headmistress had restored her shapechanging ability.

Ardrey took her outside and shoved her into the back seat of the black limousine. He climbed in beside her, and his gifted assistant got in on the other side, so that she was hemmed in by the two men. The secretary slid behind the wheel and started the motor. The big vehicle swung out into the road and sped toward Millville.

"I didn't kill anyone," Lina said.

"It hardly matters whether you did or didn't." Ardrey chuckled. "As your Headmistress observed, you are a convenient scapegoat."

"While the real killer goes free to kill again," Lina snapped.

"Oh, we'll get the real killer, too." Ardrey stared out the window. "This is a case where the bird in the hand is the bait we need to catch the whole bush. We've never found a legal basis for closing your witch school, but I think the problem is about to take care of itself."

What he intended, Lina wasn't sure, but she could imagine several possibilities, all of which boded ill for the school and for her. She studied the shackle on her wrist. It would be a tight fit, but she thought a panther's paw could slip through. She checked the road. A truck rumbled toward them. She waited for it to pass. The road had better be free of oncoming traffic when the driver lost control of the car.

The gifted man leaned down, pulled something out from under the seat in front. "Watch her," he said, unscrewing the top of a brown bottle.

As she tensed, ready to change, the man pressed a cloth against her face. A sickening sweet smell filled her nostrils. She struggled, but both men held her. She tried to hold her breath. The cloth was clamped tight over her nose. She grew dizzy; her head reeled.

Change! she willed. The blackness descended too soon.

* * *

Instead of returning to her room when the peace officers took Lina, Rehanne had dashed upstairs to Headmistress's office. She had to help Lina, and Giselle had to be found.

She had pounded on the door, not really expecting to find Headmistress so easily. But the door had opened, and Headmistress peered out at her. "You were ordered to stay in your rooms," she said.

"I know," Rehanne said miserably. "Please, don't make me explain. We don't have time. The peace officers have Lina. They said they were detaining her."

With a glare, Headmistress shoved her aside and hurried down the steps.

Rehanne started after her, but Headmistress glanced around, said, "Go back. Wait for me."

So she had gone back to wait in Headmistress's office, the door having been left open. She was too nervous to return alone to her room.

She was also too nervous to sit for long. She got up, but the cramped office provided no room to pace. To distract her racing mind, she read the titles of the books on the shelves. One drew her attention. She plucked it from its place and read the title again to be sure she'd seen correctly.

Transformations, Transmutations, and Transmogrifications. That was the title of the lost library book Britnor had been so worried about. So it hadn't been stolen; Headmistress had borrowed it.

Rehanne flipped open the front cover, saw inscribed in a neat hand "Miryam Vedreaux." She recalled vaguely hearing that as Headmistress's name, though the woman was rarely referred to by anything except her title. If this was Headmistress's own book, it was not the missing library book. That would have been another copy.

She checked the title page, the inside back cover, the spine. The book was not marked as a library book.

She sat down, leafed through the pages, and despite her preoccupations soon became fascinated by the curious compendium of spells. The first section dealt with alchemy and described processes for transmuting base metals into more valuable ones, detailing a complicated procedure for producing gold. The second section contained a variety of spells for transforming objects into other objects: a nail into a silver brooch, a woolen shawl into a lace mantilla, a sow's ear into a silk purse. And spells for transforming objects into animals, and vice versa: a spool of thread into a mouse, a twig into a grasshopper, a rod to a serpent. Each of these spells bore the warning that the transformation was temporary, and the transformed object or animal would revert to its original form in no more than an hour's time.

But it was the third section that especially intrigued Rehanne. It spoke of ways of changing one's own appearance. The spell-caster could make herself beautiful or make himself young and handsome for an evening. He could transform himself temporarily into the likeness of another person. Could alter the appearance of another person for a brief time. And—Rehanne sat bolt upright and stared at the page—a spell could transform a demon into the likeness of a human being for a period not exceeding eighteen hours!

The person who stole the library copy of the book might have worked that spell. It was possible that it had not been Kress at all in Oryon's room, but a disguised demon. Someone may have wanted Kress blamed for the demon's deeds.

Lina must see the book. She thrust the small volume into the waistband of her skirt and tugged her blouse over it, went to the door and looked out. Headmistress was not yet on the way back. Good.

Thrusting aside pangs of guilt, she ran upstairs to Lina's room. They'd left the door unlocked. Rehanne darted inside and took the book from its hiding place. She opened Lina's desk drawer and thrust it inside. The lists Lina had made lay on the desk. Rehanne added them to the one she'd made, folded all three together, and put them in her skirt pocket. After carefully closing the door behind her, she went back downstairs and reentered Headmistress's office.

She'd been back only a couple of minutes when Headmistress returned. She walked past Rehanne, rounded her desk, and slumped into the chair behind it. For a long moment she sat with downcast eyes, not speaking.

"They've taken Lina," she said at last. "I couldn't stop them."

Rehanne sat up in alarm. "What will they do to her? They won't hurt her, will they?"

"They could. They'll use her to discredit the school, I'm certain of that. We chose a remote location for the school so that the nongifted would perceive it as less of a threat, and we've worked to create a positive image, to lead the nongifted to see us as an asset. But these murders have destroyed all the goodwill we've built up in the past five decades. They've convinced the provincial authorities that we're dangerous and should be suppressed. I'm afraid they'll provoke Lina into a display of power, then use that as an excuse to punish us all."

A tide of anger rose in Rehanne. The woman was only worried about the school, not about Lina. How like her! But Headmistress looked so beaten and dispirited that the tide ebbed. "You can protect her, can't you? And rescue her?"

Headmistress shook her head. "We have the power, of course. But to use it would turn the whole province against us. I did restore her shapechanging ability. I probably shouldn't have, but I couldn't leave her without that means of defending herself."

Rehanne found a bit of comfort in that news. Lina was clever. She'd find a way to evade her captors and get back to the school.

Headmistress gazed at Rehanne. "I'm afraid this leaves you in a vulnerable position, Miss Zalos. Please exercise extreme care. You had been told to remain in your room. Had you done so . . ."

She didn't need to finish. Rehanne understood that she and Lina had brought this disaster on themselves. "We were looking for Giselle," she said. "We hadn't seen her for several hours, and we were afraid she might be another victim."

Headmistress sighed. "If only you had waited and confided that fear to me, I could have reassured you. I have Miss Dorr hidden in my apartment. You were correct in believing that she might be in danger but quite wrong in assuming that I had not anticipated that danger." She stood. "Come with me."

She'd gathered strength, pulling around her that cloak of authority and invulnerability that for a short time she had let slip. Rehanne followed her from the office to the apartment next to it. Headmistress led her inside.

The small sitting room was empty. "Miss Dorr," Headmistress called, crossing into the room beyond it.

She gasped, clutched the doorframe. Behind her, Rehanne peeked under her arm.

The room was in disarray, bedding torn from the bed and strewn around the room, a chair overturned, toiletry items swept off the dresser and smashed on the floor. Giselle was gone. Bloody prints marked the windowsill.

Headmistress rushed to the window and looked down. "Not there," she said with clear relief. "But what kind of prints *are* these?"

Rehanne gazed at them. Clearly marked in blood were what appeared to be prints of a large animal. They were unquestionably not human, but neither were they catlike. They couldn't be Lina's. She thought of the book she had taken. It might explain the peculiar prints. She should admit to Headmistress that she'd taken it, bring it back, and let Headmistress discover whether it held the answer to the puzzle.

When Headmistress turned away from the window, she looked stunned. "I've been wrong, so wrong," she muttered as though to herself. "I must consult with Veronica right away." Her eyes focused on Rehanne. "I've made a terrible mistake," she said. "I'm sorry. I shall do what I can to make it right."

"What do you—?"

"I was wrong in thinking Gray was possessed by the demon, misled by signs I don't have time to explain. I must see Veronica, and we must search for Giselle. Go to your room and wait."

She pushed Rehanne toward the door. When Rehanne tried to resist, to plead, and to tell of the book, Headmistress used her power to prevent Rehanne's speaking and to force her from the apartment. The door slammed behind her, and Rehanne found herself at the top of the stairs to the third floor before Headmistress's power released her.

She stopped, furious. The woman had admitted to one mistake; she had just made another. Rehanne no longer regretted taking the book. Her faith in Headmistress had been crushed. The woman had made a total mess of everything. She'd let Lina get arrested, Gray get lost in alternate time lines, Giselle get abducted and probably murdered. Rehanne would place no more reliance on her.

She would *not* obey meekly and wait in her room. On her own she faced the daunting challenge of trapping the demon and tracking the murderer. How she could do those things, she had no idea. But she would do what she could.

* * *

Lina woke with a throbbing head and a foul taste in her mouth. When her eyes adjusted to the dim light, she saw that she was in a tiny cell, its only light coming through a narrow, vertical slit just below the ceiling. The walls were thick stone; the door was heavy steel with a small, barred window. She lay on a narrow stone bench jutting out from the wall. The cell held no other furniture. A drain in the far corner reeked of urine.

She shuddered, tried to rise, fought off a wave of nausea. She refused to be ill. After a few minutes she sat up again, slowly, and slowly pushed herself to her feet. On unsteady legs she crossed to the door, tested the lock.

Secure. Warded, too. They weren't taking any chances.

Ardrey's eyes and nose appeared in the window of the door. "Ah, awake at last. Good. We'll have that talk now, Miss Mueller."

She moved back, away from the door, ready to change and spring when he entered.

He laughed. "I won't be opening the door. I'll talk from here."

"I have nothing to say to you." Lina backed to the ledge and sat down.

"You will," Ardrey said. "When I finish, you'll be glad to tell me about the things you've been doing at the school—studying witchcraft, consorting with demons, sacrificing your schoolmates. This hypno-gas will put you in a submissive frame of mind. You'll soon give me the whole sordid story."

His face retreated, and a rubber hose snaked through the window and wound toward Lina. Gas hissed from the nozzle on its end.

18

IN THE PRESENCE OF THE ENEMY

Gray stared at the scratched and bleeding face of his enemy. What power had brought Oryon to him? And in this condition? No need to worry about Oryon's greater talent. He lay unconscious at Gray's feet, so easy to kill. Gray could get the revenge he'd dreamed of. He could rid himself permanently of the hated dark one. In this mysterious and hidden place, he could do it with impunity: no one would find the body; no one would know.

Look at him, in the black shirt and black trousers he affects to flaunt his wickedness. His arrogance won't do him any good. Gray nudged him with the toe of his shoe.

Oryon groaned. Should he let him wake, let him see his death coming? No, that would only give him a chance to summon his power and strike back. Better to act quickly, to grab the opportunity Fate had presented.

He knelt beside Oryon, placed his hands on Oryon's shoulders. Blood welled up between his fingers. Was Oryon already dying? Was he to be cheated of his vengeance?

It required little thought to guess what had wounded his enemy. Oryon had pursued Kress. The demon in Kress must have turned on Oryon and attacked him as he had earlier attacked Gray.

Oryon saved me.

And what did he say just now? "Gray! Thank the Power-Giver!" He must have thought that somehow I summoned him to save him from the demon.

I've been swearing all along that no demon possessed me. Who'll believe me if I finish what a demon began?

He eased Oryon's shirt off the bloody shoulder and found the injury, a deep stab wound in the upper back. "Got to stop the flow of blood," Gray muttered. He drew the edges of the wound together, pressed hard. The flow slowed, but not enough. Oryon's breathing was rapid and shallow.

"Why couldn't I have been a healer?" He saw his efforts doomed to fail. And now he wanted Oryon to live as much as he had wanted him dead mere moments ago.

A powerful healer like Headmistress could close the wound and knit the torn flesh together in seconds. But Headmistress wasn't here. Nor was any other healer.

He thought of the highly talented healers among last year's graduating class. So far as he knew, no one had replaced them. The only student who claimed to have the talent was Giselle Dorr, but she had no great ability.

Any healer would help. Glumly he regarded the blood bubbling between his fingers. Without meaning to, he shaped the crimson bubbles into a rough likeness of Giselle's face. The sculpture lasted no more than a second or two before it melted over his hands. "It isn't your bloody image I need," he muttered. "It's *you*."

Screams. Cries. A loud thump. Giselle landed beside him, kicking and flailing. She rolled away from him and scrambled to her feet, screaming. Bloody scratches marked her face and arms.

"Giselle, don't run," Gray called. "I need your help. Look here. It's Oryon. He's badly hurt."

Giselle teetered on tiptoe, ready to flee. She eyed Gray

with suspicion and terror. Her gaze traveled to Oryon. She shrieked. "I can't. It's a trick."

"He'll die without a healer," Gray said. "It's no trick. I can't stop the bleeding."

"There was a thing, like a bear. It tried to kill me . . ."

"It's not here. You're safe. Come on, girl."

Slowly Giselle crept toward him, her eyes darting about as though she expected an ambush. She stopped just beyond his reach and stared at Oryon. "He's alive?" she asked tremulously.

"Yes, but he won't stay that way if you don't help him."

She looked around as if taking in her surroundings for the first time. "Where am I? How did I get here?"

"Does it matter? Hurry, for the Power-Giver's sake!" *Now I'm sounding like him.*

Giselle stared at Oryon. "I'm no good, you know. Everybody I've tried to heal is dead."

Gray lost patience. "Try anyway, damn you."

She took one step closer. Another. Oryon coughed; a trickle of blood flowed from his mouth.

Giselle gasped and hurled herself down beside him, brushed away Gray's hands and placed her own over the wound. "Power," she said. "Try to channel power to me."

"I don't—" He stopped. *I don't have that talent,* he'd been going to say. But he'd somehow shared power with Lina and Oryon. And he'd brought Giselle here. And Oryon. He wouldn't have thought he had the power for that.

He didn't know how to channel power. All he could do was stare at Giselle, try to summon strength, pass it to her. He pictured a tube, like a large umbilical cord, linking them together, pictured his talent as a precious fluid flowing through it into her body, into her hands. He closed his eyes, squeezed the lids together in fierce concentration. The visualization became clearer. He saw a tube of tough, transparent membrane, a golden liquid pulsing through it. Giselle's hands glowed with its light.

He grew weak, dizzy. It was hard to sustain the picture. His brain seemed to be shutting down. As from a great distance he heard Giselle's voice. "We did it!"

His ears were ringing and he seemed to be spinning in a void. He tried to sit up, to orient himself. Dark spots whirled before his eyes, and he couldn't tell which way *was* up.

Giselle's face swam above him. "Don't move," she said. "You passed out. You sent me so much power. I didn't realize . . ."

He was lying flat on his back. He couldn't move. His muscles refused to respond. He tried to speak, finally managed a faint whisper. "Oryon?"

"I'm here." The dark one's face bobbed into view beside Giselle's. "You saved my life."

And put myself at your mercy, Gray thought, remembering, trying again to move. His limbs were heavy, useless. Helpless, he could only gaze up at Oryon and wait for the mocking laughter, the cruel taunts.

Oryon got down on his knees beside him. "The rotten thing is that I don't have any power left, either. I threw all I had into fighting Kress. And Giselle's used up, too. We'll have to rest and give ourselves a chance to recharge. We're stuck here until we get enough power to shift somewhere. I don't suppose you know where 'here' is?"

Gray's head wobbled a weak negation.

"He needs food and water," Giselle said. "His body has to have fuel to rebuild its strength."

"Doesn't look like we have any chance of finding anything around here," Oryon said. "I'll go explore if you think it'll help. The Power-Giver knows I owe it to him."

"No." Gray wagged his head from side to side—more forcefully this time. "You'll get lost. Like before. Give me time. Let me rest awhile."

"I think he's right," Giselle said worriedly. "We'd all better rest."

Gray fell asleep as soon as he heard Oryon agree to follow Giselle's advice. He awoke feeling stronger. He could and did sit up and look around. Giselle lay sleeping a short distance away. But where was Oryon? He might have betrayed them and found a way of escape while they slept.

A shadow drifted out of the emptiness, resolving itself into Oryon's dark figure. "Feeling better?" he asked, hurrying to Gray.

By way of answer, Gray tried to stand. Oryon grabbed his arm and helped him up. Giselle stirred, blinked, and rubbed her eyes. Seeing Gray and Oryon, she jumped to her feet. "Should you be up?" she asked Gray.

"Got to be," he said. "We have to find a way out of this place."

"I've been testing my power," Oryon said. "It's come back a little. Not enough. How about yours, Giselle?"

She squinted at him and at Gray. "I can see faint auras around each of you. So mine's back a little, too. But when it's at full strength, the auras are bright, easy to read."

Gray had forgotten that she had that talent. He didn't ask what the auras told her.

"I've been thinking," Oryon said. "If we share power, we might be able to muster enough strength among the three of us to send *one* of us back to the school for help."

Giselle shuddered. "The school . . ." She clasped her hands tightly in front of her. "I don't want to go back." She looked at Gray. "A demon's loose. It was attacking me when you brought me here. You saved my life."

"Yours, too?" Oryon sounded incredulous. "A demon had

stabbed me and was about to finish me off when Gray pulled me away. How did you do that, Gray?"

"I—I'm not sure." Gray rubbed his chin, felt a growth of beard. How long had he slept? "I—pictured you. And you came."

"Did you know about the demons?" Giselle asked, her eyes wide.

"I knew Kress was possessed, and that Oryon had been chasing him. I don't know anything about another demon."

"Tell us about it," Oryon said.

Giselle hesitated, spoke slowly. "I was so upset about Dwayne that I was hysterical. Veronica took me to her apartment. She spoke to me, calmed me down. She asked me if I'd felt anything or—or seen anything in Dwayne's aura that might explain what happened to him. His aura had all but faded away when I got to him. I could read fear. And surprise. That was all until I tried to breathe life back into him. I couldn't; it was too late. But I smelled something. A faint odor of perfume and a stronger odor of—I'm not sure—something like sulfur. Veronica seemed to think that was important. After a while she took me to Headmistress's office and had me tell *her*. Headmistress said I could be in danger. She hid me in her apartment while she went to talk to the peace officers. I'd be safe there, she said. But I wasn't. That's where the demon found me." She stopped and looked away and shuddered as if she were seeing it again.

"What was it like—that demon?" Gray asked.

She shuddered again and went pale. Oryon put out a hand to steady her. Finally, she said, "It was man-sized and shaped like a man, but it had black hair all over it, like an ape or a bear. Its hands were like paws. And its face—its face was horrible." She shut her eyes. "It had a little, flat nose and long, sharp teeth in a squished-in face. I couldn't see its eyes. It had hair all around them, and big shaggy brows that hid the eyes. But it could see me.

"It chased me into Headmistress's bedroom. I jumped onto the bed to try to get away from it, and it snatched up all the covers and pulled me toward it. I jumped off, and it chased me and kept swiping at me with its claws. I grabbed a pair of scissors off Headmistress's dresser and stabbed it as hard as I could. It howled and let go of me to clutch its shoulder. I tried to run away, but it pounced on me and hauled me to the window. I think it was going to throw me out. Only—only it didn't. All of a sudden I was here."

"Odd," Oryon commented.

Very odd. A black beast. Man-sized. With a shoulder wound. Gray's eyes strayed to Oryon's healed shoulder. How had Oryon gotten that injury? Kress hadn't been carrying a knife. "You haven't told us your story," he said to Oryon.

"I don't remember much," Oryon said, frowning. "I ran after Kress. I was catching up with him, but it got dark, hard to see. He turned on me, caught me. We fought. He backed me into something—some kind of stone shelf or table. I ducked under his arm and started to run. That's when he stabbed me—I think with something he grabbed off the table. I knew I was hurt bad and I couldn't outrun him, but I tried. Then, I—I saw you."

Was he telling the truth? It was impossible to know with Oryon. The dark eyes gave away nothing. It could be only a coincidence that Giselle stabbed the black beast in the shoulder and Oryon, dressed all in black, bore a stab wound in the shoulder. But Gray tended not to believe in coincidences. "I wonder what happened to Kress," he said. "Why didn't he follow you through?"

"Couldn't, I suppose," Oryon said. "We'll have to find him, though. He's too dangerous to be allowed to remain loose."

"We'd better hope he doesn't find us," Gray said. "We don't have the strength to deal with him." He turned to Giselle. "Did you know Kress was possessed?"

"Yes." She pushed her long, sun-streaked hair back from her face and gazed at Gray. "When we healed him—not that I did much—the demon made itself known. Headmistress and Veronica spun a spell to contain it and swore me to secrecy. They were afraid the students would panic if the word got out. They were sure they could keep it confined until they could figure out how to destroy it."

"They were wrong," Oryon commented unnecessarily.

"Headmistress isn't often wrong," Gray said. He locked gazes with Oryon. "I wonder how it got loose."

If Oryon read Gray's suspicions, he gave no indication. He only said, "Save it for later. We need to find a way out of here. I'll repeat my suggestion that we pool our power and try to send one of us to the school for help."

Gray didn't like the idea, but he couldn't suggest a better one. "How do we decide which one goes—if we can send even one?"

"Drawing straws would be the fairest way, but we don't have any straws," Oryon said lightly. "Giselle, could you donate some hair?"

Giselle twisted a few hairs around her finger and pulled, grimacing. She held the thin strand out to Oryon. He selected two hairs, broke one in half, making two short pieces, and left the second long.

He closed his palm around the hairs so that only the ends showed. "You choose first," he told Gray. "Then Giselle."

Gray plucked out a single hair. It was short. So was the one Giselle selected. Oryon opened his hand, showed the long hair. "Guess I'm the one," he said.

"You cheated," Gray accused.

Oryon shrugged. "You can go, or Giselle. I don't care."

But Giselle was too afraid to go, and Gray didn't like the idea of leaving her alone with Oryon. "No," he said. "You're the one."

Oryon would probably leave them stranded, but Gray would have to take that chance. "How do we go about this?" he asked.

"Join hands," Oryon instructed, and when they did so, forming a circle, he went on. "Focus on a center point." He released Giselle's hand to indicate with his index finger a spot in their midst. Three pairs of eyes focused on that spot. Oryon reclaimed Giselle's hand. "Project power at that point," he said. "Let it build up until we all feel its strength. Draw it back on my signal. We may have to repeat the process several times."

Gray tried to follow the instructions, though he wasn't sure he had any power to project. He didn't feel anything. The whole thing felt like a charade, a silly game. When Oryon said, "Draw in, now!" Gray wanted to laugh.

He didn't know how to draw in, any more than he'd known how to project. He imagined the power flowing back to him, but again he felt nothing.

Several more times they repeated the exercise, while Gray grew more discouraged and disgusted. He was about to call a halt himself, when Oryon said, "Enough. Let's see what we've done."

Gray was sure they'd done nothing.

"It's up to you, Gray. Do whatever it is you do."

"I don't know what I do," Gray said. "I'm not convinced I did anything."

"Well, somebody did," Oryon responded cheerily. "Go on, try."

Gray *willed* Oryon to be back at the school. He pictured Oryon's room and Oryon standing in it. Nothing happened.

"Are you sure you're doing it the same way you did before?" Oryon asked, frowning.

"I think so. I don't have the power."

"You do have power," Giselle said, stepping in front of him and gazing into his face. "Your aura is a white light, brighter than Oryon's. His is blue. That means power, too, but yours is one of the brightest I've seen."

Gray stared, disbelieving. How could he have that much power and not know it, not feel it?

"Something's blocking you," Oryon said, as though Gray had spoken aloud.

"Maybe you don't trust Oryon to get help?" Giselle's soft suggestion jolted Gray.

It was true, of course. He didn't, couldn't, trust Oryon. He'd brought him here in anger. He was trying to send him away with suspicion and distaste.

When he didn't answer the accusation, Oryon said, "I give you my word, Gray, though I don't suppose you have any faith in it. But I *will* get help, and I *will* come back."

Gray nodded, shut his eyes, and re-created in his mind the picture of Oryon's room. He tried to recall every detail, to make the picture complete. The beds—they'd been made up with blankets, tucked in, military fashion. No spreads. The blankets were yellowish beige, he remembered. And the desks. Troy's had books and papers strewn over it, but Oryon's was bare. The top of the dresser was neat, uncluttered. There was no rug on the floor. Plain beige cotton curtains covered the window.

He mentally placed Oryon in the center of the room, between the beds. His black shirt and black trousers wrinkled, torn from all he'd been through. His hair uncombed, dark strands falling across his forehead. His eyes proud, his lips curved in a half smile, his—

"You did it!"

At Giselle's cry he opened his eyes. Oryon was gone.

Snakelike, the hissing hose curved toward Lina. She clamped her hand over her nose and mouth, held her breath, launched her power at the hose. It twisted around, shot out of the cell, passing between the bars of the small window in the door. She stripped off her blouse, ran, and stuffed it into the window to block the gas.

Over the loud whoosh of the gas she heard Ardrey barking orders. "Shut it off. Find the valve. Hurry!"

His last words were slurred. She heard a loud thud, and the hall became silent. After a few minutes' wait, she removed her blouse from the window and, holding her breath, stood on tiptoe to peer into the hall.

Ardrey was sprawled in the corridor. In one hand he held the key to her cell. Holding her blouse over her nose, scarcely breathing, Lina used her power to free the key from the limp fingers and insert it into the lock on the outside of the door. After a few seconds, she was able to swing the cell door open.

A few feet from where Ardrey had fallen, the note-taker, Adjutant Canby, sat slumped, giggling, his hand on the valve of a gas canister. He'd got it partway closed, but gas was still escaping from the hose. Starting to feel dizzy, she hurried to the end of the corridor and passed through a door into an office.

The gifted man stood waiting for her. He smiled an ugly smile, and his serpent eyes glittered. He spread his arms to block her path. "I knew you'd outwit those fools," he said. "You're exactly the tool I need. I've waited a long time for this chance."

"Chance?" She'd breathed too much of the hypnotic gas. She felt heavy, stupid.

He laughed and his hands shot out and clamped her

wrists. He dragged her from the office into another corridor, this one leading to the building's entrance. Short of the entrance he stopped and released her wrists. "Better put your blouse on before we go outside."

She was still holding it wadded up in her hand. From her waist up she wore only a brassiere. She shook out the blouse and put it on, her mind too fuzzy to feel embarrassed. She thought of disobeying and trying to escape, but couldn't muster the energy.

He took her wrist again and led her outside. The limousine was still parked against the curb. He opened the door and shoved her into the front seat, slammed the door, and hurried around to the driver's side.

Jump out. Run away, an inner voice urged. Her sluggish muscles refused to respond. The man slid behind the wheel.

"I'm Drake Shardan," he said. "I've been working for those fools for years, keeping my best gifts hidden, waiting for someone with power that would mesh with mine. You have that kind of power. We'll make a splendid team."

19

POWER PLAYS

Gray felt uncomfortable alone with Giselle in this featureless, empty place. He sat down and clasped his hands around his knees. Hunger gnawed at him, and the expenditure of power had brought back his earlier weakness.

Giselle sat gracefully, her legs curled beside her. Her face glowed. "I really did it, didn't I? Healed Oryon, I mean?"

Gray nodded.

"Of course, I couldn't have done it without the power you gave me, but the talent was my own. You don't heal, do you?"

"No." Feeling she deserved more than a single syllable, he added, "You've healed before, haven't you?"

"Cuts and scrapes and bruises. Nothing life-threatening." Her smile vanished. "I couldn't save my brother. I tried so hard, but I didn't have the power. If only you'd been there then."

"No healer can save everyone," Gray said.

"And I couldn't save Dwayne."

"Dwayne was dead when you reached him. But Kress was healed."

"That wasn't my doing," Giselle said. "Headmistress and Veronica healed him. Oh, they let me stay, let me think I had a part. But I wasn't needed; they could have done it without me."

"I think they would have sent you out if you really weren't doing any good."

"And look what came of that healing. We saved a demon."

She was upset again. Inwardly, Gray agreed that it would have been better to let Kress die, but she needed comfort. "You *are* a healer," he said with careful emphasis. "And you are luckier than most healers. You have other talents, too."

Brightening, she said, "That's right. Maybe my healing talent would be stronger if it was my only one. But I can do several other things. Call animals, calm them, predict the weather, read auras." She frowned. "Yours has faded again. I hope Oryon hurries."

So did Gray. "What color's my aura now?" he asked.

"A dull green." She bit her lip before adding, "Not healthy."

He lapsed into silence. He didn't have to read an aura to know that she, too, was tired and weak. If Oryon didn't return, they would die here where no one would ever find them.

His eyes closed, he nodded, might actually have slept. At Giselle's glad cry his eyes opened, he raised his head.

Oryon stood in front of him holding a large basket. "I'm back," he said. "I've brought dinner, courtesy of Headmistress and Veronica."

"I thought you were going for help," Gray growled.

"This is help," Oryon answered with a grin. "We're all nearly starved."

"Yes, but why didn't Headmistress bring us to the school instead of sending you back here?"

Oryon's smile vanished. "She didn't think it was wise right then. There's been another death, and the school is swarming with peace officers. They've arrested Lina."

"Aha!"

At Gray's triumphant cry Oryon scowled and shook his head. "They just wanted to arrest someone—anyone. Lina didn't do it. Headmistress knows that."

Gray didn't believe it. However, before he could argue, Giselle said, "Another death? Who?"

"Ferene K'Sere."

Giselle shuddered. "The demon . . ."

"Yes," Oryon said shortly. "That's another reason Headmistress feels that we're safer here. Now, do you want to eat or don't you?"

He set the basket down, opened it, pulled out a tablecloth, and spread it on the ground. Glasses and a big jar of lemonade were followed by dishes, silverware, and, wonder of wonders, a whole baked, stuffed chicken, an array of raw and cooked vegetables, and a whole loaf of fresh bread. "This should replenish your power."

Gray's hunger overcame his doubts. He attacked the feast, scarcely waiting for Giselle to serve herself before piling his plate high and working his way to the bottom of it only to fill it again.

Oryon and Giselle ate too, though somewhat less heartily. When they finished, nothing was left but chicken bones and greasy plates.

Satisfied, Gray leaned back, yawned, and let his eyelids drift shut.

"Don't get too comfortable," Oryon warned as he packed the remains of the feast back into the basket. "This dinner had a price attached. We've got work to do."

Gray sat up. "What do you mean? I thought we only had to wait long enough for the peace officers to leave."

"No. Headmistress gave orders. You're to send Giselle back, now that we've eaten. You and I are to go after Kress."

Rehanne left Headmistress's apartment knowing that Headmistress would search for Giselle, and her methods would be more effective than any *she* could employ. She did not want to encounter the thing that had breached wards, entered Headmistress's apartment, attacked Giselle, and left its prints on the windowsill. *I'm a coward,* she acknowledged. The thing must be what was responsible for the killings. She had little hope that Headmistress would find Giselle alive.

But if some kind of evil creature did the killings, it wasn't a student. So it's pointless to look for the killer among the student body. Unless . . . Rehanne thought of the book she'd taken. She needed to study it carefully.

She went to Lina's and Giselle's room, locked the door, and sat at Lina's desk. She removed the book from the drawer, but didn't open it right away. Remembering the lists she and Lina had made, she took them from her pocket, smoothed them out, and spread them on the desk. It might help to review them. Lina's bold, flowing script was easy to read. Rehanne scanned the list of missing items and the list of people to talk to, re-examined the questions she'd scrawled on the third paper.

Maybe I'll find answers to some of these questions in the book. She opened it, turned to the last section, and read.

The supper bell rang. She ignored it; she wasn't hungry and had more urgent matters to worry about than eating. If only Lina were here to study the book with her. The catgirl was cleverer than she and would see connections Rehanne might overlook.

But she isn't here. I don't think like she does, but I'm better at spells. I might see something she'd miss.

Though she conscientiously looked at every spell, the only one that seemed to relate to the killings was the one for transforming a demon.

Why would someone want to transform a demon? One answer came to mind: to use the demon to commit a crime and cast the blame on the one impersonated by the demon. That hadn't happened. No one had seen the murders committed, and no one knew whom to blame. If the demon had killed while in human guise, wouldn't it have allowed itself to be seen? If the demon had impersonated Kress, why had Kress been its first victim? Kress was the one person who could be eliminated as a suspect for the other crimes. It didn't make sense!

Nevertheless, Rehanne read the spell carefully. Her finger ran down the list of materials, which included many obscure items, stopped at the most obscure. *An object brought from the Dire Realms or previously handled by a demon.* How would someone obtain such a thing?

Unless . . . Kress had been captive for a short while in the Dire Realms. He might have brought something back, or he himself might fit the definition. In either case, he was clearly implicated, and again Rehanne asked herself why he had become the demon's first victim.

She wondered briefly whether it had not been Kress but the demon sprawled across the bed, abdomen torn open, blood everywhere. Had it been a demon-inspired delusion?

She rejected the theory. Headmistress and Veronica would have detected such a delusion and would not have labored throughout the night to heal Kress, as Giselle said they had.

Nothing made sense. She went back to reading the spell. The other materials would not be difficult to obtain. Invoking a demon always required blood. In this case, only two or three drops were sufficient, but they must come from the one the demon would be called on to impersonate. It wouldn't be hard to get such a small amount—an "accidental" jab with a pin would do it, or stealing a cloth used to clean a cut from shaving.

The spell procedure was not complicated, but it was extremely dangerous, as was any summoning spell. Rehanne shuddered, remembering the disaster that had resulted two years ago when Lina and Tria had attempted to summon a Dire Woman. A wise spell-caster shunned such foolhardy undertakings. Rehanne had refused to participate.

Following the spell, after a space separating it from the end of the instructions, someone had written a short sentence in ink now faded and difficult to read. Rehanne struggled to decipher the script, caught her breath when the import of the words became clear.

The sentence issued a warning: *This spell must not be repeated.*

The handwriting did not look like Headmistress's. Rehanne wondered whether the library's copy had contained the same warning. If not, the spell-caster might have attempted to repeat the procedure. Rehanne's grandmother had warned her about spells that could be worked only once. If repeated, they could backfire, injuring or killing the spell-caster.

That could have been what happened to Kress. He might have attempted the spell a second time and been ravaged by the demon he'd summoned. It seemed a likely explanation for Kress's injury and possession, but it didn't explain the killings. Or when the spell had first been performed.

She sat at the desk a little longer rereading the lists and thinking.

If all this had happened last year, it would have been easier to deal with. Wilce was here then to help Gray, and Tria could have worked with us openly from the beginning.

Why *hadn't* it happened last year? If Gray had brought back a demon from the Dire Realms, why had it taken almost two years to manifest itself? That didn't make sense. Everybody involved in the plot of two years ago had been here last year as well as this one.

Everybody except Reece.

The chain of tragic events started with the vandalism of Reece's and Gray's room. *Reece's room.* She added another question to her list: *Could it be Reece who summoned the demon?*

The sound of people passing in the hall told her supper was over; the girls were returning to their rooms. She'd accomplish nothing more by continuing to sit here. Armed with her list of questions, she set out to interview the people on Lina's second list: Chantal, Britnor, Vanita (to find a way to retrieve the jewel), Headmistress (to ask who had the gift of invisibility). She added Reece's name.

Headmistress wasn't likely to give out any information, and if Vanita knew a way to find her missing jewel, she'd have done so. Since finding the copy of the book, Rehanne saw little need to talk to Britnor.

That only left Chantal and Reece. Rehanne locked Lina's door and went to her own room to question her roommate.

Chantal was seated at her desk, head bowed, face resting

in her hands. Was she crying? Rehanne stepped behind her and placed her hands on the girl's shoulder. Chantal jumped and swung around, clenched fists beating at Rehanne. Her face was white, terrified, her eyes wide.

Rehanne ducked out of the way of the flying fists. "Whoa! I'm sorry. I didn't mean to startle you."

Chantal's fists dropped to her side. Slowly her rapid breathing returned to normal, and a faint flush gave color to her cheeks. "Why did you sneak up on me like that? How did you expect me to react after all that's happened?"

"I wasn't sneaking up on you," Rehanne said. "I thought you'd heard me come in."

"Well, I didn't," she said sullenly.

Rehanne repressed a sudden urge to slap the pouting face. Chantal had a right to be frightened—they all did. She had no reason to be angry and to broadcast that anger for Rehanne to pick up.

"Where've you been, anyway?" Chantal asked. "We're all supposed to stay in our rooms."

"I've been in Lina's room." Rehanne didn't see any need to divulge what had happened to the catgirl.

"I never knew you and she were such great friends. Was Giselle there?"

Rehanne frowned. She'd come to ask questions, not to answer them. Chantal's anger continued to worm into her brain. She would not provide an explanation. Telling her what had happened to Giselle would only add to her fear.

"No. Did you find your other earring?" Rehanne asked it casually as though merely wanting to change the subject.

Fear. More anger. Suspicion. The emotions struck Rehanne with the force of falcon wings.

"I—yes, I did." Glaring, Chantal slowly opened one fist to reveal the earring. "I found it in your drawer, stuffed under your stockings. I would have found it earlier if that spider hadn't appeared."

"*My* drawer! How did it get in there? And what were you doing going through my drawers?"

"Looking for the earring. And I found it. Now I want to know where the other one is."

"You think I stole it?"

"What else should I think? Who had a better chance than you?"

This was too much. She would have searched the drawers herself, had Chantal asked. She had gone through them when they were looking for the first earring. The small crescent could have fallen into the drawer, but Rehanne didn't think it had.

"Why would I steal one earring? I wasn't even in the room when the other one turned up missing. You know that. You know how hard I tried to help you find it."

"But we didn't find it." The girl's tone was cold, accusing.

"I'm not a thief. How do I know you didn't put the earring in my drawer yourself?" Rehanne spoke in anger, not caring what she said, only wanting to toss Chantal's unjust accusation back at her.

A sharp needle of fear pierced and withdrew. The words spoken in anger might have hit on the truth.

"Tell me about your earrings, Chantal," Rehanne said, pressing her advantage. "All the other things that have disappeared had magic properties. What magic is in the earrings? What do you use them for? They didn't really belong to your mother. You lied about that. I know it, and I want to know why."

She expected Chantal to call her bluff. Instead the girl went white again. "How do you know? Who told you?"

Bull's-eye! Rehanne decided to try for a higher score.

"Kress," she said, taking a wild stab. "He paid us a visit." She expected Chantal to ask who was included in *us* and was straining to come up with an answer that would give nothing away.

But Chantal leaped to her feet, screaming hysterically. "Where is Kress? What have you done with him? What did he tell you?"

Sudden fear chilled Rehanne. She sent a strong projection of calm and backed toward the door. "I have no idea where Kress is. I'm certainly not responsible for anything that's happened to him."

Chantal stood staring at her, a peculiar expression on her face, something between fear and anger. Holding her earring between thumb and forefinger, she raised her arm.

Rehanne ducked out of the room before Chantal could throw the earring at her, if that was what she'd meant to do. Clearly, Chantal was in no mood to impart any information. It would be better to go talk to Reece. Though what she'd say to him she didn't know. How would you ask someone if by chance he had summoned a demon?

She'd have to be indirect, ask him questions that wouldn't let him know she suspected him, yet would produce some reaction, however slight, if he was guilty.

Preoccupied with trying to formulate such questions in her mind as she reached the stairs to the second floor, she stepped onto the first step before becoming aware of a strong sense of danger.

Something behind her.

She turned, saw no one. A hand shoved her chest. Losing her balance, she fell backward. She grabbed for the side rail, missed, slid downward.

As she tried to right herself, she heard a harsh whisper: "Ghash, by this token I order thee to kill her."

A hideous beast the size of a man materialized at the top of the stairs. Snarling, it lunged for Rehanne, sharp talons extended. Its hot breath, reeking of sulfur, swirled around her. Claws caught in her blouse and ripped it open.

Use your power! an inner voice bade.

She sent a desperate blast into the creature to dampen its rage. The alienness of its mind jolted her. The beast seized her; its fangs sank into her shoulder; its claws into her sides.

Through her pain she hurled the force that stifled thought. The beast groaned. She poured her full power into the blanketing fog.

The claws retracted, leaving rivulets of blood streaming from her side. The fangs opened, releasing her shoulder. She struggled to rise. The creature slapped at her half-heartedly. She dodged the blow. "Go back where you came from," she ordered in a voice that wanted to tremble.

What was the name she'd heard whispered? *Ghash!* "Ghash, I command thee. Return to thy proper realm!"

The shaggy black fiend took a step backward and vanished.

Her shoulder and sides were a blaze of agony. The demon's fangs and claws were probably poisonous. She had to get help. She pulled herself up.

Something shoved her back. Stair risers slammed against her head. Crumpled into a dazed heap at the bottom of the stairs, she heard steps pelt down after her. She couldn't lose consciousness; she had to fight her unseen enemy. But blackness swirled around her, sucking her into its vortex.

The pressure of hands on her throat—human hands, not claws—pulled her out of the darkness. She struggled, tried to free her arm, wedged beneath her body. Hands tightened around her throat, cutting the flow of air to her lungs. The blackness swept her in.

20

TEMPTATION

Shardan drove through Millville at breakneck speed, not speak-ing, which saved Lina the trouble of trying to concentrate on conversation while her mind was woozy from the hypno-gas. She stared glumly out of the limousine window, watching the weathered storefronts whiz by. They passed through the downtown section and into the narrow residential streets. Shardan did not slow for the dogs and children that played in the streets. The car swerved around them, tires screeching, and children scattered with screams of terror. Her lethargy kept Lina from crying out.

Her relief when they passed through Millville and onto open highway was short-lived. The car sped faster, bouncing out of potholes, careening around curves. Lina guessed her captor was trying to reach his destination before the drug wore off. Her limbs felt heavy, but her mind was clearer. She thought she might be able to use her power, but at the speed the car was traveling she did not dare try. If the car went out of control, she'd be killed.

Shardan turned off the highway into a narrow lane that forced him to slow his speed. Lina's hand eased to the door handle. Before she could act, the car stopped in front of an old farmhouse.

"I want you to hear me out," Shardan said. "Listen to what I propose before you decide to turn your power against me. When you've heard my plan, I believe you'll be glad to cooperate."

She nodded, not because she had any intention of listening or cooperating, but to get him talking, put him off his guard.

"I did a dangerous thing back in Millville," he said. "Betraying Chief Ardrey and taking you from the jail. If he and Canby find out what I've done, I can't go back. They'll kill me. I tell you this so that you will understand the risk I was willing to take.

"I've waited a long time for this opportunity. I could not let it slip away. When you pulled that trick with the gas nozzle, I knew it was a sign, the omen I'd asked of the Power-Giver.

"I'm a truth-reader, as Ardrey told you. But I'm more than that. I sense the degree of power a gifted possesses. You have great power: fourth level. I was not aware that the school had students who had attained such high level. I was delighted to find you. The faculty, of course, are all fifth or sixth level, but they are too hidebound and set in their ways to suit my purpose."

He's not infallible, Lina noted. *He doesn't know about Veronica and Tria. Wonder what he'd say if he knew about two seventh-level Adepts? He'd go after Tria instead of me. But, no, he'd be too afraid of her. Well, he'll learn to fear me before this is over. Fourth level, am I? I'd thought so, but I wasn't sure. No surprise that Headmistress hadn't bothered to inform me.*

"I'm sure you noticed how Ardrey treats me."

Lina gave a noncommittal shrug, feeling it wiser not to admit that she'd been too preoccupied with her own problems to notice Shardan much at all.

"He despises the gifted," Shardan went on. "Not because he's jealous of our powers. I could understand that. But he thinks he's morally superior to us. In fact, he regards us as a lower form of life."

"So why do you work for him?"

"Not because I need the job. I've been waiting for an opportunity to discredit him and get control of the Peace Officers myself."

Lina scowled. She couldn't see that the Peace Officers would fare any better under Shardan's leadership, but that had nothing to do with her. "Why don't you get to your point?" she said crossly.

"Very well." He ran a finger around the steering wheel. "My point is this. The gifted are too willing to stay on the sidelines and not use their power to full advantage. I'd like to see not only myself but other gifted have the place we deserve. We have the ability, the intelligence, and, most importantly, the power. I know—my talent tells me—that you have no loyalty to any group or person other than yourself. You are the type of person who wants power and doesn't care how she gets it."

"So?"

"So, that is the type of gifted person I want to see in government. With your power and my knowledge and experience, it would be an easy matter to take over first the Peace Officers, then the Millville Council, and then the provincial government. Who knows, maybe eventually the Triumvirate."

"You're crazy!"

"Not at all. The nongifted are easily influenced. It has been their hostility and the scruples of the Gifted Community that have kept the talented from taking over all of Arucadi. But the hostility has lessened considerably in recent years. Ardrey is a throwback to the old days. And for that reason, he is ideal for our purpose."

"Your purpose," Lina corrected, tiring of this fool's ranting.

"Don't tell me you aren't ambitious. I know better. Listen!

I'm offering you a chance to become one of the most influential among the gifted. The first step in my plan is to thoroughly discredit Ardrey. I can't believe you'd be adverse to that."

Lina shrugged. She fancied she'd already discredited Ardrey by escaping and leaving the chief and his adjutant semiconscious in the jail corridor.

"I resent him for dragging me around with him as his tame talent, though his prejudice against the gifted is well known. He intends to use the trouble at your school, the murders, to build his case against the gifted and launch a pogrom. But we can turn his plan against him. Show how he interfered with the solving of the crimes, prevented the true murderer's being brought to justice, maligned the school, and concealed its great contribution to the county and to the province."

So it got back to the school and the murders. "And how do you propose to do all that?"

"We reveal the true murderer, offer proof that Ardrey was derailing the investigation and plotting against the school, and present to the provincial council an irresistible opportunity to augment its treasury by discharging Ardrey and placing me in his position." The man expounded this wild scheme with mounting enthusiasm, a glitter of insanity in his lashless eyes.

"We don't know who the murderer is," Lina pointed out. "And how would solving the murders benefit the provincial treasury?"

"*You* don't know who the murderer is, and neither do I. But your headmistress almost certainly does. My gift enabled me to see that she has a large store of knowledge that she conceals from her students and faculty. She has access to other dimensions where vast riches are waiting to be tapped. To produce the murderer and mine the wealth, we have only to control Headmistress."

"Hardly simple," Lina said, fascinated by these mad concepts. "Headmistress has great power." She did not add that Headmistress's power was buttressed by two Adepts.

"She does, indeed," Shardan agreed, nodding vigorously as though she had correctly answered a difficult examination question. "I, however, have the means of neutralizing that power. I told you I had gifts I have never revealed to my employers. Behold!"

His left hand had dropped unobtrusively to his side. He raised it with a suddenness that made Lina jerk at the door handle. She got the door open, but before she could leap out, strands of light darted from his outspread fingers and became a net around her. In seconds it closed her in, trapped her in a white haze. Though he had spoken no spell words, Shardan had worked a spell identical to the one Ferene had used on her. As before, Lina was sealed into a cocoon that allowed no signals from the outside world to reach any of her senses. Veronica had declared this man a mere second-level talent, but no second-level could produce such a prison. Lina's efforts to shatter it only wasted her power.

Not by her doing the net dissolved and she tumbled back onto the car seat. Shardan beamed with satisfaction. "That is how Headmistress can be rendered harmless," he said. "I can teach you that little trick."

Lina gasped. *Little trick!* Yes, she'd like to learn the secret. *Must* learn it, though it meant playing along with Shardan for a time.

Shardan smiled. "Now that you know how easily I can prevent your escape, come inside the house with me, and I will demonstrate one more of my hidden gifts."

He got out of the car, and she followed him into the farmhouse. The interior was unadorned and sparsely furnished with plain, hand-fashioned wooden furniture of the most utilitarian kind. She guessed that no one lived in the house but Shardan made use of it for his own nefarious purposes. The house had no electricity; Shardan lit a candle and, carrying it in a candleholder, led Lina into a bedroom. The rough wooden bed frame held a bare, dusty mattress. On a wall hung a full-length mirror in a frame of polished pine, better crafted than the other things she'd seen. Shardan directed her to stand in front of this mirror.

She wasn't pleased with the image she saw reflected—the wrinkled clothes, the uncombed hair, the smudged face. But those things faded into insignificance when Shardan, candle uplifted, stood behind her. Wary, she watched him in the mirror, but it was her own image and not his that wavered, changed. She cried out in shock as she saw Headmistress's familiar features replace her own.

Shardan chuckled. "You see that I made no idle boast. I may not have many talents, but the ones I have are quite useful. This one I mastered only recently. I can enable you to replace the headmistress while we extract the necessary information from her. I can sustain the transformation only for short periods of time—not more than an hour or two—so we will have to plan carefully to make full use of that time."

He lowered the candle, and again the mirror image wavered. Lina welcomed the reappearance of her own reflection.

"With that kind of power, why do you need me?" she asked. "Why haven't you simply transformed yourself into the appearance of Chief Officer Ardrey and taken over his position long ago?"

"Had I been able, I would have done so. Sadly, I cannot transform myself. I can only employ my talent on another. That is why I need a gifted confederate who is not burdened with principles."

Lina knew that many talents could only be directed outward. His story could well be true, but it did not dispel her suspicions. "I'll have to have proof that I can trust you. How do I know you won't betray me when you get what you want?"

"Trust!" He spat. "Trust is something the Community prattles of. I will not speak of trust but of safeguards. I will give you the weapon I showed you so that you can entrap your headmistress. I know you covet that little trick. In return I'll take something of yours and hold it as guaranty to insure your cooperation—something you will not wish to lose. I think you will follow my plan."

Lina whirled around to face him. More than ever he resembled a snake. She tensed, tried to shift to her panther form. She could not.

He smirked. "Ah, yes. I know of that gift and how much you value it. When your headmistress returned it to you, I easily read that transaction. Indeed, I could see the panther form within your own. And I traced the process by which the headmistress had gathered that form and withheld it from you as well as the way she replaced it." He rubbed his hands together in glee. "I can't tell you how delighted I was to witness the exchange. I grasped its value to me immediately."

Lina's temper exploded like a volcano. She launched herself at him, clawing and kicking. And suddenly found herself cocooned in the white net once more. This time when it released her, it dumped her unceremoniously on the bed. Shardan remained near the mirror.

"Calm yourself," he said. "Your gift will be returned to you when you return mine to me. You will not need your panther form to carry out the task I set you. You will need only this." He opened his hand and showed her what looked like a ball of luminous twine. "This gift in exchange for yours."

He tossed the ball to her; she caught it, and examined it dubiously. "How does it work? Can anyone use it?"

He nodded. "Anyone with even the smallest degree of talent. Squeeze it in the palm of your hand, point your hand toward the person you wish to hold fast, open your fingers, and let your mind direct the threads. They will move with the speed of thought to encircle the victim."

Lina squeezed the ball in her hand, held that hand out toward Shardan, and opened her fingers as he'd directed. Threads of light spun toward him, then snapped back into her hand with a force that made her palm tingle.

He laughed. "I've set up a defense against it," he said. "Did you think I would be so careless? But your headmistress won't be expecting it. You shouldn't have any trouble using it against her."

"Where did you get this? Did you make it?" Lina was burning now with curiosity.

"It was a—ah—shall we say, a reward, for a favor I did in Tirbat for a highly gifted man. He had an unfortunate run-in with a high official in the national government several years ago, and I helped him escape a death sentence in exchange for this device. Of course it was then necessary for me to leave Tirbat."

"You said it required little talent to use it. Could it be used by someone with no talent—a nongifted?"

"No. If it had been of any use to the authorities, I would have been unable to acquire it."

Lina rolled the marvelous ball around in her hand. Wherever it had come from, it was an astounding bit of magic and she longed to have it for her own. She knew it was not what Ferene had used to capture her; that had been genuine magic, not any sort of device. But owning this thing would give Lina the same ability without Ferene's special talent.

Yet she also knew that however badly she wanted it, she would never give up her shapechanging ability in exchange for it. Shardan undoubtedly understood that; it was the reason he was willing to entrust her with this wonderful thing.

"Now I must return to Millville and see if my confederates have come out of their trance," he said. "If they have, I will have a tale ready for them. You will wait here until I come back. You will have to spend the night. I will give you sheets and a blanket for the bed. In the morning I will take you back to the school, and we will put our plan into action."

She nodded sullenly, and, pocketing the magical ball, she watched in silence while he puttered about, digging bed linens out of a closet, showing her where a chamber pot was kept, and producing from a kitchen cabinet a sealed jar of blackberry preserves and a loaf of bread, which he placed on a white enamel-topped table.

"I'm sorry I have nothing better to offer you," he said. "I'll bring better fare tomorrow. And soon we'll feast on the best of the land."

He left her. She heard the click of the door lock and a few moments later the roar of the limousine engine. She waited until the noise faded into the distance. Then she picked up the jar of preserves and hurled it against the wall, where it smashed and spattered into a satisfying mess. The loaf of bread she dropped onto the floor and ground beneath her feet into a pile of tiny, hard crumbs.

Too bad Gray isn't here to sculpt something with these, she thought.

She tried the windows and the doors, was not surprised to find them all securely locked. No matter. Shardan hadn't taken all her talents.

She scooped up a handful of blackberry preserves and used it to write a message on the white enamel tabletop: *I'll meet you at the school.*

At the front door, she called up her power, shrank the bolt and hinges until the door fell loose, lowered it to the ground, and strode over it and down the lane to the highway.

She walked along the side of the highway watching for an

oncoming car or truck. One would come by before long, and when it did, she was sure she'd have no difficulty persuading the driver to stop and give her a ride.

Gray argued with Oryon only briefly about going after Kress before yielding to the inevitable. He'd known subconsciously from the time he made the decision to save Oryon's life that he was thereby committing himself to an involvement in the dark one's affairs. Oryon's folly had unleashed the demons; they had to be vanquished. The attempt might kill him; he considered that a strong probability. His life was worth little. If he spent it battling the evil that threatened Simonton School, his death would at least have value.

He joined with Oryon and Giselle in another exchange of power. The first time he'd felt nothing, but this time the power traced a tingling path as it flowed outward from him, and its return spread a fiery heat throughout his body. He could not tell whether he had become more sensitive or the increased perception measured an increase of power. If he could send Giselle back to school, he would know his power had grown.

He pictured the hall outside Headmistress's office, recalling in vivid detail the floorboards worn by the scuffing feet of the countless students who'd waited there, the heavy door, the nearby landing from which one flight of stairs ascended to the third floor and another led down to the first. In the midst of this scene he imaged Giselle, standing at the office door, poised to knock.

He suppressed a strong urge to transfer himself and Oryon along with her. He could, he was certain of it, but he'd find no peace at the school until he'd seen this ordeal through.

Something seemed to tug at him, though, calling for his presence on the landing. He shut his eyes against the temptation and refused to edit himself into the scene.

This time he knew when Giselle left. The transfer sent a

ripple coursing along the channel he'd created. His mental image of her acquired motion. He saw her start, whirl around to look at something on the stair.

Oryon jogged his arm; his eyes popped open; the vision vanished.

"Good work," the dark one commended him. "Now, can you find Kress?"

"I don't know," Gray said. "I'll try, but first, how are we going to protect ourselves? What weapons do we have to use against the demon?"

"Headmistress gave me two things. The first is the demon's name. While she had it prisoner in Kress, she used her power to discover it. Knowing it will give us some control over him. The name is Grimgrist. And the second thing . . ." Oryon dug into his shirt pocket, brought out a tiny object clamped between his fingers. "Headmistress thought you might recognize this."

He held out for Gray's inspection a silver crescent earring with a diamond in its center.

Gray stared in disbelief. "Where did Headmistress get that?" He reached for it, jerked his hand back. "It's one of the earrings I bought for Rehanne as a date gift. I had them in my pocket the night of the Midwinter Ball when I . . . when you . . . when the Dire Women . . ." The painful memories flooded in, bringing renewed rage.

Oryon stepped back and closed his hand over the earring. "It was found under Kress's door the night the demon attacked him. Headmistress thinks Kress found it—or them—when he was in the Dire Realms. He brought them back with him when he was rescued, didn't tell anyone about them, and, somehow, discovered that because of their association with the Dire Realms, they could be used to summon a demon and command it. Except that he overreached himself.

He never was very smart. He let his control slip; the demon tore into him and then possessed him."

The explanation calmed Gray. It made sense. And though the blame still fell on Oryon, it shifted the responsibility for the current mess squarely onto Kress. "So we have to rescue Kress from his own stupidity?"

"We have to either destroy the demon or send it back where it came from with safeguards that will prevent its return."

"And the earring can help us?"

"The earring can help us find the demon; the knowledge of its name *might* help us control it. Headmistress could promise no more than that."

A premonitory shudder spidered up Gray's spine. Again he fought down the temptation to transfer himself back to the safety of the school. Safety would be only an illusion as long as the demon remained free.

"All right," he said. "Let's get on with it."

21

ESCAPE

A shrill scream penetrated Rehanne's fading consciousness. The hands around her throat loosened their grip. Moments later comforting arms cradled her head; a gentle touch eased the pain in her throat. The return to full consciousness brought with it a sharp awareness of the bruises and aches resulting from her tumble down the stairs. Then those injuries, too, subsided and were replaced by a warm sense of well-being. Reluctant to open her eyes and dispel the wonderful sense of relaxation, she tried to block the whisper insistently calling her name.

But the urgent appeal broke through her resistance. She raised her lids and gazed up into a worried face.

Giselle! It took a few seconds for her sluggish brain to register the significance of Giselle's presence.

When it did, she said in wonder, "You're not dead. We were so worried—" She stopped, struck by an eerie thought. "Unless—am I dead? Are we both—?"

"Of course not, silly," Giselle rebuked her with a smile. "It *was* close, though. Thank the Power-Giver I got here in time."

"But where were you? How did you get here? How did you know—?"

"I didn't know you were in trouble. It was mere luck that I arrived when I did. I've been with Gray. *I* was being attacked by a demon when somehow Gray winked me out of Headmistress's apartment to another place. I don't know where it was—it was empty and featureless. But Gray and Oryon were there, I don't know how, and Oryon was badly hurt, and Gray had called me to heal him."

Rehanne stared, scarcely able to believe the strange story. Why Gray was with Oryon she understood from Lina's account. But where had Gray gotten the talent to call someone to him into what Tria had described as another time line? And if he had that power, why had he sent for Giselle and not *her*?

With a guilty start she issued a mental rebuke to herself for that jealous thought. He'd sent for Giselle because he needed a healer.

But Giselle was not a strong healer. Why hadn't he sent for Headmistress? Or Veronica? Or Tria?

But Gray didn't know about Tria, and—

"Gray sent me back so that he and Oryon could go after

Kress," Giselle explained. "I saw you lying here, and you seemed to be strangling."

"I was *being* strangled," Rehanne corrected. The last shred of lethargy fell away. She'd already wasted too much time. She sat up, looked around. "Someone—the murderer—has the gift of invisibility. Whoever it was would have killed me. And that person probably isn't far away. We're in danger here."

Rehanne headed down the stairs.

Giselle caught her arm, tried to hold her back. "Hadn't we better go to Headmistress for help?"

Rehanne shook her head. "Headmistress has already made too many mistakes. We need to find Veronica. She's the one who can help us, if anyone can."

Gray's newfound talents gave birth to a pride that grew with each use of power. For the first time, he knew the desire to test his strength and to experiment with ways to increase it. For the first time, he understood how Oryon had been led astray by power's seductive appeal.

He grew eager to confront Kress, confident that he'd be able to control him and subdue the demon. It was Oryon who urged caution, who delayed. No doubt he was thinking of the nearly fatal wound Kress had given him. (If it *had* been Kress. Gray couldn't dispel his doubt.)

"If we bring him here, the transfer will take him off guard and give us the advantage of surprise," Oryon persisted with the argument they'd been having.

"It will also deprive us of a vital weapon." Gray pointed out in different words what he'd said twice before. "Our sudden arrival where he is will surprise him. But if he does have a weapon and attacks us, I can send him back here, and we can follow and grab him while he's disoriented from the change."

"Kress might be disoriented, but will the demon be?" Oryon asked. "And we know he has at least one weapon, the one he stabbed me with. We won't surprise him twice. If we use the earring to lure him here and use his name to bind him, we won't spend power we can't spare. Your way could leave us dangerously depleted."

Gray stubbornly refused to yield. The power built up by their sharing glowed and pulsed within him, coursing through his veins, demanding release. He felt invincible, omnipotent. "If you won't come, I'll go alone." He ignored the small inner voice whispering that his haughty declaration sounded like something the old Oryon would have said.

"I'll come," Oryon said with quiet dignity.

Gray savored the victory. He made a show of flexing his arms and squeezing his eyes tightly shut to evidence his concentration. He could not visualize Kress's surroundings as he had done in sending Giselle back to the school, so he visualized Kress as he had last seen him and mentally constructed his own and Oryon's images on either side of Kress. Forced to leave the surrounding area blank, he relied instead on sending the flow of power outward in search of Kress rather than drawing it in toward himself as he would do to bring Kress to him.

He did not feel the transition. Oryon's muttered "Power-Giver help us!" made him open his eyes.

They had transferred to a high-ceilinged stone chamber. Its rough walls suggested it might be a cave. In its center on a wide stone table directly in front of them lay Kress, bound, eyes full of terror. Behind the table three hideous, grinning demons capered and chortled. One Gray recognized as the demon he had sculpted, the one Headmistress had called Gruefell. That one held a stone blade poised over Kress's chest. The place reeked of sulfur.

That sight was horrifying enough, but Gray raised his eyes to behold a sight that held him frozen in terror.

Behind the demons, on raised thrones, sat the two Dire Women who had captured him, tortured him, and transformed him into a beast. Their death-mask faces wore hungry grins. They gestured, and two fiends leaped around the table and grabbed him and Oryon. Daggerlike claws sank into Gray's arms.

"Gray, whip us back," he heard Oryon shout.

But pain and fear paralyzed him, leaving him helpless in the demon's grasp.

The demon tossed him effortlessly across the table to one of its fellows. That one in turn tossed him to another. Making a game of it, they threw him back and forth, catching him in stabbing claws until he bled from wounds all over his body.

"Grimgrist, by your name and by the token I hold, I order you to free me and my companion." Oryon's voice, loud and bold, cut through his agony.

The Dire Women's hideous laughter crushed Gray's hope. Too near fainting to resist, he was rolled about while the fiends wound wire around him, binding his arms to his side and banding his legs tightly together. The wire cut into his already abused flesh. The demons dumped him onto the table next to Kress. Seconds later Oryon, similarly trussed, thudded onto the table on Kress's other side.

The Dire Women came and stood over them, their great batlike wings overshadowing the table. "So, Gruefell, you have served us a feast. Well done."

At her words Gruefell and his two companions leaped and cavorted around the table, filling the air with shrieks of glee.

"Gray." Oryon's whisper reached him through the din. "I'll feed you all the power I have. Get us out of here."

He couldn't! Not with the Dire Women hovering over him. He felt his sanity slipping away.

"Try!" Oryon urged again, and he felt power flow into him. Oryon was doing what *he* could. Gray had to try. He'd brought them here. He had to redeem himself.

Closing his eyes, he tried to drive out the cacophony assaulting his ears, the pain of his wounds, the wire that cut off the circulation in his arms and legs, and with it the free flow of power. He tried to picture his room at school, but even with his eyes shut all he could see was the terrible faces of the Dire Women.

A Dire Woman scraped her taloned hand across his cheek. The memories revived by that touch drove out all other thought.

"Hurry!" Oryon's cry reached through his private darkness.

He tried again, desperately visualizing his bed and Reece's, unmade as they usually left them. He imagined feeling the bed beneath him instead of the hard stone table. The wrinkled sheets, the rough wool blanket. His pillow beneath his head. Oryon stretched on Reece's bed. The quiet of the school replacing the screeching fiends.

"Whew! You did it!" Oryon's voice boomed into the silence. "But where's Kress?"

Gray looked around him at the familiar room. Against all odds he *had* done it!

But he'd never thought of Kress. And his power was spent.

Oryon writhed and struggled in his bonds. "You've got to bring him. They're going to kill him. Hurry!"

"I can't. No strength left."

"What's happened? Where'd you guys come from?" Reece's trembling voice came from the front of the room near the door. Gray could move his head enough to see his shaken roommate cowering against the wall.

"Reece! Focus your power on Gray. Let him draw it."

At Oryon's sharp command, Reece stepped closer. "Why—?"

"No questions," Oryon barked. "Do it!"

A weak probe touched Gray like the brush of a feather. *No! How can I save Kress? I can't!* Then he thought with shame of his own recent arrogance. His stupidity in rejecting Oryon's advice.

"More!" he said to Reece.

The touch grew stronger. Gray pulled at it, drew it in. His mind painted the image of Kress lying on the stone table. *Here,* he thought. *To me!*

Reece leaped aside barely in time to avoid being crushed by the heavy stone table that crashed down between the beds, splintering the floorboards, shaking the room. The massive table teetered dangerously before stabilizing. Kress's body slid back and forth on the wide top, the handle of the stone knife protruding from his chest.

The thunder of the table's descent echoed around the room. When it died away, Oryon again spoke into the silence. "Reece, for the gods' sake, man, untie me!"

Gray heard Kress's voice, weak and broken. "It's too late. I'm gone. But so's Gruefell. The Dire Women killed him when you got away."

Then silence. And moments later Oryon announced what Gray already knew: "He's dying."

Gray scarcely felt Reece struggling with the tight bonds. He didn't care about being freed. He'd failed again. Kress was dying because of his pride and his folly. Oryon, whom he had despised, had kept his head and acted bravely, while he'd played the part of a sniveling coward. And although he deserved all the censure that could be heaped on him, Oryon uttered not a word of reproach.

When at last the wire fell away, Gray sat up and rubbed his bleeding arms and legs. Reece had yet to free Oryon. He edged around the table and went to work at that task. Gray got to his feet and squeezed past the table, trying not to look at Kress's bloody face. He stumbled from the room and wandered toward the stairs. He had no destination in mind; he only wanted to get away.

Someone—he didn't look to see who but thought it might have been Veronica—hurried past him, and a voice he thought was Veronica's said, "Wait. Don't go any farther."

He paid no attention. He had to get away. But where could he go to escape himself?

22

The Dead Speak, the Lost Are Found

Rehanne and Giselle reached the bottom of the stairway and started toward the patio. The halls, which would normally be busy in the early evening, were deserted. All the other students seemed to be obeying the order to stay in their rooms.

"How are we going to know if the murderer's near if he's invisible?" Giselle's plaintive voice slowed Rehanne's steps.

"I think I'll be able to sense a presence," Rehanne answered, concealing her doubt. "I've felt it before, but I didn't know what it was."

She couldn't be sure she would feel that invisible presence in time to evade a trap. She should not be leading Giselle into danger. But Giselle was already in danger. The murderer had sent the demon to kill her once before and wouldn't hesitate to do it again.

"What do you plan to do if you sense him?"

"Shhh!" Rehanne could not bring herself to admit that she had no plan. Tiptoeing to emphasize the need for silence, she led Giselle past classroom doors.

Glancing toward the intersecting corridor, she saw instead an archway through which a wide, gleaming marble stairway was clearly visible.

She gasped. She had seen glimpses of the hidden and mysterious rooms that formed part of the larger school, that edifice which spanned dimensions and opened into alternate worlds. She had entered one or two small, exquisitely decorated chambers for a quick look around before they vanished into their usual invisibility.

This was different. It had none of the shimmering air of unreality that had characterized those other rooms. It stretched before her solid and inviting. She glanced at Giselle and knew by her wide-eyed stare that she was seeing it, too.

Go through every door that opens to you, Master Tumberlis had said many times. Rehanne remembered too well the lectures in which Old Tumbles had expounded on the multidimensional nature of the school and how the ability to see and explore the halls and chambers that appeared suddenly and unexpectedly before one was an indication of reaching a higher level of giftedness.

Despite her haste to find Veronica, she was drawn toward this marvelous stairway. Giselle must have felt the same attraction. She passed through the archway while Rehanne hesitated. "We've got to go in," she said in an awed whisper, and started up the stairs.

Rehanne followed slowly, afraid she was making a grave

mistake. She was only halfway up the stairs when Giselle reached the top. "Wait, Giselle," she called. But her friend paid no attention.

She glanced behind her and was alarmed to find that she could no longer see the familiar school corridor. Golden doors, tightly shut, closed off the archway. They might have been drawn into some kind of trap. "Giselle," she shouted urgently.

Giselle only called back, "Hurry, Rehanne. Come and look at this." The words were fading into the distance.

Rehanne sped up the rest of the stairway. She stood in a corridor lined on one side with windows of amber-hued glass that tinted the light streaming through them a rich gold. The corridor led to a chamber into which Giselle had already disappeared. Rehanne hurried to find her.

It was a circular chamber, with no furniture, no windows, no other door. Inset in the white marble floor were concentric rings that looked to be of some sort of metal, each painted a different color, spaced so that a long stride would carry an average-sized person across it to the white marble flooring separating it from the next circle. In the center of the rings was a golden disk just large enough for one person to stand on.

Arms at her side, Giselle stood on that disk and gazed upward with a rapt expression. Rehanne followed her gaze. The domed ceiling was painted with colored rings matching those on the floor, and in its center a golden disk seemed to be suspended in space below the actual top of the dome directly above the disk on the floor.

"What is it? What do you see?" Rehanne called.

Giselle didn't answer, didn't give any indication she'd heard.

Rehanne had to reach her, but she was strangely loath to cross those bright metallic rings. She stood before the first, a yellow band, took a deep breath, and stepped over it, taking care not to let her foot touch it. A tingle like a mild electric shock passed through her as she crossed. It was not unpleasant, but it did not relieve her mind.

The next ring was blue, and as she stepped over it a cold chill shook her, slowed her, and increased her fear.

Crossing the third ring, a pale green, brought a gut-twisting nausea that sent her to her knees on the far side of the ring, retching, her stomach wracked with cramps. Weak and shaken, she staggered to her feet and moved forward.

Two more rings lay ahead of her, the closer a bright red, the innermost a deep purple. She shouted again at Giselle, got no response. Her friend stood immobile, as though carved of stone.

Rehanne took several running steps and jumped across the red band. Fiery heat lanced her. Her flesh burned. If she stopped, she might not be able to force herself back into motion; she dashed onward over the purple band.

The horror of death seized her. Screams tore from her throat. She felt as though she were sliding into an open grave. Sobbing hysterically, she scrabbled across the floor to the golden disk and threw her arms around Giselle's legs.

She was in an island of calm. Her fear vanished. She stood and confronted Giselle, reached into the circle, grasped her shoulders, and shook her. Giselle wrenched free and shoved Rehanne away without speaking a word.

Fear and urgency drove Rehanne forward again. She grabbed Giselle, grappled with her, and yanked her off the disk.

Giselle blinked and groaned. "No!" she shouted. "You've no right to do that. I was talking to my brother."

She struggled, but Rehanne held tight. "Wake up, Giselle," she gasped. "Your brother's dead. You weren't talking to him."

"I was. He was right there." Giselle was crying and pointing at the upper disk.

With a sudden, sharp twist Giselle broke free and hurled herself back onto the disk. Rehanne leaped after her and fought with her, trying to drag her out. She caught Giselle off balance and, in pushing her off the disk, placed herself in its center.

Calm. Warmth. Wonderful peace. She stood and lifted her face to the upper disk.

A face stared back at her. Fenton's. Familiar wide grin. Red hair mussed as it had always been in life.

"Rehanne," he called down to her, his voice cheerful. "I wanted to tell you something. I never got the chance. Can't leave unfinished business."

He paused and the grin faded. "I'd remembered something Kress said. It wasn't easy, being his roommate. He was always bragging about something or other, and I didn't pay much attention. But I remembered that earlier on the night he was ripped up he'd bragged about how he'd soon have more power than he'd ever had before. I asked him how he planned to manage that, and he said, 'Chantal's going to help me. She's a little gold-digger, but she's got some useful talents. I bribed her with a pair of earrings and promises I don't plan to keep.' He laughed, but I guess he realized he'd said too much. 'Keep your mouth shut about this,' he said. 'If you don't, I'll shut it for you permanently.'

"I wasn't really worried, though I did keep what he'd said to myself." The face was grim as he added, "It wasn't Kress who killed me. It was a demon. I think—"

Giselle pushed Rehanne off the disk, and they fell to the floor, wrestling and kicking. In their thrashing around, they rolled across the purple band.

On its far side Rehanne sat up, dazed, shaken, filled with

dread. Giselle lay curled in the fetal position, moaning and trembling. Rehanne put out her hand and touched Giselle's shoulder. Slowly she uncurled and sat up. The gaze she turned on Rehanne was bleak but sane.

"We've got to get out of here," Rehanne said.

Giselle nodded. They helped each other to their feet and supported each other across the remaining rings. Rehanne felt their effects, but not as strongly as she had on coming in, and Giselle seemed too stunned to be fully aware of the strange and disparate sensations.

When they reached the door and passed into the corridor with the amber windows, they stopped as if by mutual consent.

"I *did* talk to my brother," Giselle said wonderingly. "I saw his face in the gold disk. He said I mustn't blame myself for his death. He'd been in a bad mood and had raced the horse across a dangerous field, been thrown, and got his foot caught in the stirrup and dragged over the rocky ground. He was dead long before I got to him, so of course I couldn't heal him." She gazed into Rehanne's eyes with an expression that defied Rehanne to express disbelief.

"I believe you," Rehanne assured her. "I saw Fenton when I was in the circle." Quickly she shared with Giselle what Fenton had told her. "He was still speaking when you pulled me out of the circle. I'm not sure what else he was going to tell me, but I hope he said enough to let him rest."

Giselle nodded. "It's as though we were meant to come here and talk to them. For their sakes and for ours."

Rehanne started to agree, stopped, struck by the implications of Giselle's observation.

Of course they were meant to come here. Otherwise the door to this place would not have opened for them.

Rehanne did not regret the experience of speaking with

the dead, but she did resent the sense of being a pawn in a game she did not understand.

The light provided by the amber windows was much dimmer than it had been earlier. It was growing late. She hurried toward the marble stairway, and Giselle followed.

A loud meow halted her. She spun around. A silver cat strolled toward her, its tail raised like a banner. Purring, it rubbed against her legs.

"Maridel's cat! It has to be!" Rehanne reached down and scooped up the animal, cuddling it in her arms.

"Where did it come from?" Giselle said wonderingly.

"I don't know, but that's one lost item found. Let's take it to Maridel."

They hurried down the stairs and into the familiar hallway. They went directly to Maridel's room.

The cat's loud purring comforted and soothed Rehanne. Holding the cat in her arms, she petted its soft silver fur as she and Giselle stood waiting for Maridel to respond to their knock. Too much time went by. Worried, Rehanne knocked again, louder.

Finally a timid voice called out, "Who is it?"

Of course they would be afraid to open, after all that had happened. She should have thought. "It's Rehanne. And Giselle," she called. "We found Maridel's cat."

The door eased open a crack. A pair of frightened eyes peered out. Rehanne held the cat out so it could be seen.

The door swung open. "Moonbeam!" Maridel snatched the cat from Rehanne's hands and hugged him against the flannel robe worn incongruously over a silk nightgown. "Oh, Moonbeam, I've been so worried about you. Where have you been, you naughty kitten?"

She looked up and swung her hair out of her face. "Where did you find him?" she asked in a sharp tone, as though she suspected Rehanne of having hidden the cat.

"In the hall near the stairs," Rehanne answered without explaining *which* hall and *what* stairs. She only wanted to get away, now that she had delivered the cat.

Maridel backed into the room and put her hand on the door, but before she could shut it, the cat gave a loud meow and stretched a paw toward Rehanne.

The door stayed open. Maridel buried her face in the cat's thick fur for a moment, then looked up. "Moonbeam says I'm being rude," she announced. "I'm to invite you in. But Debra's in bed. She doesn't feel well, and—"

"That's all right," Rehanne said quickly. "We have to go."

Moonbeam yowled and twisted from his owner's grasp, leaped toward Rehanne, and rubbed against the back of her legs, pushing her toward the door.

"I think you'd better come in," Maridel said. "Moonbeam insists."

"I think we should," Giselle whispered. "The cat has a positive aura. Maybe he can help us."

Gray wandered through the empty rooms of the aged, abandoned school, neither knowing nor caring how he had come there again. The place suited his mood. The dust, the broken furniture, the smell of rotted wood. Most of all, the emptiness.

Loneliness suited him. He didn't deserve to be with people. He couldn't face their accusations. Or their pity.

Poor Gray. Poor foolish Gray. He has power he didn't know he had, doesn't know how to use, can't learn to control. Stupid and inept, that's what he is.

Or, Gray's to blame. Not only for Kress's death. For everything. For not using his power earlier. For using it in the wrong way. For refusing to help Oryon when Headmistress first proposed it, before any of the murders had occurred.

If he'd done what she'd asked, if he hadn't been so stubborn, all the deaths could have been prevented. Jolly, good-natured Fenton. Dwayne, who'd been little more than a child. And Kress. Kress, who was not an innocent victim as the others had been. But he had not deserved to die like that.

Sacrificed by demons! Killed to satisfy the Dire Women's hunger. At least the demon Gruefell was also dead, if Kress's dying words were to be believed. But that left the two other demons who'd been terrorizing the school.

Could he do anything to stop them, or would any effort of his only make matters worse? Maybe if he stayed out of it, let the others handle it . . .

In the parlor he picked up a broken chair leg and idly drew designs in the dust that coated the floor. Preoccupied with his despair, he failed to notice what he had drawn until a shaft of light from the setting sun passed through the front window and for a few seconds illuminated the sketch.

It was a rough depiction of the satyr.

The satyr. What was he? Gray felt sure he was not evil. Would he help Gray? Could he? It was worth a try.

He recalled the hall of mirrors where he'd seen the satyr. Shutting his eyes, he tried to remember and image every detail—the mirrors in their ornate frames, the party-goers in the dress of a long-past era, the satyr himself, peering over his shoulder at his mirrored reflection.

Painstakingly he recreated the scene in his mind. When he had included everything he could remember, he opened his eyes.

Before him he saw his mirrored reflection. Behind him the satyr grinned into the glass.

When Lina reached the school, darkness had long since fallen. Supper was over; the school was quiet, its doors locked. She did not wish to knock and advertise her return.

If she only had her shapechanging ability, gaining entry would be an easy matter. Without it she could see no way of getting in. The talent she'd used to escape from Shardan's farmhouse would do her no good here at the school; it was warded against such sorcery, and she didn't have her talisman.

She'd probably have to roust someone to open the door, but first she'd go around to the back of the building and check the rear entrances. They'd be locked but possibly not as strongly warded. Her talent might work on one of them.

She found her way by the light that fell from the second- and third-floor windows. No light shone from any of the first-floor windows, so the parlor remained closed and Head-mistress's order for students to stay in their rooms was still in force. She shouldn't find that surprising, but she felt as though she'd been gone for days instead of hours. It was hard to believe that so much could have happened in a single afternoon.

She glanced up at the second-floor windows and was startled to see a light in Oryon's room. She'd supposed Oryon was still lost in some alternate time. But of course, his room-mate, Troy, would be there.

A dark shadow moved in front of the window. She stared. That *was* Oryon, not Troy. She was certain of it. If she could get his attention . . .

She bent and scrabbled about for pebbles. When she'd gathered a handful, she stood and lobbed them at Oryon's window, using her power to be sure they reached their target. With one she miscalculated the force, and the window cracked when it struck the glass.

She saw Oryon draw aside the edge of the curtain and peer downward from the side of the window. She waved. "Oryon, it's Lina," she called softly. "I'm locked out. Help me find a way in."

He stuck his head all the way out and gazed down at her. "Can you climb a rope?" he asked.

"Yes."

"Wait."

He withdrew from the window, and she glanced nervously at the other lighted rooms, hoping no one had heard the exchange. The wait grew long. She checked around her constantly to be sure she wasn't observed. At last Oryon reappeared and tossed her the end of a long rope. He'd made knots at intervals along it to provide her with hand- and footholds. She ascended easily, and he grasped her hand and helped her over the windowsill. Together they hauled in the rope.

"What's been happening here?" she asked, casting a swift glance around the room. "When did you get back? How?"

Troy, Oryon's roommate, stood by his desk, wide-eyed and clearly ill at ease. He shifted his gaze uncertainly from her to Oryon. "Should I leave?" He backed toward the door as he asked, either assuming or hoping for an affirmative answer.

"No. Stay," Oryon said quickly before Lina could offer the opposite advice.

She frowned, and Oryon said, "There've been too many secrets. That's what caused the deaths. We all—the whole school—are involved in this thing. We've got to work together."

Lina decided not to waste time arguing, though her doubts remained. Troy was only a second-year student, and she could not remember all his talents, but she was sure one of them was the ability to block the operation of power. That gift might come in handy, but she didn't want it to prevent her from sharing power with Oryon.

"He's a quencher," Oryon said, as though picking up her thought. "If things get rough, we may need that talent on our side. We can't expect him to help us if he doesn't know what's going on."

She shrugged, conceding the point without aligning herself with Oryon's view.

"Kress may be dead," Oryon said abruptly. "Demons did it. They nearly got me and Gray, too. Gray shifted himself and me out in time, but by the time he could get Kress, they'd stuck a knife into his chest and he was dying. Gray blames himself. He's wandered off, and I don't know where. Veronica came in and sent me to look for him while she did what she could for Kress. She had her assistant with her. I tried to find Gray, but he probably shifted again. Guy's got tremendous power. Funny how it showed up so late."

Lina thought Veronica and Tria might have saved Kress, but she didn't care, and it was clear Oryon didn't know. Other things were more important. "What about Rehanne? What's she been doing?" Rehanne was a good follower but a poor leader. Lina could not imagine her finding the initiative to act on her own.

"I don't know. I tried to find her at the same time that I went looking for Gray. Couldn't find her, and she's not in her room. Maybe Gray called her to him and took her with him, wherever he went."

Lina grimaced. She'd counted on Rehanne's help, though that was before she'd known Oryon was back. She could work with him, but she wouldn't be able to manipulate him as she would Rehanne.

"I'm a finder, too," Troy spoke up unexpectedly. "I can't locate a person in another plane, of course, but if they're here on this plane, I can find them."

Lina glared in exasperation. "Why didn't you say so before? We could have used you to find Giselle. Has she turned up?"

"I don't know where she is now," Oryon said, "but she was with Gray and me for a while. She healed me when a demon sliced my shoulder open. Gray sent her back here before he and I went after Kress, and I haven't seen her since."

"I can see there's a lot you haven't told me, but the details will wait," Lina said. "We'd better get busy."

"In a minute," Oryon said. "You haven't told me where you've been and why you got locked outside."

Lina flopped into a desk chair and summarized the afternoon's adventure, describing how she'd escaped first from Ardrey and later from Shardan. She explained Shardan's ambition but did not disclose either the weapon he had given her or his ability to transform her into Headmistress's likeness.

Oryon said, "Should you report to Headmistress and tell her about Shardan?"

"Not until she asks. She doesn't tell us things."

"All right. Let's get to work." Oryon turned to his roommate. "Troy, do whatever you need to do to find Gray and Rehanne."

"I've already done it," said the sandy-haired youth. "I can't find Gray, but Rehanne and Giselle are together upstairs in Maridel's room."

Lina jumped to her feet. "Let's go."

"It's late," Troy objected. "The stairs will be warded."

"Oryon can break the wards. He's done it before."

"Yes, but . . . Wait a minute. I'll be right back." Oryon dashed from the room and returned a couple of minutes later with Reece in tow.

"My power's at low ebb," Oryon explained. "Reece is an enhancer. He'll give me a boost if I need it. And by the way, he says Veronica and her helper shooed him out of his room while they took care of Kress, and when he went back later they were all gone—so we don't know whether or not they were able to heal Kress."

"Even the stone table had disappeared, along with the mess it made," Reece put in.

"Never mind that now," Lina said. "Let's get upstairs."

Reece, in slacks and undershirt, looked no more enthusiastic for this adventure than did Troy. But he fell into step beside Troy, and the two of them followed Lina and Oryon down the hall toward the stairs.

23

A GATHERING, A SCATTERING

Gray turned slowly from the mirror to face the spot where the reflected satyr had seemed to stand. As before, the room was empty, party-goers and satyr visible only as reflections in the mirror. He swung around and viewed the satyr in the mirror. The creature smiled and pointed behind it, pivoted, and wound its way through the crowd to a door on the far side of the room. At the door it paused and looked back at Gray, beckoned, and passed through.

Gray turned to gaze across the empty room. There *was* a door on the far side, a door he hadn't seen before. It stood open, waiting. He hurried across the room.

The door led to a narrow, dark stairway, nothing more. Gray felt his way down it. At the bottom a second door led outside to what seemed to be a small, enclosed garden. Night had fallen, and faint starlight provided the only illumination, so Gray could see only dimly. Something like a boulder rested in the center of the garden, and perched on it was a shadowy figure. The satyr!

It raised its hands to its mouth and the high, sweet sound of pipes filled the night. The music entranced Gray, drove out his anxiety.

How long the satyr played, Gray couldn't guess. The music drifted around him in timeless splendor. When the pipes ceased to play, Gray felt that their notes would stay with him forever.

The figure slid to its feet and moved toward him, and it was human, not a satyr. "Time to go in," it said.

Gray blinked and recognized the place where he stood. Even in the darkness he should have known it for the school patio. What he had taken for a boulder was the side of the fountain. And the classroom corridor light revealed the person he followed inside as Viad, the first-year student with the gift of transmitting music.

"Veronica sent me to fetch you," Viad explained. "Your friends are waiting for you on the third floor in Maridel's room."

"The third floor? The women's floor? It's warded."

"Hurry, and you'll find the wards down."

"Who's Maridel? I don't know her. Why would my friends be with her?"

"She's a first-year student. Your friends know her. Hers is the second room on your left when you come off the stairs. Go. Before the wards are put back."

Gray was halfway up the stairs when he realized that Viad had not come with him and that he had not asked Viad which "friends" were waiting.

Rehanne entered Maridel's room, Moonbeam purring at her heels. Maridel motioned her and Giselle to seats in the desk chairs. She sat on a bed; in the other her roommate lay with the covers tucked under her neck, her face wan in its frame of cropped dark hair.

Giselle had scarcely sat down when she jumped up again and headed toward the bed, saying, "What's wrong? I'm a healer. I can help."

Moonbeam raced toward her, hissing, leaped in front of her, and hurled himself at her, scratching and biting.

"Ow! No! Stop!" Shouting and striking at the cat, Giselle backed away from the bed.

Maridel leaped up and grabbed the cat. "Bad kitten!" she scolded.

Giselle eyed the cat warily and continued backing to the desk chair. "He doesn't want me to heal—what's your room-mate's name? Debra?"

Maridel nodded.

"Why? Can you find out?" Rehanne asked, intrigued by Moonbeam's strange behavior.

"I'll try." Maridel returned to her seat on the bed, keeping a firm hold on the cat. Again she buried her face in the sil-very fur.

After a time she raised her head. Her hair obscured her eyes. "He won't tell me," she said. "The only thing I got from him is that Debra's illness isn't serious."

Rehanne was skeptical. Debra's eyes were closed, her skin waxen. She seemed unaware of the arrival of visitors, though Rehanne's shouts at the cat should have awakened her from a normal sleep. It was as if she was in a coma. Maybe Giselle should try again while Maridel held Moonbeam.

A knock on the door kept her from making the sugges-tion. Lina's voice called out, "Is Rehanne there?"

Rehanne jumped up and ran to the door. Ignoring Maridel's cry of "Be careful!" she flung the door open.

Lina did indeed stand in the hall, but not alone. With her

were Oryon, Troy, and Reece. Rehanne stared in shock until Lina said, "Well, are you going to let us in?"

"No!" Maridel called, but Rehanne ignored her and stood aside, allowing them to enter.

Troy and Reece were plainly embarrassed to enter a girl's room at night. Rehanne saw Reece's gaze settle for a moment on Debra and flee away, while his face reddened.

Lina walked into the area between the beds and pointed at Debra. "What's wrong with her?"

"She's ill," Rehanne said.

"The cat won't let me heal her," Giselle added.

"The cat?" Lina pivoted and stared at Maridel and the animal in her arms.

Moonbeam yawned and turned his head away from Lina.

"I can't offer you a place to sit. I'm sorry." Maridel's awkward apology sounded more like a plea for her unwanted guests to leave.

"We'll sit on the floor," Oryon said. "We need to talk."

"It's late," Maridel objected. "Debra's sick."

"Forget about the time," Oryon snapped. "People have been killed, demons are loose, we're all in danger, and if we're to prevent more deaths we've got to act tonight." He settled himself on the floor between the desks, and Lina dropped down beside him. Reece and Troy remained standing, Troy resting his hip against the corner of a desk.

"But why are Debra and I involved?" Maridel wailed. "We have nothing to do with the killing or with demons."

"Do you think you're safe?" Lina asked. "We're all involved: everyone at the school."

Maridel stood, holding Moonbeam. "Then let's rouse everybody and have a general meeting. With Headmistress—she should be here."

Lina shook her head. "Headmistress seems to be leaving matters to us. And we're going to handle it."

"Do you have a plan?" Rehanne asked, afraid to hope that Lina could really do anything but wanting desperately to believe that there was something to be done.

The catgirl leaned forward. "I have an idea—"

A knock on the door kept her from saying anything more. Maridel groaned. Reece, closest to the door, eased it open a crack and peered out, then swung it wide.

Gray stepped into the room.

His tired, beaten look alarmed Rehanne. He hadn't shaved or changed clothes. She called his name and pushed toward him through the crowded room. He seemed not to hear or see her. His gaze settled on Oryon.

But Lina captured his attention by shooting a question at him with a sharpness that made Rehanne cringe: "How did you know where we were?" He didn't need to hear that accusatory tone; he'd been through so much.

He blinked and turned slowly toward Lina as though awaking from a dream. "Viad sent me."

"Viad! How did—?" Lina stopped and snapped her fingers. "Veronica! She's orchestrating this whole thing. Well, not the murders, of course. But our solving them and stopping the murderer and defeating the demons. That's the way she works; I've figured out that much. She doesn't do anything directly, but she manipulates people. She runs this school and moves us all around like chess pieces. Headmistress is only a figurehead."

She stopped, breathing hard and glaring at the bewildered faces around her. She was right, Rehanne was sure, though the others probably thought her mad.

Rehanne squeezed between Reece and Troy to reach Gray. She put her arm around his waist. "I've been so worried about you."

He didn't react, didn't look at her. Instead, he said to Lina, "I don't believe that of Headmistress."

"It's true, whether you believe it or not," Lina said. "To-morrow I'll prove it. I have a couple of tricks that Veronica doesn't know of. I think I'll arrange for Headmistress to surprise her."

Rehanne didn't like the way Lina was taking charge, but the others seemed ready to accept Lina's direction.

"What are you talking about?" Giselle asked.

Lina shrugged off the question. "Later. We're here to find the murderer before he or she or it finds us."

"He, she, or it doesn't seem to have any problem finding us when it wants," Rehanne said.

Maridel whimpered and hugged Moonbeam to her chest. Troy glanced nervously toward the door.

"*It*," Reece repeated speculatively. "The demon."

"The demon or demons are doing the killing," Oryon said, "but someone summoned them. Someone was controlling them—trying to, at least. They aren't easy to control. Kress learned that the hard way." He stopped and turned to Reece. "What happened after I left? Kress died?"

"I don't know. Maybe not. Veronica and the other maid carried him away."

Gray shuddered and turned even paler, if that was possible. Rehanne tried to hug him. Gently but firmly he pushed her away and sank down onto the free desk chair.

Oryon said, "If he died, it's not your fault, Gray. You did all you could."

"You know that's not true. If I'd listened to you and done it the way you wanted, we could have saved him."

"You can't know that. Don't torture yourself with what might have been."

"Right," Lina interposed. "We don't have time to hash over past mistakes. We've got to keep from making new ones."

"So what do you propose?" Giselle asked.

"First that we pool our knowledge. I want to know anything that's happened while I was in Millville. And I picked up a bit of interesting information there that might mean something." Lina turned to Rehanne. "Oryon's already filled me in on what happened to him and Gray. What have you done? What ideas have you come up with?"

Rehanne glanced at Reece. Heat crept over her face as she told of wondering why none of this had happened last year and of heading toward the boys' floor to question Reece.

"You suspected *me*?" Reece asked, his voice squeaking.

"Why not? Nobody is free of suspicion," Lina snapped. "Go on, Rehanne."

Rehanne told of feeling the presence behind her too late to keep herself from being pushed down the stairs, described the demon's attack, and told how Giselle had saved her. "So," she finished, "my idea about Reece was wrong. The attack came from behind me—from the girls' floor. I'm sorry, Reece."

He nodded, still looking pained.

"Don't be sorry," Lina said. "It was a good thought. Why *didn't* this happen last year? We all know what happened the year before last."

Gray stared at the floor, Oryon and Reece nodded unhappily, and Troy grunted an embarrassed assent. Only Maridel merely looked perplexed. As a first-year student, she probably *didn't* know.

Lina went on. "What I learned in Millville might have a bearing on that question. Shardan told me that Chief Officer Ardrey badly wants to discredit the school, and to help him with that delightful project he enlisted a student to spy for him. That may not have anything to do with our troubles this year, but it could. Ardrey would have recruited his traitor toward the end of last year.

"We'll keep it in mind as we review everything else we

know about the murders, the circumstances surrounding them, and the missing objects."

Rehanne scarcely listened as Lina recounted the now familiar facts. A memory was teasing her mind and she had to track it down. Vaguely she heard Lina tick off the list of missing items and speculate again on why they might have been taken.

Then Lina mentioned the missing book, and everything clicked into place. "I have it!" Rehanne announced.

For the first time Gray met her gaze, his eyes suddenly eager. "You know who it is?"

"Yes. It has to be." Rehanne scanned the faces now turned toward her. "Remember last year toward the end of the year when three students got into trouble in Millville? Eula and Bettina should have known better. They were both first-year students when . . . when we had the other trouble, and they dropped out after that first term, but last year they came back. After the trouble in Millville, they left again—I don't know whether they dropped out or were expelled; it doesn't matter. The third student was Chantal, and she was allowed to stay in school. She was only a first-year student then, and she claimed that she had just gone along with Eula and Bettina. I doubt that. Anyway, she would have had contact with Ardrey, and he could have frightened her into doing whatever he wanted."

"Yes, that fits," Oryon said.

Gray frowned. He looked disappointed. "She might be a spy, but that's hardly the same as summoning demons to commit murder."

"No, but listen," Rehanne continued rapidly. "She's secretive about what talents she has. Coral told me that Chantal's a reverse empath, but she might also have the gift of invisibility."

"That's only a guess," Reece said.

"It's a good guess," Lina offered. "What else?"

"The book that was missing. I found a copy of it in Headmistress's office." Rehanne told of the last spell, the one for transforming a demon into the likeness of a person, and of the handwritten warning below it. "So," she concluded, "we all know how cozy Chantal was with Kress. Suppose for some reason they used the spell at some time before Kress was hurt. They didn't know you couldn't use the spell twice. I don't know when they used it the first time or what their plan was, but whatever it was, it back-fired when they tried it a second time and the demon tore Kress up."

"I can guess when they first used it," Gray put in abruptly. "The day I got here. I was leaving the parlor to go upstairs when Kress shoved into me and knocked me into Jerrol. I thought it was Jerrol. He didn't say anything, just growled and started to attack me. He would have lured me into a fight, but Veronica stepped in and stopped us and sent me on to Headmistress's office. I'll bet it wasn't Jerrol at all, but the demon, and they were trying to get me—and the real Jerrol, too, I suppose—into trouble. There was a peace officer on duty in the parlor, watching us. I think it was Ardrey. If we had fought, we'd have played right into his hands by making the whole school look bad."

"That's exactly what Ardrey wanted," Lina said. "It sounds like a reasonable theory."

"There is one thing," Rehanne said, absentmindedly chewing at a fingernail. "The spell requires something from the Dire Realms. I don't know where Chantal would have gotten such a thing. But I suppose . . ." Her voice faltered and she looked at Gray. "I suppose Kress could have."

"Could have and did." Oryon turned to Gray. "The earring I showed you, remember?"

Gray nodded. "I'd bought earrings for you, Rehanne, for

your date gift. I had them with me . . . then. Kress must have found them and brought them back."

Then! Rehanne flinched. She put her hand to her mouth; her teeth tore at her nails, bit one below the quick.

"Hah!" Lina said. "And he gave them to Chantal. The little weasel. We should have guessed."

Rehanne pulled her hand away from her mouth. "She was lying about losing the first one," she said, excited again. "She wanted to divert suspicion from herself. But then she really did lose one—the one they used to summon the demon that tore Kress up. So she made a big production out of finding the first one in my drawer and blaming me for taking it."

"This *is* making sense so far," Oryon said, resting his arms on his knees. "It explains what happened to Kress. But what about the murders of Fenton and Dwayne?"

Rehanne considered. "*If* Chantal has the gift of invisibility, she could easily have pushed Dwayne down the stairs. And I think she could have summoned a demon to kill Fenton, even though she couldn't use the transformation spell again. That would be why she had to get him outside where no one could see what she did."

"But Kress," Giselle, said, frowning. "How did she free him—if she did. How could she even find him where Headmistress had him hidden?"

Rehanne saw Gray gaze intently at Oryon. But it was Troy who answered. "I think I might be to blame for that," he said, pushing away from the desk, his face flushed with embarrassment. "Chantal came to me crying because she didn't know whether Kress was alive or dead. She begged me to try to find him. She realized that I wouldn't be able to locate him if he'd died, so if I found him, it would mean that he was still alive. And I did find him, though I couldn't pinpoint his location. It was weird—at first I thought he was somewhere on the third floor, though it didn't make sense that he would be on the women's floor. But then I realized that he was higher than that, maybe in an attic room. Though even that . . . if the school had towers, I would have said that he was in a tower room. I didn't understand, and told her so, but she seemed satisfied. She said it was enough to know he was still alive."

"I still don't see how she could have gotten to him," Gray said. "And even if she did, how could she have set him free? Oryon couldn't."

That drew puzzled glances and questions that had to be answered. Quickly Oryon explained that Headmistress had revealed Kress's hidden location to him and Gray. "She asked me to try to break the wards, and I couldn't," he finished.

"But she could," Gray added. "She did, just long enough to let us see what he'd become."

Lina jumped to her feet. "I'll bet Ferene could find him *and* break the wards," she said. "She had tremendous power. And somehow Chantal persuaded her that it was the right thing to do. The gods know what the lying little creep told her."

"We've got to find Chantal," Giselle said, also standing.

"That won't be easy if she's made herself invisible," Lina said.

Troy had been hanging back, looking as if he wanted to fade into the wall. Now, though, he stepped forward and said excitedly. "Invisibility! I can counteract that gift."

Oryon broke into laughter. "Of course! That's part of being a quencher. That's why you were assigned to room with me. Though I haven't used the talent of invisibility since . . ." His voice trailed off. He shrugged.

He really does regret what he did, Rehanne thought.

"What will we do with Chantal when we find her? She's dangerous." Giselle shuddered and her face was pale.

Only Maridel remained seated. She hugged Moonbeam to

her breast. "Whatever you're going to do, I wish you'd go somewhere else to do it. You have no right to be here when Debra is so ill."

"What's Debra's talent?" Oryon asked, ignoring her plea.

Maridel's arms fell away from the cat, which jumped to the floor. "Why do you ask? You surely don't expect *her* to be able to take part in—"

"Tell me," Oryon snapped. "This isn't a game. We'll need all the help we can get."

"Well, Debra can't be of any use to you. She controls animals. That's her only talent."

"If she can control animals, why couldn't she find Moonbeam for you?" Rehanne asked, the question slipping out before she thought.

"I guess because Moonbeam's special. He's not like an ordinary cat."

The silver cat looked up at her, his head cocked. He pivoted and strolled to Lina, sat on his haunches and stared at the catgirl, ears erect.

Lina gave him a scornful glance and turned her gaze to Oryon. "We're wasting time," she said.

He nodded. "Troy, see if you can locate Chantal."

"I'll need quiet."

"You'll have it." Oryon's stern gaze swept over the group, commanding obedience.

The room fell silent. Everyone watched Troy, who did nothing more than stare off into space, a look of concentration on his face.

Rehanne ticked off the seconds in her mind. They stretched into minutes. No one moved.

"She's in the first room on the other side of the hall, the room closest the stairs," Troy announced with a suddenness that made everyone jump.

"That's the empty room," Rehanne said. "The one where Ferene was hanged." And where, she remembered, she had first felt the invisible presence.

"Can you break the invisibility spell from here?" Oryon asked Troy. "Or do you have to be where she is?"

"I can try to do it from here." He sounded doubtful.

"Wait." Oryon turned to Gray. "Can you transfer her here? At the same time that Troy makes her visible?"

Gray rubbed his whiskered chin. "I don't know. I'm not sure I can transfer someone within the same time stream. I'll try, but . . ."

"Trying's not enough," Oryon snapped. "It's got to happen. Reece, do what you can to enhance his power. And Troy's. Gray and Troy, act on my signal."

No one questioned Oryon's orders or asked by what right he'd assumed command. *He's always had that air of authority,* Rehanne thought. *That's what got him into trouble before. I hope this time he knows what he's doing.*

"Now!" Oryon barked the command, pointing one hand at Gray and the other at Troy.

Maridel gave a cry of fear. Moonbeam, in his place by Lina, yawned, showing sharp, pearly teeth. Debra moaned and tossed as though gripped by fever.

With a shriek of anger Chantal plopped into their midst, in front of Rehanne and so close that she trod on Rehanne's toes.

"Grab her," Oryon shouted.

Rehanne caught her by the shoulders. Shrieking, she twisted and squirmed in Rehanne's grasp. Reece jumped to Rehanne's side and helped hold her.

Chantal stopped struggling. She looked ludicrous wrapped in an old, deep-pocketed pink flannel bathrobe. Standing motionless, she cast her glance over the room full of her fellow students and rested her gaze on Lina. "What's the meaning of this?" she demanded. But her shoulders trembled beneath Rehanne's hands.

"I think you know," Oryon said.

Her gaze darted from face to hostile face. She pulled something from her pocket and shouted, "Ghash, I summon thee!"

Rehanne tightened her grip and Gray jumped to help her, while Oryon stepped in front of Lina as though to protect her.

Long seconds passed and nothing happened. Relief showed on several faces.

A loud groan drew everyone's attention to Debra. She jerked up to a sitting position as though she were a marionette lifted by strings. Her eyes were closed, but her mouth opened wider than Rehanne thought any human mouth could have stretched. Black smoke flowed from the mouth and solidified into the hideous bearlike form of the demon Ghash.

Maridel screamed and stared in terror at her roommate. A cinerous fog flowed from the open mouth and gave shape to a second demon, this one with the head of a crested, long-beaked bird, a ropy neck, and a man-shaped body, naked, its flesh the hue of old bones.

Debra fell back onto the bed and lay as if dead. Maridel scooted back on her bed and pressed herself against the wall. Moonbeam jumped up beside her. Giselle fell to her knees and crouched partway under a desk.

The first demon stormed past Lina and wrenched Chantal from Rehanne's grasp. The second thrust Reece aside and loomed over Rehanne and Gray. Rehanne shrank back in terror, and Gray slid in front of her, shielding her with his body. Reece and Troy ducked behind Rehanne and Gray.

"Grimgrist," Oryon called, recovering before the rest. "And Ghash. I name you and order you to do us no harm."

The two whirled around and faced Oryon, Ghash still holding Chantal. Rehanne looked past Gray, scarcely daring to hope that the demons would heed Oryon's command.

The hideous creatures glared at Oryon and gnashed their teeth. Poised to attack, they hovered in precarious balance between stillness and deadly motion.

Chantal twisted one arm free of Ghash's hold and plunged her hand into a pocket of her robe. She drew it forth holding a black wand.

"Here," she said, thrusting the wand toward Ghash. "It's his. Use it against him."

Ghash clutched the wand awkwardly in his taloned paw and waved it toward Oryon, then dropped it and stomped on it, crushing it. As though a cord had snapped, Grimgrist completed his lunge, snatched Oryon by the neck, and dangled him above the ground. Oryon's face purpled.

Lina rose from her place on the floor beside Maridel's bed and lifted her fist as though to throw something.

With a dreadful roar Ghash cast Chantal aside and caught hold of Oryon's arm and leg. Grimgrist kept his grip, and the two demons tugged at Oryon. He'd be torn apart if they kept it up.

"Stop!" Gray pushed Rehanne behind him and stepped forward.

"No, Gray!" Rehanne caught at him, trying to hold him back. "They'll kill you."

But Gray kept moving, dragging Rehanne with him. He launched himself at Grimgrist and tried to pry those brutal fingers from Oryon's neck. The demon snarled and slashed at Gray with its teeth.

"Use your power," Lina shouted, circling them, her fist in the air. "Reece, help him focus."

How did she expect Gray to summon his power while

struggling with a demon? Grimgrist's beak sank into Gray's shoulder.

A howling, hissing, spitting cat hurtled into Grimgrist's face. The demon opened its beak, snapped at the cat, missed. Moonbeam dug his claws into the demon's bare chest and clung. Ghash let go of Oryon's leg and swatted at the cat.

The confusion and terror were enough to explain the sudden dizziness Rehanne felt, the nauseating sense of disorientation.

She thought she was seeing double until, as her mind cleared, she realized that she faced a wall of mirrors that reflected the struggling demons, Oryon, Gray, her, and Moonbeam.

None of the others.

She had no idea how they had come here, unless Gray had somehow transported them.

She hated this place where the mirrors multiplied the demons' hideous shapes and captured in repeated images their mauling of Oryon and Gray.

Blood dripped onto a marble floor. Gray's blood. Oryon's. Grimgrist's.

Ghash's mighty paw dislodged Moonbeam. The cat fell to the floor and scampered out of the demons' reach.

Rehanne saw her reflected self, pale, trembling, her arms linked around Gray's waist. *Like a leech,* she thought. *I'm not helping him. I'm holding him back.*

She forced herself to break her grip and back away from him. She had to find a way to help him battle the demons.

Use your power, Lina had said.

She'd used her mental coercion on Ghash when Chantal had sent him to attack her. She wasn't sure she could do it again, not on both demons at once.

She had to try.

24

THE OTHER SIDE OF THE MIRROR

Lina circled the demons, trying to find a vantage point from which to hurl Shardan's binding-net. But with Oryon between them she could not capture them without binding Oryon as well. Gray, too, was in the way, and Rehanne. How far would the binding-net stretch? Maybe she could capture them all, then find a way to release the others while holding the demons. If she'd only had more chance to practice with the net.

She'd called out to Gray to use his power, but she had little hope that he could while he was struggling with the demons. He was too involved in his struggle to heed a shout to get out of the way.

Maridel's cat leaped onto a demon. Good. Maybe the silly cat was worth something. If it distracted the creatures enough to give her a chance to hurl the net—

Demons, Oryon, Gray, Rehanne, and cat disappeared. Just winked out, leaving an empty space in the center of the room at which everyone gaped in startled bewilderment.

Slowly Lina lowered her arm. Gray must have used his power to transport them all somewhere. She regretted suggesting it. She didn't like the feeling of helplessness she got from knowing that she could do nothing, now, to aid Oryon. She should have tried the power-net while she had the chance.

Her gaze fell on Chantal, who was cowering by Debra's bed. An outlet for her rage and frustration! She opened her fist and tossed the net at Chantal. It touched her, enveloped her in a gauzy white cocoon attached by a glowing thread to Lina's fingers. She tugged on the thread and the cocoon floated toward her as though it weighed no more than a feather.

Giselle crawled from her hiding place beneath the desk. "What happened? Where'd they go? What did you do to Chantal?" She delivered the questions in a tremulous voice.

"Chantal's in here," Lina said, tapping the cocoon. It was wispy and unsubstantial as a cloud. "She won't do any more mischief. But I don't know where Gray took himself and Oryon and the demons." She tried to sound offhand, but her worry came through; her own voice was none too steady.

If she could only think of something, do something. "Troy," she said, "can you find them?"

Troy stood near the door, a dazed look on his face. She had to repeat her question twice before his gaze focused on her. He opened his mouth and started to speak, but the crash of Reece's fist into the wall drowned his words.

"This school! This damn school!" Reece shouted. "It's going to kill us all."

Lina shot him a withering glance. "Panic like that, and you probably will be killed. To stay alive, you've got to think straight."

"I want to leave," he moaned, leaning his face against the wall.

"Well, you can't. Snap out of it. We'll need your help."

But he kept his back to her and clapped his hands over his ears. The fool! He almost deserved to die.

"Troy?" she asked, dismissing Reece. "Can you find them?"

"I'm trying," he said. "I'm not getting anything. They're out of range."

It was what she'd feared. No way to reach them, no way to help Oryon.

If anyone could take care of himself, Oryon could. Why should he, not Gray or Rehanne, haunt her thoughts? Had he, through those times of power sharing, made himself a part of her? She shook her head to rid it of the unwelcome idea.

No point in fretting over the fate of the vanished ones. She couldn't do anything about them. Better to occupy her mind with what she *could* do.

She moved to Giselle's side, pushed her toward the bed on which Debra lay pale and still. "See if Debra's alive. How could those demons use her as a channel like that?"

Giselle stumbled toward the bed and laid a trembling hand on Debra's forehead. "She's alive," she reported.

"Can you heal her? Bring her around?"

"I'll try." She sat on the bed and looked at her patient as though reluctant to touch her.

"Go on," Lina urged. "Don't be so slow about it."

"Suppose . . . suppose the demons come back?"

"They won't!" Lina snapped, not sure they wouldn't, but losing patience with the cowardice everyone was displaying.

She turned to Maridel. "What are you sniveling about?"

"Moonbeam," the girl sobbed. "I finally got him back, and he's gone again, and those things will kill him."

"Three people are gone with those 'things,' and you worry about a stupid cat? Get off your backside. I want you to go with me."

"Where?" Maridel wailed, using her hair to blot the tears from her face.

"To the empty room. I want to find out what Chantal was doing there."

"Why can't they go?" Maridel pointed at Troy and Reece.

"I'm going to get Headmistress," Reece said. "Nowhere else." He jerked the door open.

"Get back in here!" Lina used her power to pull the door shut again and hold it shut against his pushing.

"But shouldn't we?" Troy asked timidly. "Get Headmistress, I mean?"

"Not yet." She recognized the possibility that Headmistress—or Veronica, or Tria—could find and rescue Oryon and the others. They had power she didn't.

Veronica had said she couldn't trace Gray through the time streams, but Lina didn't trust the little maid.

Maid! That was a laugh. Veronica, not Headmistress, ran the school and controlled everyone in it. Lina had long known and resented that fact.

She'd captured Chantal. She should turn her prisoner over to Headmistress. But she'd have to reveal Shardan's gift, and she wasn't ready to do that. "It wouldn't do any good to get Headmistress," she told Troy. "There's nothing she can do. Giselle, you getting anywhere with Debra?"

Giselle was bent over the sick girl. She shook her head without looking up. "I can't wake her."

"Keep trying. Troy, stay here with Giselle. Reece, you'll come with Maridel and me."

She walked toward Troy and Reece, drawing the cocoon with her. Maridel followed, dragging her feet as though every step cost effort.

Reaching Troy, she nudged him toward Giselle. He stopped an arm's length from the bed. No doubt he, too, feared the return of the demons. But Lina trusted him to keep guard here, as she could not trust Reece.

She grabbed Reece's arm. "Come on. You're in no danger." She pushed the door open and shoved him out.

He resisted briefly, yielded, and walked beside her, glowering and casting nervous glances at the long white shape that floated at Lina's other side.

The empty room was locked, as Lina had expected, but

the lock was no challenge to her. In seconds she had the door open, the light on, and her charges all safely inside.

"Chantal had Oryon's wand," Lina reminded her companions. "She probably had it hidden in here somewhere, and the other stuff she stole might be here, too. We're going to look for it."

She didn't expect either Reece or Maridel to be of much use in the search. She'd brought them with her only because she didn't trust them. But Maridel looked around, pointed at the half-open bottom drawer of one dresser, yanked the empty drawer all the way out, and gave a cry of triumph.

In the space beneath the drawer lay an array of articles: Lina's talisman, Vanita's fire jewel, candles, the book, items Lina recognized as being spell ingredients, and a few things that were probably stolen but had not been reported missing. Among these were a lovely white lace shawl, a small dagger with an embossed silver hilt, and a man's heavy gold ring in the form of a serpent swallowing its tail. She was sure it belonged to Master Hawke.

"Quite a collection," Lina said, bending to reclaim her talisman. She started to straighten, but stooped again to snatch up Vanita's jewel.

She slipped the talisman into her pocket but cradled the large gem in the palm of her hand. Gleaming with reflected light, it did seem filled with fire. "I think we should return this to Vanita immediately," she said.

"It's late," Maridel objected. "She'll be sleeping."

"We'll wake her." Lina led her entourage toward the door. "With this she may be able to tell us whether Oryon and Gray and Rehanne are alive."

She expected Reece to protest, but he'd fallen into a sullen silence. He moved along with her as though walking in his sleep. It occurred to her that his hysterical reaction might be due in large part to the depletion of his power by having shunted so much to Gray and possibly to Oryon as well. It didn't matter; she had no sympathy to waste on him. She had to find out about Oryon.

She pounded on Vanita's door.

"Who's there?" The call came almost immediately.

"Lina. Are you dressed? Reece is with me. We've found your seeing jewel."

An angry sniff from Maridel reminded Lina she had forgotten to mention the first-year student's presence. She did not bother to correct the omission.

The door opened and Vanita stepped out into the hall. She had slipped on an elegant red silk robe that, with her shoulder-length dark hair, gave her an exotic look.

"Shadoe's asleep," she said. Spotting the jewel, she broke into a delighted smile. "You *do* have it! Where did you find it?"

"I'll explain later. First we need you to use it."

Vanita took the jewel from Lina's hand. It flared a brilliant red as though greeting its owner, though probably it was merely reflecting the red robe. She held it to her face and peered into its depths. "I'll need a quiet place to do a reading," she said.

"We can go to my room," Lina said. "Giselle's somewhere else."

Vanita nodded. "What's that?" she asked, pointing at the white cloud drifting at Lina's side.

"No time to explain," Lina said again, her impatience growing with her anxiety. "Come on!"

Vanita gazed dubiously at Maridel and Reece. Reece maintained his stupefied silence, but Maridel launched maddeningly into an excited explanation.

"It's Chantal. She was the thief, and Lina caught her and

put her into that . . . whatever it is . . . and Rehanne found my cat Moonbeam, but demons came and—ouch!"

The hard pinch Lina gave her arm stanched the hemorrhage of words. She glared at Lina until the kick that followed the pinch propelled her toward Lina's room.

"Explanations later," Lina said firmly. "We need you to try to contact Oryon and find out if he's alive or dead. Also Gray and Rehanne."

"Where are they?" Vanita asked as Lina unlocked her door and found the light switch.

"We don't know. In another time stream where no one can reach them if they're alive." Lina maneuvered Chantal's cocoon into the room and stood aside to let the others enter. "If they're dead that won't matter, will it? You'll be able to reach them?"

"Probably. The dead are outside of time." Vanita went to Giselle's desk, which was cleaner than Lina's, and set the jewel on it. She seated herself in the desk chair, leaned forward, and hunched over the jewel. "You want me to try Oryon first?"

"Yes." Lina dragged the other chair close so she could observe the procedure.

Maridel went to sit on a bed, and Reece slumped against the wall. Lina paid no more attention to either of them. Her gaze remained riveted on the fire that blazed within the gem, shifting and flaring like real flames.

Abruptly Vanita sat up and threw her head back. Her mouth opened, her lips moved. Maridel gave a squeal of terror as Vanita spoke with Oryon's voice.

"Who calls me back? I've only just crossed over. I—No, I—"

The voice faded. Vanita's shoulders slumped. The light waned within the jewel.

"What happened?" Lina asked, clutching the edge of the desk. "He's dead?"

"He—he was. I reached him. Then he wasn't there anymore. I don't know why. That's never happened before." Vanita peered into the darkened gem as if trying to fathom the mystery.

"Try again," Lina urged, her heart pounding. He couldn't be dead. Not Oryon.

Vanita nodded and this time cupped her hands around the jewel, hiding its light from Lina's anxious eyes. After several minutes she looked up and shook her head. "I can't reach him. I don't know what it means."

Dared she hope? But he had spoken through the channel open only to the dead. Lina bit her lip. She felt tears gathering that she would *not* allow to fall. When she was sure she could hold her voice steady, she said, "Try Gray. Or Rehanne."

Again Vanita bent over the jewel. Again Lina waited. And again the waiting seemed endless.

The jewel flared so brightly the glow shone through Vanita's encircling hands. And again Vanita's mouth spoke.

"No! You can't—" Rehanne's voice, filled with terror.

"Let me go! Let me go!" Gray's voice, sharp, clear, determined.

Then silence, a silence dreadful in its incomprehensibility.

Vanita, pale and trembling, stared blankly at the dulled gem.

Lina, trying to make sense of the troubling cries, absently brushed tears from her cheeks.

Gray fought to free himself from Grimgrist's hold. Oryon hung limply in Ghash's hairy arms, and Gray could not tell whether he lived.

The creatures had not attacked Rehanne, but once they finished with him and Oryon, they'd go after her. Maybe he could send her back, though the effort would deplete his remaining strength.

Grimgrist twisted Gray's arm behind him with a force that shot pain up his shoulder and through his body. The demon's grip tightened; the bone of Gray's upper arm snapped with an agonizing jolt. Waves of nausea rushed through him. He battled the blackness that threatened to envelop him.

His twists and kicks did no more than cause Grimgrist to shift around in an awkward ballet until captive and captor faced the mirrored wall. Gray's glazing vision settled on his reflection in the glass. He saw Grimgrist's other hand crunch down on his shoulder and knew he was witnessing his own death.

But the demon let out a howl of rage as it raised its eyes and glimpsed its reflection. Its reaction distracted Ghash from torturing Oryon. It, too, looked up and, roaring, lifted Oryon and hurled him at the mirror.

Oryon passed through the glass and blended with his reflection.

With another furious cry, Grimgrist dropped Gray and charged the mirror. The charge carried it through, and it began grappling with its double. Ghash followed and attacked *its* double. As a bizarre backdrop to the surreal vision, elegantly clad men and women gathered behind the intruders and watched with expressions of horror and loathing.

Arms supported Gray's shoulders and head. Rehanne had dropped beside him. She rested his broken arm on his chest. He screamed with the pain of the movement.

"We've got to get you to a healer," she said.

"No. Got to save Oryon." He tried to rise. "Help me up."

"Lie still. You're badly hurt. You can't stand."

"Have to." He tried again, and nearly fainted.

"Please, Gray, save your strength to get us out of here."

"Can't leave him . . . like I did Kress."

"Why should you risk your life for Oryon?"

He didn't answer but mustered his strength for a third attempt to get onto his feet. Rehanne held him back.

He wrenched free of her grasp and, choking back screams at the agony that lanced his arm and shoulder, humped toward the mirror, drawing near enough to touch the glass with his good arm. But Rehanne hovered over him like a protective mother hen.

"Got to do this," he grunted, desperate to make her understand. "Don't . . . help . . . demons."

"I'm trying to help *you*." Her tone was indignant.

"Then don't . . . stop me." He pressed his hand against the glass. It felt cold beneath his feverish touch.

"Let me do it." She placed herself between him and the mirror and leaned against the glass, trying to go through. The glass remained solid, and her position blocked Gray's view of Oryon and the battling demons.

He rolled against her, sending his broken arm flopping against her calves. The agonizing impact tore a cry from his throat. Blackness swept over him.

He felt as though he was being sucked into a whirlpool. Blindly he struck out with his good hand, grabbed something, wrapped his fingers around it, held on.

"Gray, don't! My ankle!"

Rehanne must have straddled his body and bent over him. His clutch on her ankle unbalanced her. She toppled across him; her weight falling on the arm sent him into unconsciousness.

He was floating before the mirror, and its reflected figures beckoned to him. The demons still wrestled, but they seemed to be shrinking, losing substance. Oryon lay where he had fallen, and a man of the company of dancers approached him, walking well around the demons to reach his side. The man bent over him and grasped his shoulder. Oryon stirred.

The group around the demons parted and the satyr stepped into view. He grinned at Gray but stayed among the dancers. His gaze filled Gray with a heaviness that drew him downward. He sank back into his body and its pain engulfed him. He retched from the agony and his mouth filled with bile.

"Gray!" Rehanne's relieved cry only added to his misery. He could not let her hold him back. He *had* to reach Oryon. Because suddenly he understood that world beyond the mirror and why Oryon had entered it. It was a world of the dead, and if Oryon took his place among the dancers, Gray could perhaps join him, but neither would be able to return.

He got onto his knees, supported himself with his unbroken arm, and crawled toward the mirror, his broken arm dragging the floor.

Rehanne's arms circled his waist. "No!" she said.

"Help me stand," he begged, forcing the words out through clenched teeth.

This time she did as he asked, but his shaking legs refused to support his weight. He toppled toward the mirror. Rehanne caught him, kept him from crashing against the glass.

But his injured arm swung forward. He braced for the anguish of the shock, but the arm passed painlessly through the glass. He lunged forward and followed the arm into the mirrored chamber. Rehanne moved with him but was halted halfway through the glass. She hung like a fly caught in resin, leaning forward, her fingers grasping Gray's shirt. "No! You can't—"

"Let me go!" he shouted at her. "Let me go!"

It was not his plea but his returning strength that pulled him from her grip and drove him forward, toward Oryon. His arm no longer pained; it responded to his urgent command, its injury healed.

He dove between the wrestling pairs of demons, reduced to mere wraiths, and caught up with Oryon. "You can't take him," he shouted to the man who led him to the dancers.

The man turned in anger. Gray raised his arm and struck out with his fist, landing a blow on the man's chin. The man staggered back, and Gray caught hold of Oryon and dragged him toward the mirror.

Oryon moved along with him as one dazed. He stumbled but did not resist. Gray steered him between the demons and into Rehanne's outstretched arms. "Draw back," he told her. "Take him with you." He accompanied the command with a shove that sent Oryon and Rehanne tumbling backward, through the mirror. He saw them crash to the floor on the other side. He leaped toward them, was brought up short by solid glass. He was trapped.

"Well done," said a voice behind him. "A life for a life."

He turned to confront the smiling satyr.

Rehanne lay shivering on the floor. Her captivity in the glass had been a nightmare; she couldn't shake the horror of it. She'd experienced the same fearful sensations as when she'd crossed the purple band in the round chamber where she'd spoken to Fenton. She felt again the terror and chill of death, the illusion of slipping into a bottomless abyss. And Gray had walked away from her, abandoned her. Her panic had expanded, filled her, beat on the bars of her mind.

When something fell against her, she grabbed it and hung on with the strength of a drowning person. The weight sagged against her, shoving her back, out of the entrapping glass. She fell hard; her senses swam. The weight pressed her down; she couldn't breathe. Instinctively she pushed it off her and, rolling over on her side, drew great, shaking breaths. She curled into the fetal position and hugged herself for warmth and to halt the trembling.

Near her someone groaned. The sound startled her back to sanity. She straightened, sat up, looked around. "Gray?"

But it was Oryon she saw lying on the floor, his hand to his head. He moaned again. She scooted to his side. "Oryon," she said. "Wake up. We've got to find Gray."

His eyes opened. He seemed to have trouble focusing. "The demons?" The question was a hoarse whisper.

She pointed toward the mirror, gasped to see nothing in the glass but her own reflection and Oryon's. "He's gone!"

She lurched to her feet and threw herself against the mirror. Solid, hard, cool but not icy, it was simply—glass.

She leaned against it and sobbed. "I've lost him. He saved you; he couldn't save himself."

After a time she turned back to Oryon. He was sitting up, staring at her and the mirror, looking confused and bewildered. "What happened?"

She pointed at the reflected room. "You don't remember? Being in there? You were dead, I think." She spoke slowly, sorting out her idea. "Gray went after you, brought you back. But he—he couldn't get back with you."

"Maybe he transferred himself somewhere else?"

Rehanne shook her head. Gray had had no strength left to do that, she was sure.

"Are you saying that he's dead?" Oryon scrambled to his feet and stood in front of her.

"I don't know." Her eyes filled with tears again. She blinked them back. "I'm afraid so."

Oryon stared at her for a few moments, then slowly swung

around to survey the whole room. "Where is this?" he asked. "Where did the demons go? Tell me what happened."

Rehanne wiped her face with her hands and described Gray's fight with the demons, their reaction to the mirror, how Ghash had thrown Oryon through the mirror and passed through it after him, and how Gray, despite her attempts to stop him, had gone after Oryon and thrust him back. "And now I've lost him." Another bout of sobbing made it impossible for her to say more.

"And we're lost," Oryon said. "Without Gray we have no way of getting back to the school."

The words sounded callous. Didn't he care that Gray had sacrificed his life to save him? He was only worried about finding the way home.

"I can't do anything for Gray here," Oryon said softly. "At the school we can find help. It might not be too late to save him, if we can only get back quickly."

His words made Rehanne feel ashamed. He was right. They had to get back and get help. But how?

The image of a silver cat flashed into Rehanne's mind. Moonbeam. The cat had come with them. Where had it gone?

"Moonbeam," she called. "Here, kitty. Here, puss."

A distant meow answered her calls. Together she and Oryon moved toward the sound. It seemed to come from the far wall, away from the mirrors.

As they neared it, Rehanne saw the door, scarcely noticeable, so perfectly did it blend with the wall. She hurried to it, afraid it would be locked. It opened to her touch.

Stairs lay beyond the door, and halfway down Moonbeam sat as though waiting for them. When they started down, Moonbeam rose and bounded to the bottom of the steps. They hurried after him along a narrow corridor and through another door.

This one led them outside. It took Rehanne only a few

seconds, even in the darkness, to recognize the school patio.

Rehanne grabbed Oryon's arm and pointed toward the Faculty Residence Hall, a shadowy bulk beneath the stars. "Veronica!" she said. "She'll know what to do."

25

EXCHANGE

Rehanne pounded on the door of Veronica's apartment and waited impatiently. Maybe no one was in. Or maybe Veronica was asleep in a back room and hadn't heard. She banged again.

Oryon put a restraining hand on her arm. "I hear footsteps. Someone's coming." His calm voice steadied her.

The door opened. Tria stood framed in the rectangle of light.

"Veronica. I need Veronica. It's Gray. She's got to help." In her grief and panic she couldn't assemble her thoughts.

Tria seemed to understand the incoherent babble. "Come in. She knows. She's working on it."

Rehanne followed Tria into Veronica's parlor, and Oryon stepped in after her.

Veronica was seated at a small table that held a crystal globe. Beside her, Headmistress sat stiffly, hands clenched together, face grim, eyes intent on the crystal. Neither woman acknowledged the arrival of their visitors.

Rehanne remembered her earlier certainty that she was being manipulated, her resentment at the way Headmistress had withheld information from her and the others. Maybe she'd been wrong to come here. But she had no other hope of rescuing Gray.

She stepped up to Veronica and shook the woman's shoulder. "Gray," she said. "We lost him. You've got to bring him back."

"It's too late." Veronica nodded toward the crystal.

Rehanne peered into it, saw a swirl of shapes. She dropped to one knee for a closer look. A scene shimmered, small and distant, in the crystal's depths. She concentrated to resolve the bits of moving color into objects and people.

First to come into focus was a central figure seated on a boulder, a reed pipe held to his mouth. Not a human figure— its hairy legs ended in cloven hooves; horns crowned its head. A demon? What was it doing?

A crowd gathered around it, listening, perhaps, to the music of the pipes. People, not demons. Dressed as the folk in the mirror had been dressed, in formal gowns and suits of a bygone era.

The creature on the boulder lowered his pipes and smiled—a warm, joyous smile, not an evil one. The crowd applauded, their expressions rapt.

Squinting to sharpen her focus, Rehanne studied the faces. In the front row, directly in front of the piper, she saw Gray. He looked happy like all the others, and he applauded as enthusiastically, his arm showing no trace of injury. He turned toward a young man standing beside him and nodded. The youth with the dark red hair looked familiar, though Rehanne couldn't place him.

"Les!" Headmistress breathed the name as though it were a prayer.

Rehanne glanced at Headmistress, was startled to see the woman's eyes fill with tears, her hand stretch toward the globe.

On her second, close look at the crystal, Rehanne recognized Gray's companion as the subject of the dark portrait that hung in the school parlor. Then the scene swam out of focus, dissolved into iridescence.

She lowered her other knee to the floor and swiveled to face Veronica. "Why can't you save him? You must have been watching him for some time. You know where he is. And the demons are gone—aren't they?"

"The two most dangerous demons are gone—Ghash and Grimgrist. Gruefell was destroyed earlier. At least for the present no others have access to the school. By transporting Ghash and Grimgrist to the Hall of Mirrors and forcing them to face their mirror opposites, Gray discovered the best way to destroy them. Demons can't tolerate contact with their counterparts in the realm of the dead. The pity is that Gray passed through the mirror and into that realm. He's safe but beyond our reach."

"Why?" Rehanne clutched at Veronica's skirt. "You have tremendous power. I know you do. You've been manipulating all of us."

Headmistress made a strange, choked sound, and Veronica said, "I admit to arranging some challenges for you. I did nothing that would cause deaths. Nor did I send anyone or cause anyone to be sent into other dimensions or time lines. What you fail to realize is that the Power-Giver is a great manipulator of events and of people, and that he abides in a place that cuts across time lines and planes of existence."

While Rehanne hesitated, overtaken by doubts, Oryon stepped forward. "The Power-Giver—he *is* alive then?"

Tria placed a hand on Oryon's shoulder and said gently, "Yes, Oryon. The Power-Giver still lives."

Talk! They all did nothing but talk—and ignore her need.

Rehanne clutched Veronica's arm. "You *do* have the power to rescue Gray."

Veronica placed her hands over Rehanne's. "My dear, not even I can call back the dead."

"Dead!" Rehanne rocked back on her heels. "But Gray isn't—his arm was broken and twisted, and the demon had taken a bite out of his shoulder, but he wasn't dead, he could be healed, he—"

Oryon turned away from Tria. "*I* was dead. Ghash strangled me." He rubbed his neck. "My throat still aches. I'm the one who belongs beyond the mirror. Gray came after me and exchanged himself for me. He traded his life for mine."

"Gray did that!" Headmistress said in an awed tone. "I always knew he had the power. Like Les." She stood, towering above them all. "Because he was alive and exchanged himself willingly, another exchange should be possible."

Gripped by a cold fear, Rehanne swallowed and forced herself to say, "I'll go."

"Alone you could not reach that realm," Headmistress said, gazing tenderly at Rehanne. "I have the power to take you, but Gray will need a reason to return, and you must supply that reason. If you can persuade him to go, I shall stay behind in his place."

Veronica tilted her head back and glared at Headmistress. "You are needed here. You cannot be spared."

"Fifty years ago when I wanted to follow Les, that argument convinced me. For fifty lonely years I have done my duty, but the pain of losing him has not lessened. It is enough. Tria!" She looked over her shoulder. "Tria, fetch Viad. Hurry!"

Rehanne heard running footsteps, the slam of a door.

Veronica kept her gaze fixed on Headmistress. "The Community that you profess to care so much about is in grave danger. These murders have hurt it badly. Had we not lost

Ferene K'Sere—she had tremendous power, potentially greater even than Tria's. If only I'd foreseen . . ."

"You can't blame yourself," Headmistress said. "I, too, deeply regret Ferene's death, but no one is irreplaceable, including me."

"No one can defend the Community as you can," Veronica insisted. "The crimes here have given the civil authorities an excuse to attack it. Chief Officer Ardrey will do all he can—"

Headmistress interrupted. "It's time for others to defend the Community. I have done my part. Let me join the Community on the other side."

Veronica bowed her head. "So be it then, Miryam. I will not stop you."

Tria returned so quickly with Viad, Rehanne guessed she had used her power to fetch him. Rehanne started to rise, and Oryon helped her to her feet.

"I need your music, Viad, to forge us a path," Headmistress told the young man. "And if we reach him, Gray and Rehanne will need it to guide them back."

He nodded as though understanding completely what she required.

"You will come with me," she told Rehanne, taking her arm. "But only as far as the door."

It was not toward the apartment door that she led her, but toward a wall, newly interrupted by a wide ramp stretching far beyond the confines of the residence hall. Headmistress and Rehanne ascended the ramp, followed by Viad. Music filled Rehanne's mind, a melody so painfully sweet it tore at her heart.

The walk was long; the ramp stretched on so far that when Rehanne glanced behind her, Veronica's parlor had vanished into a shroud of haze. The air grew cold as they climbed, though no wind blew. Ahead of them and on either side of the ramp Rehanne could see nothing but a clear, bright emptiness. She tried to look down, shuddered, and drew away from the void that seemed to reach into infinity.

They came at last to a wavering curtain of light. Headmistress halted. "You may go no farther." Each word sent a puff of steam into the icy air. "I can enter only if Gray agrees to the exchange. We must summon him to the other side of the curtain."

"How do we do that?" Rehanne found herself trembling so that it was hard to get out the words. "How will he know we're here?"

"Viad's music will draw him close enough so that he will be able to hear us. You must persuade him to pass through."

A shadow fell against the curtain. "He's here," Headmistress said. "Speak to him."

Though she strained to see, Rehanne could not distinguish the form. But she called out, "Gray, it's Rehanne. I've come to take you home."

The music continued to play in her head. She heard no other sound. "You defeated the demons," she said, projecting her voice to reach through the shimmering barrier. "You're a hero. You must come back. The school needs you."

No sound came from beyond the veil of light; the shadow did not move.

"*I* need you, Gray," Rehanne cried. "I love you. Please don't leave me."

The curtain shimmered, the shadow behind it darkened, but no one passed through.

Headmistress reached toward the shadow. "Gray, most of your life lies ahead." She spoke urgently. "Mine is past. Let me come through in your place. Come to Rehanne and let me go to Les. Don't make Rehanne know the loneliness I've known for fifty years."

"Come, Gray. Please, come," Rehanne begged, her tears freezing on her cheeks. Desperate, she extended her power of coercion, transmitting the urge to step forward, to join her, not sure the sending would pass through the veil.

Viad's music keened and sobbed and pleaded. The curtain fluttered. A hand reached through. Rehanne clasped it, drew it toward her.

A voice that was not Gray's spoke through the curtain. "Come to me, Miryam."

Like a young girl, Headmistress sprang forward. Her extended arms passed through the curtain. For an instant the veil of light parted. Gray crossed through and, at the same moment, Headmistress, youthful and vibrant, threw herself into the waiting arms of Gray's red-haired companion. Before the curtain closed, Rehanne had drawn Gray into her arms.

His flesh was cold, and when her lips brushed his, she found them so chill and unresponsive that she drew away without completing the kiss she'd intended. His eyes seemed unfocused, blank.

Viad proceeded steadily down the ramp. Rehanne followed in silence, guiding Gray. He walked as if in a dream. Gripped by a fear that he had returned to her no more than a living corpse, she kept bottled within her all that she had wanted to say to him.

The haze in front of them cleared, and Veronica's parlor became visible; they were near the end of the ramp. Oryon stood waiting for them; Veronica remained seated at the table with the crystal globe. Viad's steps quickened. He stepped off the ramp, and the music ceased.

As he crossed from the ramp onto the faded carpet, Gray stumbled and one arm went limp. Rehanne screamed at the sight of the bone poking through torn and discolored flesh. Blood spread from the jagged tear on his shoulder.

Oryon leaped forward and caught him as he sagged. Viad helped lower him gently to the floor.

"He was healed," Rehanne said. "He was all right until now."

"All hurts are healed beyond the mirror," Veronica said. Her voice sounded tired, old. "He has reverted to the condition in which he passed through. Someone will have to go for Giselle. She's the only healer we have left."

26

OF DRAMA AND ART

Lina sat alone at a table in the dining hall. Few other students had ventured out of their rooms to breakfast. No announcement had yet been made either of Headmistress's disappearance or of the capture of the murderer and the defeat of the demons, so the student body remained nervous and fearful. Master Tumberlis, looking especially solemn, presided over the meal and announced that a convocation would be held at two that afternoon and that all students must attend. Until that time the order to remain in their rooms except for meals continued in effect.

Lina was still eating when Tria, in her maid's uniform, came to her and announced Shardan's arrival. He'd come early. Lina left her plate of hotcakes and ham to answer his summons.

They took seats in the parlor in chairs near the fireplace, well away from the door. Shardan's lashless eyes stared at Lina with the intensity of a cobra. Ardrey would come later, the truth-reader explained. He had been sent ahead to set up the appointments Ardrey required with Headmistress, certain of the faculty, and various students.

"You should have followed my instructions and waited for my return," he said. "You took a foolish and dangerous chance coming back here on your own."

Lina grinned. "It worked out well. I know the school routine. What you wanted I could accomplish more easily at night. In the daytime it would be impossible to deceive Headmistress and get her alone."

He leaned forward. "You've already done it?" he whispered.

She nodded. "Would you like to see her?"

"You have her in the net? And no one knows?"

With another smug nod Lina said, "It was simple. And after being in that cocoon for several hours, I'm sure she'll tell you anything you want to know."

"Get her for me."

"Not with so many people around. If I bring her down in the cocoon now, it'll arouse suspicion. Anyway, you have to keep your part of the bargain. I want my shapechanging talent restored."

"First you'll play the part of Headmistress when Ardrey comes. I'll tell you what to say and do so that he'll be discredited and I'll be a hero."

He outlined his plan. It sounded workable, and the danger was no more than she was willing to risk. She contributed several ideas of her own. He accepted so readily her declaration that Chantal was the murderer that she guessed it came as little surprise to him.

"I'll follow your plan," she said. "But not until you restore my panther form. Only when I have it back will you get your vengeance on Ardrey. You can read me; you must know I'm telling the truth."

The bare lids blinked. His lips spread in a grim smile.

"And I will know if you attempt to deceive me. All right. You'll have your talent when you deliver my net to me—with your headmistress inside it." He hefted himself out of the chair's soft cushions. "And you'd better bring it quickly. Ardrey will be here at any moment."

Lina shook her head. "I'll deliver it to you *when* Ardrey is here. I'll convince him that the murderer is imprisoned in it and is too dangerous to be released. You can take charge of it and claim to know a way to release the prisoner safely. You can go to the seminar room across from the stairs. I'll have Chantal tied and hidden there, waiting for you. Hide the net with Headmistress in it, and come back with Chantal. Take her in, turn her over to Ardrey, and reclaim the net and Headmistress later."

His eyes glittered with menace. "If you try to trick me, I'll know," he warned. "If I read any hint of deception, I'll destroy you before you can betray me."

"You must be reading me. You'd already know if I intended treachery."

"You read true," he acknowledged. "I'll trust you. You'd be a fool to pass up what I'm offering you. Just be careful. Stick to the plan."

She rose to her feet. "You'll be pleased with my performance."

She left the parlor and went upstairs. When she reached the third floor, Rehanne was waiting for her.

"It went all right?" Rehanne asked anxiously. "He couldn't read you?"

"He read me perfectly." Lina grinned at Rehanne's dismayed gasp. "Relax," she said. "Your work held. He couldn't read the thoughts you suppressed. I spoke the truth as I knew it. I'll let you do some reinforcement before I go back. But first we'd better get everybody together and go over the plans."

* * *

Slowly and carefully Lina descended the stairs and entered the parlor where the men waited: Ardrey, Canby, Shardan, and four members of the provincial council. She felt awkward mimicking Headmistress's stride, carrying herself as if she were much taller than her actual height. She wished she could check a mirror to assure herself that the illusion was holding.

She reeled in the strand of power-net by which she guided the cloudlike cocoon, drawing it closer to her, and paused to compose herself before addressing the visitors.

Ardrey's gaze fastened on the floating white shroud. "What's that? Where is my prisoner?"

"Your prisoner is recovering from the effects of the harsh and illicit treatment she received at your hands, Chief Officer Ardrey." Lina had practiced Headmistress's tone and manner of speech. She read no suspicion in the faces turned toward her. "Miss Mueller had nothing to do with the crimes of which you accused her."

"If she was innocent, why did she use her witchcraft to flee before we could question her?"

"She was badly frightened. You had chloroformed her. When she awakened, you threatened her with torture and attempted to render her helpless with hypnotic gas. Your truth-reader will verify that I speak truly."

"Nonsense!" Ardrey turned to direct his gaze in Shardan's vicinity.

While Canby scribbled in his notebook, the four council members leaned forward in their seats to hear Shardan's verdict.

Shardan cleared his throat and lowered his lashless eyes as though embarrassed. "I read no falsehood in her words," he said.

"That's impossible!" Ardrey thundered, glowering. "Look more deeply. She must be deceiving you."

"I'm sorry, Chief Officer. The truth is quite clear."

The councilmen shifted uncomfortably and frowned at Ardrey. Canby ceased writing and stared at Shardan.

"Terrible crimes have been committed here," Ardrey said, his voice growing louder as his agitation mounted. "The girl could not have been the only one involved, but she was certainly not innocent. I think you've corrupted my truth-reader."

"Not at all. Your truth-reader has done nothing more than offer an honest evaluation, as his position requires." She turned to the councilmen. "Gentlemen, I am happy that you have accompanied Chief Officer Ardrey. I deeply regret the tragic events of the past days, and I have devoted my time and my skills to unmasking the murderer."

"And you have done so?" a councilman asked.

"Indeed I have." She crossed to stand in front of Shardan. "Sir, will you take custody of this and verify that I testify truly to its contents?"

She held out to him the thread that served as a leash and gazed into his face, waiting. This was the moment of greatest risk. She did not think his power could penetrate the net, but if he noticed the single strand she kept wound around her little finger . . .

Her hand touched his. He took the leash, and in the same instant she felt the rush of power as the panther essence flowed into her. Its strength staggered her, and she was sure her disguise had wavered. But as she stepped back from Shardan, she saw everyone's gaze riveted on the cocoon. The slender strand that linked her to it was no more visible than spider's silk.

"This is trickery," Ardrey declared. "Whatever that thing is, there's no killer in it."

"It does seem, ah, insubstantial," said the councilman who had spoken before. "We must insist on proof. The truth-reader's word is not enough."

She nodded. "I will provide proof. But first let me explain." She returned to her place near the door. "We have always been a law-abiding institution with the aim of producing graduates of the highest caliber, young men and women who contribute in positive ways to Arucadian society. However, the gifted have often unfairly been the target of prejudice and misunderstanding."

She lifted a hand and pointed at Ardrey. "The chief officer's prejudice led him to place a spy, an informer, among our student body in the hope of finding evidence of wrongdoing with which he could discredit us."

Ardrey raised clenched fists. "I won't listen to this nonsense."

"Let her speak," the oldest councilman said sternly.

"The spy," Lina continued, "was a young lady named Chantal Navarese. Miss Navarese could not discover any faults or crimes, so she decided to create some. She sought out a young man whose moral strength was not as great as it should have been and persuaded him to join her in robbing other students and vandalizing their rooms. She tempted him to seek power from demons. Their scheme backfired; the demons possessed them and led them to kill. When they had done the demons' work, the evil ones destroyed the young man. But the young woman lives and is captive within the power-net I delivered to the truth-reader."

Again everyone turned toward Shardan—everyone except Ardrey, who was livid. "You accuse without proof!" he shouted.

"Her words read true," Shardan said.

"Release her from that—that power thing. Let us see her."

The other three councilmen nodded agreement with the one who had spoken.

"She is dangerous," Lina said, still following the script.

"Precautions must be taken. A premature release could allow her to unleash demons again."

"Ridiculous! There's nothing in that thing. How could there be?" Ardrey struck the shroud with his fist. "It's nothing but some kind of balloon disguised by witchery."

Shardan swung it away from him. "I tell you, she speaks the truth," he insisted.

"Traitor!" Ardrey bellowed. "You lie!"

A councilman stood and clasped Ardrey's arm. "Calm yourself." To the supposed headmistress he said, "Madam, you have made serious charges. You must show us proof."

"I will do so." To this point Lina had followed Shardan's script. She hoped that her act thus far had assured him that she was cooperating and put him off his guard.

Ardrey stood glaring at her, his hands on his hips.

She met his gaze. "You and your men," she nodded at Shardan and at the adjutant, who was again writing furiously in his notebook, "examined the bodies of the three murder victims, did you not?"

"You know we did. You were with us."

Careful, she thought. *Can't afford many mistakes like that.* "Quite so," she said. "You will therefore recognize my witnesses." She turned toward the doorway and waved her hand.

Framed in the entrance, pale against the darkened hallway, stood a fearful apparition—a corpse whose red hair was matted with twigs and dried blood, its face bruised, its throat torn open and the flesh around it blackened.

Gasps came from the councilmen. One gagged. Another cried out, "Sorcery! I won't have it."

"The dead make truthful witnesses, gentlemen," Lina said. "They cannot lie. Fenton Rhoze, tell these gentlemen who killed you."

Slowly the phantom lifted its hand and pointed at the

shroud beside Shardan. A gurgling sound rose from its throat. Bloody bubbles seeped from the gaping wound. Words came in grating croaks: "Chantal Navarese. Lured me outside. Called a demon. To slit my throat."

The apparition glided from the room into the darkened hall. "Next witness," Lina called.

A second visitor from the dead materialized in the entranceway. "Dwayne Echols," Lina addressed it. "Name your slayer."

Eyes stared blankly from the pudgy face; head wobbled loosely from side to side. "I could not see her," it said. "She protected herself with a spell of invisibility when she jerked my head back and made me fall and break my neck. I felt her hands and smelled her perfume. And after death I knew it was Chantal Navarese who killed me."

It drifted from the room and was replaced by a third specter, its long hair tied back so that the marks of the rope were plain on its neck, its face purple, its eyes bulging, its swollen tongue protruding from blackened lips.

"Ferene K'Sere, you died by your own hand. Who drove you to that act?"

"Chantal Navarese." The rasping whisper was barely audible. "She persuaded me to use my power to free Kress. I didn't know he was possessed of a demon. When I realized what I'd unleashed, I was consumed with guilt. Chantal used her power to enhance that feeling, until I was driven to hang myself."

Lina was glad they'd used Vanita's fire jewel to speak to Dwayne and Ferene so that these testimonies were accurate. That last bit of information from Ferene answered a question that had nagged at Lina. She hadn't understood why Ferene, as strong as she was, would have taken her own life.

The dead witness left. Lina turned toward her audience. "You have heard the testimony of the victims. You—"

"Wait," called out a voice behind her. She looked back at the entranceway.

Kress stepped into the light, the handle of a stone knife protruding from his chest. "I, too, have the right to accuse Chantal. She led me to consort with demons. They sacrificed me, but she bears the blame. I demand vengeance."

He stepped forward, toward Shardan and the cocoon. Ardrey recoiled from the walking corpse. The secretary's notebook clattered to the floor. Shardan stood his ground.

"Enough of this charade," he growled.

The phantom touched the cocoon. Lina pulled on her single strand and wound it around her fingers, unraveling the net. Chantal tumbled to the floor. She gazed up at the vision of Kress, screamed, and her eyes rolled back so only the whites showed. Her body thrashed and jerked.

The ghost retreated. Shardan glared at Lina across Chantal's writhing body. "You betrayed me!" He shouted, gathering in the threads of the power-net, including the one that Lina had withheld. She tried to hold on to it but could not.

Concealing the net within a closed fist, he turned to the others. "She deceived you. She is not the headmistress. Look!"

Lina's flesh crawled as he tried to strip the illusion from her. The tug of his power was strong. But the illusion held. It had not been created using Shardan's power; like the specters, Headmistress's appearance was maintained by a spell cast by Rehanne, who'd found it in the book she'd taken from Headmistress's office.

Shardan's face crimsoned. "She's an impostor," he yelled. He vaulted over Chantal and charged Lina.

A handsbreadth from her face he halted and fell back as

though he'd slammed into an invisible barrier. Lina smiled. Oryon hadn't lost his touch.

"Gentlemen," she addressed the councilmen, "I think you can see that not only has the murderer been revealed, but your peace officers have been shown to be corrupt and inefficient. They are responsible for placing this viper in our midst." She gave a scornful nod toward the writhing Chantal. "I trust you will deal with them appropriately and take measures to ensure that my school will suffer no further harassment."

"Liar! Cheat!" Shardan yelled.

Again Lina felt the tug of his frantic effort to unmask her. Crazed with wrath, Shardan jumped up and down and shouted gibberish. The spell held.

She feared he'd use the power-net on her, but before he could try, the councilmen scrambled to their feet, and the four of them hustled Ardrey and Shardan from the room. Canby followed with the air of a whipped dog. A councilman turned back to ask, "What about her?" He indicated Chantal. "Shall we send other officers to take her?"

"If you will trust us, we shall deal with her," Lina answered. "It is the custom of the gifted to discipline our own. I promise you that we will render her incapable of causing harm to others."

The councilman nodded, obviously relieved to be rid of the responsibility.

When they were safely out the front door, Lina collapsed into a chair and let the illusion slide from her. A few moments later the room filled with her confederates. Under Tria's direction, Vlad and Todrick carried Chantal from the room.

"You were spectacular, Lina," Maridel gushed. Beside her, Moonbeam purred.

"I could have sworn you were really Headmistress," Giselle enthused. "Every word, every movement was *her*."

"Thanks." Pride dispelled some of the weariness she felt.

"You all were pretty great, too. Rehanne, the spells worked exactly as they were supposed to. I couldn't guess who was who."

"Britnor was Fenton, Troy was Dwayne, and Petra was Ferene," Rehanne said.

"We would have been hurt if you hadn't let us have a part in it," Petra said, standing with Britnor, who grinned and nodded.

"And *Kress*." She turned to Oryon. "We hadn't planned that one. It must have been you."

He shook his head. "I only added that little touch with the knife."

"Excellent," she said. "Properly gruesome."

"Except that the dead aren't gruesome," Gray put in. He slouched against the wall, one arm in a sling, the usual glum look on his face. "Not after they've crossed over."

"If we'd portrayed them all healthy and happy, that wouldn't have produced the effect we needed," Lina said. "But who did play the part of Kress?"

"I did," said a voice from the doorway.

Tall, handsome, looking perfectly healthy, Kress walked into the room and crossed it to stand by the fireplace. Only Oryon looked unsurprised by the dramatic entrance.

Everyone moved back, away from him, except Gray, who walked slowly toward him. "Is it you? Really you? You aren't dead?"

"Do I look dead? Now, I mean?" Kress clearly hadn't lost his arrogance. "Headmistress healed me—she and Veronica." He frowned as if puzzling that out. He probably had yet to figure out the true role of the supposed maid. Kress really wasn't very bright, Lina reflected.

"Thank the Power-Giver," Gray said. "I've been blaming myself for your death."

Kress did have enough sense to look ashamed at that. "You've blamed *yourself,* after all I did?" he asked. Then, hurriedly, he went on, "I didn't know . . . I mean, I didn't intend for the demons to come. That was all Chantal's doing, you know, and—"

Oryon cleared his throat loudly and Kress stopped, flushed, and then said, "All right. I did a lot of things I shouldn't have. I didn't mean for anyone to get killed, though, and . . . and I've learned my lesson. I have, really. After all, the demons tried to kill me, twice. They would have if it hadn't been for our healers. And for Gray. As it is . . ." He stopped and looked off into the distance, and his face suddenly looked bruised, creased with lines that had never been there before. No one else spoke, and after an awkward pause, he went on. "The things they did to me—I never want anything to do with demons again."

"And *I* want nothing more to do with peace officers," Lina said, feeling the need to take everyone's mind off the demons.

"I think they'll leave us alone after this," Oryon said.

"What'll happen to Chantal?" someone asked.

"Veronica will handle her. Probably strip her of her power and confine her somewhere. In another world, maybe." Lina relaxed, letting a contented lassitude sweep over her.

"Good riddance." Debra shuddered. She was perched on the arm of the chair Maridel sat in. Her color was back, her eyes clear. "I didn't like being a channel for demons. She had no right to use me like that."

"She'd bespelled Debra after Kress was killed," Giselle explained. "She was afraid the demons might come for her, too. She made Debra a channel, thinking she'd drive them into Debra to save herself. Instead they came through Debra to get to her."

"I didn't know what she was doing," Debra said. "I had a head cold, and she told me the spell would cure it."

"Moonbeam wouldn't let anybody near Debra because he knew what Chantal had done." Maridel stroked the cat proudly. "He wanted the demons to come through because he was sure we'd defeat them and make the school safe again."

Lina smiled at Maridel's "we." Moonbeam *had* played an important part, she grudgingly admitted. But Maridel? She might think of the cat as her familiar, but Lina was sure it was the other way around. Whatever Moonbeam was, Maridel was no more than his useful spokesperson.

"I think we ought to have a celebration," Vanita declared. "Not only for unmasking Chantal and defeating the demons, but for the way we all worked together, sharing power to carry off the show and fool the peace officers. And for Kress's recovery."

"That's a great idea," Petra seconded. "We can dress for dinner tonight and have a dance afterward."

"Yeah! Let's do it!" chimed in several voices.

"If the new headmistress or headmaster lets us." Reece's comment sobered the group.

"That's right," Troy said. "Convocation's this afternoon. Wonder who it'll be."

"Probably Old Tumbles. He's the senior faculty member."

"Ugh! He's practically gaga," Maridel said.

"I'd guess Mistress Dova or Mistress Blake," Vanita said. "If it's Mistress Blake, she'll let us party."

"Just so it isn't Master San Marté," Britnor said with a grimace.

"He likes dances, though," Petra said.

Lina glimpsed Tria standing unnoticed by the door. Tria smiled and nodded, and Lina winked. "I'd guess whoever the new head is, we'll be able to have our celebration," she told the group.

"I'll wear my chiffon frock," Maridel proclaimed, bouncing from her chair. "Debra, you can wear that clingy blue thing that looks so good on you."

"I think Oryon ought to honor the occasion by wearing something besides black," Giselle suggested.

The group chorused assent, and everyone gazed at Oryon. He looked down at his feet. "I—uh—don't have anything but black," he said.

"Borrow something," someone shouted.

"Yeah, Oryon. Time you stopped dressing like an undertaker," Britnor said.

Oryon's face reddened. "Well, I—to be honest—I'm color-blind. I'd look ridiculous if I tried to match colors."

"Color-blind!" Gray pushed himself away from the wall, stared at Oryon, and laughed uproariously. "Color-blind!" He slapped his knee with his good hand. "Come on. I'll fix you up with something of mine. I'm an artist; you can trust me to have good color sense."

Still laughing, he grabbed Oryon's arm and led him out. Others followed, giggling and chattering. Lina stayed where she was. Rehanne stood near the fireplace, staring up at the portrait hung above it.

"That's the first time I've heard Gray laugh like that since two years ago," Lina said. "He'll be all right, Rehanne."

Rehanne continued to gaze at the portrait. "She went to him. It took her fifty years, but she went. I didn't have her courage. Instead of going to him, I made Gray come back to me. He'll be all right, but—" She turned to Lina. Tears brimmed in her eyes. She blinked them back. "Headmistress always told me I had to learn to let him go, and I wouldn't listen.

"Giselle could have healed his arm. He wouldn't let her. He only wanted it set, he said. He wanted it to hurt, to take his mind off the other pain—the pain of coming back. He doesn't blame me. He praised me for helping him fight the demons and all that. But it won't be the same between us. It can't be."

"Things never stay the same, Rehanne," Lina said sleepily. "They change. People change. Look how different Oryon is.

"You were there for Gray when he needed you. If he doesn't need you anymore, it's because he's finally healed. He's strong. If you only loved him because he needed you, that wouldn't have been enough anyway. Give it time. See what happens. Maybe you'll be surprised."

Her eyes closed. She heard Rehanne's footsteps leaving the room. She was tired, but pleased with her success. Except for losing the power-net. She'd hoped to keep that useful item. No point in dwelling on the loss. Someday, she resolved, she'd either recover that one or find another.

"I don't get it, Gray," Reece said, straddling his desk chair and leaning toward the suitcase into which Gray was placing his folded clothes. "Why leave now, when everything's settled down?"

Gray didn't answer. He'd heard all the arguments—from Lina and Oryon, from Giselle, and above all from Rehanne.

But Reece persisted. "You've just found your full power. You need to develop it. And this is your last year. Why throw everything away?"

Gray straightened to meet Reece's gaze. "I'm not throwing anything away." He'd make one more attempt to explain, though he knew Reece wouldn't understand. "I don't have the power. It's gone. And I don't want it back. I had it when I needed it. That's enough. I'd be wasting the year if I stayed. No—let me finish," he said when Reece tried to interrupt. "I don't know where I got the power to transfer to alternate time streams and to transport others. Maybe it was a loan and the lender took it back after it accomplished its purpose." He set the last stack of shirts into the suitcase.

"What I do know is that my true gift is my art. That's what I want to develop, and I can't do it here." He snapped his suitcase shut. "The art I produce with my power only lasts a few seconds. I want to create work that endures. I've learned of a school of art and sculpture in Stansbury that will accept me on Mistress Blake's recommendation." He couldn't yet think of her as Headmistress. For him there was only one "Headmistress."

"But you're leaving Rehanne," Reece persisted.

Gray merely shook his head, not wanting to talk. He picked up his suitcase and headed for the door. The bus wouldn't arrive for another hour, but he could go outside to wait for it.

"She loves you, you know," Reece said.

Gray turned and leaned against the door with a weary sigh. "That's why I've got to leave," he said. "For two years I've been leaning on her, drawing her strength. I can't keep doing that. I've got to find my own strength."

He opened the door, stepped into the hall, paused, and turned for a last glance at the room. "Maybe, if I find what I'm looking for, I'll come back to her. Although I'm not sure she'd want me then."

He walked down the hall, past the office that used to be Headmistress's, down the stairs, and out the big double doors. At the curb he set down his suitcase and sat on it to wait for the bus.